Warwickshire County Council

This item is to be returned or renewed before the latest date above. It may be borrowed for a further period if not in demand. **To renew your books:**

- **Phone the 24/7 Renewal Line 01926 499273 or**
- **Visit www.warwickshire.gov.uk/libraries**

Discover • Imagine • Learn • *with libraries*

Warwickshire County Council

Working for Warwickshire

did not play in his own gaming house. He would have to find a gentleman willing to be her partner, but he'd gain n

Rhys

013789675 3

Welcome to...

THE MASQUERADE CLUB

Identities concealed, desires revealed…

This is your invitation to Regency society's
most exclusive gaming establishment.

Leave your inhibitions at the door,
don your disguise and indulge your desires!

This month club proprietor Rhys, the most renowned
gambler in London, finally meets his match…

A REPUTATION FOR NOTORIETY
June 2013

Rhys's friend Xavier, the most devilish rogue in town,
prefers to gamble with ladies' hearts.

Don't miss his story, coming soon!

A REPUTATION
FOR NOTORIETY

Diane Gaston

First published in Great Britain 2013
by Mills & Boon, an imprint of Harlequin (UK) Limited.
Harlequin (UK) Limited, Eton House, 18-24 Paradise Road,
Richmond, Surrey TW9 1SR

© Diane Perkins 2013

ISBN: 978 0 263 89830 9

Printed and bound in Spain
by Blackprint CPI, Barcelona

As a psychiatric social worker, **Diane Gaston** spent years helping others create real-life happy endings. Now Diane crafts fictional ones, writing the kind of historical romance she's always loved to read. The youngest of three daughters of a US Army Colonel, Diane moved frequently during her childhood, even living for a year in Japan. It continues to amaze her that her own son and daughter grew up in one house in Northern Virginia. Diane still lives in that house, with her husband and three very ordinary housecats. Visit Diane's website at http://dianegaston.com

Previous novels by the same author:

THE MYSTERIOUS MISS M
THE WAGERING WIDOW
A REPUTABLE RAKE
INNOCENCE AND IMPROPRIETY
A TWELFTH NIGHT TALE
    (in *A Regency Christmas* anthology)
THE VANISHING VISCOUNTESS
SCANDALISING THE TON
JUSTINE AND THE NOBLE VISCOUNT†
    (in *Regency Summer Scandals*)
GALLANT OFFICER, FORBIDDEN LADY*
CHIVALROUS CAPTAIN, REBEL MISTRESS*
VALIANT SOLDIER, BEAUTIFUL ENEMY*
A NOT SO RESPECTABLE GENTLEMAN?†
BORN TO SCANDAL

*ary *Three Soldiers* mini-series
†linked by character

And in Mills & Boon® Historical *Undone!* eBooks:

THE UNLACING OF MISS LEIGH
THE LIBERATION OF MISS FINCH

AUTHOR NOTE

A REPUTATION FOR NOTORIETY is the first of two books in *The Masquerade Club*, a series in which identities are concealed and desires revealed. The Masquerade Club is a gaming hell (a gambling establishment) in Regency London, like those where in reality many a gentleman—and lady—lost vast fortunes playing cards or rolling dice.

My own history of card-playing is not so dramatic. As children, my sisters and I played at gambling with our own toy roulette wheel and a real set of poker chips. We learned to play five-card stud and twenty-one. Game-playing, especially if for real or imaginary stakes, could easily consume a whole day, and often took up a great part of our summers.

My father had no interest in cards, but my mother and aunt (the Aunt Loraine in my dedication) loved to play. Whenever we got together with their sister and our cousins we could hardly wait to get out the cards.

The card game we played was Shanghai, a complicated rummy game that we adapted to make even more challenging. We played for money. Fifteen cents was the stake, but extra nickels could also be won (or lost). These games were competitive and cut-throat and riotous fun. Even now when we see our cousins we break out the cards and play Shanghai.

The gambling hells of the Regency were, I dare say, not anything like playing Shanghai with my cousins, but I like to think we were not too dissimilar from Jane Austen and her characters, who spent many evenings playing such card games as Loo, Commerce, and Cassino.

I hope you enjoy *The Masquerade Club*, Celia—and Rhys, who has A REPUTATION FOR NOTORIETY.

Visit my website at http://dianegaston.com or send an e-mail to diane@dianegaston.com

Dedication

In fond memory of my Aunt Loraine, who taught me to enjoy life, no matter what.

Prologue

London—June 1819

Rhys noticed the woman as soon as she appeared in the game room doorway. Taller than fashionable, she held her head high as she perused the room. Her face was half covered by a black mask reminiscent of those he'd seen in Venice, crowned with feathers and painted with gilt filigree. A large garnet was set between the eyes. Visible still were her full lips, tinted and enticing.

In her deep red gown, matching the reds, greens and golds of the game room, she might have been an item he'd personally selected. He watched as she moved gracefully through the room, stepping carefully as if uncertain the space worthy of her. Did she intend to play hazard? Or one of the other games? He was keen that this woman should admire what he'd done to the gaming hell and enjoy herself.

He wanted her to return.

Rhys intensely wished for this gaming house to be a success. He would settle for nothing less than it becoming London's most desirable place to gamble, a place both gentlemen and ladies would be eager to attend. Not for the profit it would earn, but to show he could be the best at whatever he tackled.

The challenge exhilarated him, in a way he'd not experienced since the stimulation of battle. Only this time there was no carnage in its wake.

This time there was a beautiful woman here to enjoy herself and it was his job to see that she did.

She paused in the middle of the room and he quickly made his way to her.

'Good evening, madam.' He bowed. 'I am Mr Rhysdale, the proprietor of this establishment. It will be my pleasure to assist you. What game do you wish to play?'

She lifted her eyes to him. Through the black mask he saw they were an intriguing green. Her hair, a walnut-brown laced with gold, was loosely piled on her head.

Who was she?

'Mr Rhysdale.' She nodded and her voice was surprisingly soft and reticent. 'I would like to play whist, but I do not have a partner.'

How he would relish partnering her himself,

but he did not play in his own gaming house. He would have to find a gentleman willing to be her partner, but he'd find no enjoyment in the task. His friend Xavier would play cards with her if Rhys asked, but women much too easily succumbed to Xavier's handsome features. No, Rhys would not pass her on to Xavier.

Rhys wanted her for himself.

Chapter One

~~~~~~~~~

London—May 1819, one month earlier

Rhys and his friend Xavier sat at a table in the dining room of Stephen's Hotel. They had just been served their food when Rhys glanced towards the doorway.

Two men stood there, scanning the dining room.

Rhys knew them. Had known them since childhood. Viscount Neddington, né William Westleigh, and his brother Hugh, the legitimate sons of Earl Westleigh.

His brothers.

Rhys turned back to his food.

Xavier put down his fork with a clatter. 'What the devil?' He inclined his head towards the doorway. 'Look who is here.'

Rhys glanced up. 'They are looking for someone.'

Stephen's Hotel catered to military men, or former military men like Rhys and Xavier. Not the usual stamping ground of the Westleighs.

Rhys waited for the inevitable moment one of the Westleighs would notice him and slip his gaze away as if Rhys had never existed. Over the years when their paths had crossed, Neddington and Hugh always tried to act as if he'd never existed. Certainly that was their wish.

Ned, the elder, taller brother, turned his head in Rhys's direction. Their eyes locked, but this time Ned did not look away. This time he nudged his brother and the two walked straight for Rhys's table.

'They are headed here,' Rhys told Xavier.

His friend blew out a breath. 'I'll be damned…'

Rhys continued to hold Ned's gaze. Rhys always stood his ground with the Westleighs.

They stopped at the table.

'Rhys.' Ned inclined his head in an effort, Rhys supposed, to appear cordial.

'Gentlemen.' Rhys would be damned if he'd greet them by name and pretend an intimacy that had never existed. He gestured towards Xavier. 'My friend, Mr Campion.'

'We are acquainted.' Ned bowed in acknowledgement.

'We are indeed.' Xavier's tone was sarcastic.

Rhys cut another piece of meat. 'Are you merely paying your respects, or do you seek me out?'

'We seek you out,' Hugh replied, his voice taut and anxious.

Xavier glanced from one man to the other, obviously curious as to the purpose of this unusual visit.

Rhys made his expression neutral. Years of card-playing taught him to conceal his thoughts and emotions. He certainly had no intention of revealing anything to a Westleigh. He lifted a piece of beef into his mouth.

'Forgive us for interrupting your dinner.' Ned's tone was conciliatory, if somewhat stiff. 'We need a word with you.'

They *needed* a word with him? Now this was unique.

Rhys deliberately kept his attention to his plate, but he gestured to the empty chairs at the table. 'Have a seat.'

Hugh, shorter and always more hot-headed, emitted an indignant sound.

'We would prefer to speak in private.' Ned seemed anxious to avoid offending Rhys in any way.

Xavier straightened. If his friend were carrying a sword, Rhys suspected he'd have drawn it.

Rhys gazed at the two men, seeing only the boys they once were. The bitter memory of their first encounter, when Rhys was nine, flashed through his mind. He'd confronted them with what he'd just learned—that they shared a father.

That moment, like countless others from their childhoods, had resulted in flying fists and bloody noses.

Rhys stared into eyes identical to his. Dark brown, framed by thick eyebrows. Like his, Ned's and Hugh's hair was close-cut and near-black. Rhys might be taller and thicker-muscled, but if he stood side by side with these two men, who could ever deny they were brothers?

He exchanged a glance with Xavier, whose lips thinned in suspicion.

Rhys shrugged. 'Wait for me in the parlour off the hall. I'll come to you as soon as I've finished eating.'

Ned bowed curtly and Hugh glowered, but both turned and walked away.

Xavier watched their retreat. 'I do not trust them. Do you wish me to come with you?'

Rhys shook his head. 'There never was a time I could not take on both Westleighs.'

'Just the same, I dislike the sound of this,' Xavier countered. 'They are up to something.'

Rhys took another bite of his food. 'Oh, they are up to something. On that we agree. But I will see them alone.'

Xavier shot him a sceptical look.

Rhys took his time finishing his meal, although he possessed no more appetite for it. In all likelihood this would be an unpleasant interview. All encounters with Ned and Hugh were unpleasant.

Xavier clapped him on his shoulder before parting from him in the hall. 'Take care, Rhys.'

Rhys stepped into the parlour and Ned and Hugh turned to him. They'd remained standing.

He gestured. 'Follow me to my rooms.'

He led them up the two flights of stairs to his set of rooms. The door opened to a sitting room and as soon as Rhys led the men in, his manservant appeared.

'Some brandy for us, MacEvoy.'

MacEvoy's brows rose. MacEvoy, a man with an even rougher history than Rhys, had been his batman during the war. Obviously he recognised Hugh Westleigh from the battlefield.

'Please sit.' Rhys extended his arm to a set of chairs. It gave him a perverse pleasure that his furnishings were of fine quality, even if the items had been payment for various gambling debts. Rhys was doing well, which had not always been true.

MacEvoy served the brandy and left the room.

Rhys took a sip. 'What is this about, that you must speak with me now? You've made such a point of avoiding me all these years.'

Ned glanced away as if ashamed. 'We may not have…spoken to you, but we have kept ourselves informed of your whereabouts and actions.'

Ned was speaking false. Rhys would wager his whole fortune that these two had never bothered to discover what had happened to him after his mother had died and their father had refused any further support. The earl had left him penniless and alone, at a mere fourteen years of age.

No use to contest the lie, however. 'I'm flattered,' he said instead.

'You've had a sterling military record,' Ned added.

Hugh turned away this time.

'I lived,' Rhys said.

Hugh had also been in the war. The two former officers had come across each other from time to time in Spain, France and finally at Waterloo, although Hugh had been in a prestigious cavalry regiment, the Royal Dragoons. Rhys ultimately rose to major in the 44th Regiment of Foot. After the disastrous cavalry charge at Waterloo, Rhys had pulled Hugh from the mud and saved him from a French sabre. They said not a word to each other then, and Rhys would not speak of it now. The moment had been fleeting and only one of many that horrendous day.

Ned leaned forwards. 'You make your living by playing cards now, is that not correct?'

'Essentially,' Rhys admitted.

He'd learned to play cards at school, like every proper schoolboy, but he'd become a gambler on the streets of London. Gambling had been how he'd survived. It was still how he survived. He had become skilled at it out of necessity, earning enough to purchase his commission. Now that the war was over his winnings fed the foundation of a respectable fortune. Never again would his pockets be empty and his belly aching with hunger. He would be a success at…something. He did not know yet precisely what. Manufacturing, perhaps. Creating something useful, something more important than a winning hand of cards.

Hugh huffed in annoyance. 'Get on with it, Ned. Enough of this dancing around.' Hugh had always been the one to throw the first fist.

Ned looked directly into Rhys's eyes. 'We need your help, Rhys. We need your skill.'

'At playing cards?' That seemed unlikely.

'In a manner of speaking.' Ned rubbed his face. 'We have a proposition for you. A business proposition. One we believe will be to your advantage, as well.'

Did they think him a fool? Eons would pass before he'd engage in business with any Westleigh.

Rhys's skin heated with anger. 'I have no need of a business proposition. I've done quite well…' he paused '…since I was left on my own.'

'Enough, Ned.' Hugh's face grew red with emotion. He turned to Rhys. 'Our family is on the brink of disaster—'

Ned broke in, his voice calmer, more measured. 'Our father has been…reckless…in his wagering, his spending—'

'He's been reckless in everything!' Hugh threw up his hands. 'We are punting on the River Tick because of him.'

Earl Westleigh in grave debt? Now that was a turn of affairs.

Although aristocrats in severe debt tended to have abundantly more than the poor in the street. Ned and Hugh would never experience what Rhys knew of hunger and loneliness and despair.

He forced away the memory of those days lest he reveal how they nearly killed him.

'What can this have to do with me?' he asked in a mild tone.

'We need money—a great deal of it—and as quickly as possible,' Hugh said.

Rhys laughed at the irony. 'Earl Westleigh wishes to borrow money from me?'

'Not borrow money,' Ned clarified. 'Help us make money.'

Hugh made an impatient gesture. 'We want you to set up a gaming house for us. Run the place. Help us make big profits quickly.'

Ned's reasonable tone was grating on Rhys's nerves. On Hugh's, too, Rhys guessed.

Ned continued. 'Our reasoning is thus—if our father can lose a fortune in gaming hells, we should be able to recover a fortune by running one.' He opened his palms. 'Only *we* cannot be seen to be running one, even if we knew how. Which we do not. It would throw too much suspicion on our situation, you see, and that would cause our creditors to become impatient.' He smiled at Rhys. 'But *you* could do it. You have the expertise and…and there would not be any negative consequences for you.'

Except risking arrest, Rhys thought.

Although he could charge for membership. Call it a club, then it would be legal—

Rhys stopped himself. He was not going to run a gaming hell for the Westleighs.

'We need you,' Hugh insisted.

Were they mad? They'd scorned him his whole life. Now they expected him to help them?

Rhys drained the contents of his glass and looked from one to the other. 'You need me, but I do not need you.'

Hugh half rose from his chair. 'Our father supported you and your mother. You owe him. He sent you to school. Think of what would have happened if he had not!'

Rhys glared at him, only a year younger than his own thirty years. 'Think of what my mother's life might have been like if the earl had not seduced her.'

She might have married. She might have found respectability and happiness instead of bearing the burden of a child out of wedlock.

She might have lived.

Rhys turned away and pushed down the grief for his mother. It never entirely left him.

Ned persisted. 'Rhys, I do not blame you for despising our father or us, but our welfare is not the main issue. Countless people, some known to you, depend upon our family for their livelihood. The servants. The tenant farmers. The stable workers. The village and all its people in some fashion depend upon the Westleigh estate to be profitable. Too soon we will not be able to meet the expenses of planting. Like a house of cards, everything is in danger of collapsing and it is the people of Westleigh who will suffer the most dire of consequences.'

Rhys curled his fingers into fists. 'Do not place upon my shoulders the damage done by the earl. It has nothing to do with me.'

'You are our last resort,' Hugh implored. 'We've tried leasing the estate, but in these hard times, no one is forthcoming.'

Farming was going through difficult times, that was true. The war left much financial hardship in its wake. There was plenty of unrest and protest around the country about the Corn Laws keeping grain prices high, but, without the laws, more farms would fold.

All the more reason the earl should have exercised prudence instead of profligacy.

'Leave me out of it.'

'We cannot leave you out of it!' Hugh jumped to his feet and paced the room. 'We need you. Do you not hear me? You must do this for us!'

'Hugh, you are not helping.' Ned also rose.

Rhys stood and faced them both. 'Words *our* father once spoke to me, I will repeat to you. *I am under no obligation to do anything for you.*' He turned away and walked over to the decanter of brandy, pouring himself another glass. 'Our conversation is at an end.'

There was no sound of them moving towards the door. Rhys turned and faced them once again. 'You need to leave me, gentlemen. Go now, or, believe me, I am quite capable of tossing you both out.'

Hugh took a step towards him. 'I should like to see you try!'

Ned pulled him away. 'We are leaving. We are leaving. But I do beg you to reconsider. This could bring you a fortune. We have enough to finance the start of it. All we need is—'

Rhys lowered his voice. 'Go.'

Ned dragged his brother to the door. They gathered their hats and gloves and left the rooms.

Rhys stared at the door long after their footsteps faded in the hallway.

MacEvoy appeared. 'Do you need anything, sir?'

Rhys shook his head. 'Nothing, MacEvoy. You do not need to attend me.'

MacEvoy left again and Rhys downed his brandy. He poured himself another glass, breathing as heavy as if he'd run a league.

He almost wished Hugh had swung at him. He'd have relished planting a fist in the man's face, a face too disturbingly similar to his own.

A knock sounded at the door and Rhys strode over and swung it open. 'I told you to be gone!'

'Whoa!' Xavier raised his hands. 'They are gone.'

Rhys stepped aside. 'What were you doing? Lurking in the hallway?'

'Precisely.' Xavier entered the room. 'I could not wait a moment longer to hear what they wanted.'

Rhys poured another glass of brandy and handed it to his friend. 'Have a seat. You will not believe this, I assure you…'

Sending away the Westleighs ought to have been the end of it. Rhys ought to have concentrated on his cards that night rather than observe the workings of the gaming hell on St James's Street. He ought to have slept well without his thoughts racing.

Over the next few days, though, he visited as many gambling establishments as he could, still playing cards, but taking in everything from the arrangements of the tables, the quality of the meals, the apparent profitability of the various games.

'Why this tour of gaming hells?' Xavier asked him as they walked to yet another establishment off of St James's. 'A different one each night? That is not your habit, Rhys. You usually stick to one place long enough for the high-stakes players to ask you to play.'

Rhys lifted his shoulders. 'No special reason. Call it a whim.'

His friend looked doubtful.

Rhys did not wish to admit to himself that he was considering his half-brothers' offer, although all the people who had been kind to his mother in the village kept rising to his memory. He could almost envision their suffering eyes if Westleigh Hall was left in ruins. He could almost feel their hunger.

If he pushed the faces away, thoughts of how much money he could make came to the fore. The Westleighs would be taking the risk, not Rhys. For Rhys it was almost a safe bet.

If only it had been anyone but the Westleighs.

Rhys sounded the knocker on the door of an innocuous-appearing town house. A huge bear of a man in colourful livery opened the door. Rhys had not been to this house in perhaps a year, but it appeared unchanged.

'How do you do, Cummings?' he said to the liveried servant. 'I have been gone too long from here.'

'G'd evening, Mr Rhysdale,' Cummings responded in his deep monotone. He nodded to Xavier. 'Mr Campion.'

Cummings might act the doorman, but he'd be better described as the gatekeeper, allowing only certain people in, chucking out any patron who became rowdy or combative.

Cummings took their hats and gloves. 'Nothing has changed here. Except some of the girls. They come and go. The game room is up the stairs. Same as always.'

Rhys was not interested in the girls, who often sold their favours on the side.

He glanced around the hall. Nothing appeared changed.

Three years ago he'd been a frequent patron of this place. He, like so many gentlemen at that time, had been intrigued by a masked woman who came to play cards and often did quite well. She'd been a mystery and that intensified her appeal. Soon the men were wagering on which of them would bed her first, all properly written down in the betting book. Rhys had not been interested in seducing a woman just to win a bet.

He shook his head. He had not thought of that masked woman in years. Who had won her? he wondered.

He turned back to Cummings. 'And Madame Bisou. Is she here tonight?' Madame Bisou owned this establishment.

'Aye. She should be in the game room.' Cummings turned away to store their hats.

Rhys and Xavier climbed the stairs and entered the game room, all a-bustle with activity as the time approached midnight. The hazard table was in the centre of the room, encircled by eager players. The familiar sound of dice shaken in a cup and shouts of 'Seven!' reached Rhys's ears, followed by the roll of the dice on the green baize and more shouting. Now and again a patron might win big, but the odds always favoured the bank, as they did in faro and *rouge et noir*. The two faro tables stood against one wall, nearly obscured by players; the other side held the games of *rouge et noir*. Rhys avoided all these games, where winning was almost completely dependent on luck. He confined himself to games of skill.

'I thought you came to play cards.' Xavier nudged him.

'I have,' he responded. 'But I have not been here in a year. I am taking stock of the room.'

At that moment, a buxom woman with flaming red hair hurried towards them. 'Monsieur Rhysdale. Monsieur Campion. How good it is to see you. It has been *trop longtemps,* no?'

Rhys smiled both at the pleasure of seeing her again and at her atrocious French accent. 'Madame Bisou!' He leaned over to give her a kiss on the cheek and whispered in her ear, 'How are you, Penny?'

'*Très bien, cher,*' she responded, but her smile looked stressed. She turned to greet Xavier before Rhys could ask more.

In those difficult London days of his youth Madame Bisou had been Penny Jones, a decade older than he and just as determined to free herself from the shackles of poverty. They'd both used what God had provided them: Rhys, his skill at cards—Penny, her body. But she did not spend all the money she earned on gin like so many of the other girls. She'd saved and invested and finally bought this place. She'd been running it for almost ten years.

'Why has it been so long since you have been here?' She took Rhys's hand and squeezed it.

'I am asking myself that same question.' Rhys smiled at her, genuinely glad to see an old friend.

Her tone changed to one of business. 'What is your pleasure today, gentlemen? Do you wish a woman? Or a game of chance?'

Xavier answered her. 'A game of whist, if we can manage it.'

Rhys would have preferred merely to watch the room for a little while, but Penny found them two willing high-stakes partners.

When the play was over, Rhys and Xavier collected their winnings, more modest than most nights, but Rhys had to admit to being distracted. They moved on to the supper room. One of the girls began a flirtation with Xavier. Rhys spied Penny sitting in a far corner.

He walked over to her. 'It is not like you to sit alone, Penny. Is something amiss? Might I help?'

She sighed wearily and appeared, for the moment, much older than her forty years. 'I have lost the heart for this, Rhys. I wish I could just walk away from it all….'

Rhys's heart beat faster. 'Are you thinking of selling the business?'

'How can it be done? I cannot advertise.' Her gaming hell was illegal. 'I am too weary to even think how to accomplish it.'

This was unlike her. Penny always found a way to do precisely as she wished.

Rhys's nostrils filled with the scent of opportunity.

Fate was shoving him in the direction he must go. He was the solution to Penny's problems. He could save his old village. He could enrich his coffers.

All he must do was sell his soul to the devil.

His father.

The next day Rhys presented himself at the Westleigh town house. He'd not told Xavier his intention. He'd not wanted to be talked out of it.

It was well before the fashionable hour for making calls. Probably well before Ned and Hugh rose. It was half-past nine, a time working men and women were well into their day while the wealthy still slept. But Rhys needed to do this first thing or risk the chance of changing his mind.

The footman who answered the door led him to a drawing room off the hall. Unfortunately, the room was dominated by a huge portrait of the earl. Painted with arms crossed, the image of Earl Westleigh stared down, his expression stern and, Rhys fancied, disapproving.

Let his image disapprove. Rhys knew his own worth. He was determined the world should know it soon enough.

Still the earl's presence in this house set his nerves on edge. Would he join Ned and Hugh for this interview? Rhys half hoped so. He would relish standing in a superior position to this man who once held power over his life.

But it was far more likely the earl would do anything possible to avoid his bastard son.

Rhys's brothers, to their credit, did not keep him waiting long. He heard their hurried footsteps and their hushed voices before they entered the room.

Ned walked towards him as if he would offer his hand to shake, but he halted and gestured to a chair instead. 'Shall we sit?'

Hugh held back and looked solemn.

Rhys calmly looked from one to the other. 'I believe I'll stand.'

His response had the desired effect. Both men shifted uncomfortably.

'Are we to assume your presence here to mean you have reconsidered our offer?' Ned asked.

Rhys inwardly grimaced. Ned called it an offer? 'I came to further the discussion of whether

I am willing to rescue you and our father from penury.'

'Why?' Hugh demanded in a hot voice. 'What changed your mind?'

Rhys levelled a gaze at him. 'Call it an attack of family loyalty, if you like. I did not say I've changed my mind.'

Ned placed a stilling hand on Hugh's arm, but spoke to Rhys. 'What do you wish to discuss?'

Rhys shrugged. 'Well, for one, it takes a great deal of money to start a gaming establishment. Will I be expected to invest my own money? Because I would not stake my fortune against something so risky.'

'How is it risky?' Hugh cried. 'The house always has the advantage. You know that.'

'The house can be broken,' Rhys countered. 'It is all chance.' Rhys succeeded at cards by reducing chance.

'But it is not likely, is it?' Hugh shot back.

Ned's eyes flashed a warning to Hugh, before he turned to Rhys again. 'The monetary investment will be ours.' He lowered his voice. 'It is now or never for us, Rhys. We've scraped the last of our fortune to bank this enterprise. All we want from you—all we need from you—is to run it.'

They must truly be desperate to devise a plan like this, especially as it involved him. Desperate or mad.

'A gaming house will not make much money

right away unless it can quickly build a reputation. It must distinguish itself from other places. Give gamblers a reason to attend.' Rhys paused. 'You want to attract the high-stakes gamblers who have money to throw away.'

'It must be an honest house,' Hugh snapped. 'No rigged dice. No marked cards.'

Rhys gave him a scathing look. 'Are you attempting to insult me, Hugh? If you do not think me an honest man, why ask me to run it?'

Hugh averted his gaze.

'No cheating of any kind,' Rhys reiterated. 'And no prostitution. I will tolerate neither.' He'd keep the girls at Madame Bisou's employed, but he'd have nothing to do with them selling their bodies.

'We are certainly in agreement with all you say,' Ned responded.

Rhys went on. 'Within the parameters of honesty, I must be given free rein in how the house is run.'

'Of course,' Ned agreed.

'Wait a moment.' Hugh glared. 'What precisely do you mean by free rein?'

'I mean I decide how to run it,' Rhys responded. 'There will be no countering of what I choose to do.'

'What do you choose to do?' Hugh shot back.

Rhys kept his tone even. 'I will make this house the one every wealthy aristocrat or merchant wants to attend. I want to attract not only wealthy men, but ladies, as well.'

'Ladies!' Hugh looked appalled.

'We all know ladies like to gamble as well as gentlemen, but ladies risk censure for it, so I propose we run the house like a masquerade. Anyone may come in costume or masked. That way they can play without risk to their reputation.' This had worked for the masked woman who'd come to Madame Bisou's and caused such a stir those years ago. No one had ever learned who she was.

Rhys had thought this all through. It had been spinning in his mind ever since Ned and Hugh first proposed he run a gambling house. He would call it the Masquerade Club. Members could join for a nominal fee. They could dress in masquerade as long as they purchased their counters with the coin in their pockets. If they sought credit or were forced to sign a promissory note, they must reveal their identity.

He continued explaining to Ned and Hugh. 'This is my plan thus far. It is not up to negotiation. If I come up with a better idea, I will implement it and I will not confer with you beforehand.'

'See here——' Hugh began.

Ned waved a hand. 'Leave it, Hugh. As long as it is honest and profitable, what do we care how the place is run?' He turned to Rhys. 'Anything else?'

'I want half the profit.'

'Half?' Hugh shouted.

Rhys faced him again. 'You risk money, but it is my reputation that will be at risk. We can charge a nominal subscription and call it a gaming club, but there is still the risk that it will be declared illegal. I must be compensated for that risk.' Besides, he intended to give Penny a portion of his profits, as part of the sale, and Xavier, too, if he was willing to help.

'I think your terms are agreeable,' Ned responded. 'Shall we discuss how much money you need to get started?'

Rhys nodded, but tapped a finger against his lips. 'I do have a question.'

Ned looked up suspiciously. 'What is it?'

'Does the earl know you wish me to do this?'

The brothers exchanged glances.

'He knows,' Ned answered.

And was not happy about it, Rhys guessed. Something Rhys counted upon. Besides earning a profit, Rhys wanted the gaming house to provide him another pay-off. He wanted to rub the earl's nose in the fact that it was his bastard son who pulled him from the brink of ruin. Rhys wanted revenge against the man who sired him and never, ever, acknowledged that fact, who had instead turned him away without a penny, not caring if he lived or died.

He tapped on the back of a chair with his fingertips. 'Very well, my *brothers*—' he spoke sarcastically '—I agree to run your gaming house.'

The two men who so resembled him visibly relaxed.

'On one more condition,' Rhys added.

Hugh rolled his eyes. Ned looked nervous.

'Our *father*—' Rhys spoke this word with even greater sarcasm '—Earl Westleigh, that is—must publicly acknowledge me as his son. It must seem as if I am accepted into the family as one of you, an equal member. I must be included in family functions and social occasions. I must be treated as one of the family.' What better revenge than this?

Ned and Hugh gaped back at him with horrified expressions. Apparently the idea of accepting him as a brother was as anathema to them as it would be to the earl.

'That is my condition,' Rhys reiterated.

Ned glanced away and silence stretched between them.

Finally he raised his eyes to Rhys. 'Welcome to the family, brother.'

Chapter Two

Rhys accomplished the sale and reopening of the gaming hell within three weeks of calling upon his half-brothers. He changed the décor and the menu and retrained all the workers. Madame Bisou's became the Masquerade Club and news of its opening travelled swiftly by word of mouth.

The first days had been stressful, but each night the numbers of patrons had grown, as had the profit, which made the Westleighs less fraught with worry. Rhys could count on one of them—Hugh mostly—to come in the guise of an ordinary patron. Rhys knew they were keeping tabs on what he had created.

He'd been watching for one of them when he spied the beautiful masked woman who had just told him she wished to play whist.

Rhys had experienced his share of affairs with

women. He and Xavier had enjoyed some raucous nights in Paris with willing *elegantes,* but rarely, if ever, had he been so intrigued as with this woman.

Her posture was both proud and wary, and she had come to the gaming house alone, in itself a courageous act for a woman. What's more, her lips were moist and pink and her voice like music to his ears.

'How might a lady find a willing partner?' she asked.

What man could refuse her?

For the first time since opening the gaming house, Rhys regretted that he could not play cards. He would have relished being her partner and showing her his skill.

As it was, he must find her another man—to partner her in whist.

He bowed. 'Give me a moment to fulfil your desire.' A serving girl walked by with a tray of port. He took one glass and handed it to her. 'Refresh yourself in the meantime and take a look at all the house has to offer.'

He quickly scanned the room and spied Sir Reginald, a harmless man who frequented gaming hells and flirted with the ladies, but rarely followed through. His card playing was competent, if not inspired. Sir Reginald would be forgiving if she turned out to be a poor player, but would not disappoint if she was skilled.

Rhys could not imagine her not being skilled

at whatever she tried. He wanted her to enjoy herself. He wanted her to like the Masquerade well enough to return.

He brought the unmasked Sir Reginald to her. 'Madam, may I present Sir Reginald.'

Sir Reginald bowed gallantly. 'It will be my privilege to partner you.'

She smiled at Sir Reginald, her pink lips parting to reveal pretty white teeth. Handing Rhys her empty glass as if he were a servant, she accepted Sir Reginald's arm and walked with him to a card table with two other men. After speaking with the men, the lady and Sir Reginald sat. One of the other men dealt the cards.

Rhys had no intention of being so easily dismissed by this mysterious masked woman. He had other duties to occupy him at the moment, but, before she left, he intended to speak with her again.

Celia Gale breathed a sigh of relief to finally be seated at a card table, staring at diamonds, hearts, clubs and spades.

Entering the game room had been like crossing through the gates of hell. It had taken all her courage to do something so potentially damaging to her reputation. A lady, even a baron's widow, did not go gambling alone in the dead of night.

Even worse, it meant entering a world where other, even greater, risks existed—the lure of cards and dice, the heady thrill of winning, the certainty that losing could be reversed with one more hand, one more roll of the dice.

Cards and gambling once took away everything she held dear. The road to ruin was only one bad hand of cards away.

But what choice did she have? How else was she to procure the money she needed?

She'd heard of this gaming hell at a recent musicale she'd attended and immediately thought it was a godsend. Two men had spoken of it within her earshot.

'Thing is, the ladies can attend. It is called the Masquerade Club and anyone may come in disguise,' one had said.

'They do not have to reveal themselves?' the other asked.

'Not at all. Any lady may gamble without fear of ruining her reputation.'

She could gamble for high stakes and no one would know! At last a way to earn the funds she so desperately needed.

'Your deal, my dear,' Sir Reginald said, bringing her back to the present.

She'd spied Sir Reginald at a few of the entertainments she'd attended, but they had never been introduced. There was little reason to suppose he would recognise her. The other two gentlemen, also unmasked, were unknown to her before this night.

She dealt the deck slowly and with deliberation.

'Nicely dealt.' The man on her left smiled condescendingly.

She inclined her head in acknowledgement.

Her father taught that gambling was part skill at cards and part skill with people. Let these gentlemen condescend. It was to her advantage if they underestimated her. They might become careless in their choice of cards to lay down.

When the serving girl came around offering spirits, the gentlemen accepted, but Celia nursed one glass of port. She needed all her wits about her.

She purposely played as if this were her first time at a green baize table, and, by so doing, the counters grew into a pretty little pile at her right elbow. These gentlemen were betting quite modestly and, she suspected, were sometimes letting her win.

She indulged their mistaken impression. Soon enough this room would know her skill and then the competition—and the risk—would intensify.

She glanced up. The establishment's proprietor, Mr Rhysdale, was watching her. Too often when she looked up he was watching her. It set her nerves on edge.

Her blood had raced with fear when he'd approached her after she'd entered the room. She'd thought she'd done something wrong, transgressed some secret code of behaviour that was known only to those who frequented gaming hells.

He was a magnificent man, tall and muscled and intense. His eyes assessed everything, but his expression remained inscrutable. What was he thinking as he meandered through the tables, when he turned his gaze towards her?

He raised a glass to her and she quickly looked away.

What earthly reason made him watch her so closely? There were other masked ladies playing cards in the room.

She took the last three tricks of the hand, winning the game.

'That is it for me,' one of the gentlemen said.

'And for me,' his partner added.

Sir Reginald straightened. 'Would you like to try your luck at *rouge et noir,* my dear?'

She shook her head. 'No, thank you, sir.'

She wanted to play more cards. Games of skill, not merely of chance. She was at a loss as to how to manage it. Certainly she would not seek out Mr Rhysdale to find her a new partner.

All three gentlemen bowed and excused themselves, leaving her alone. Celia rose. She busied herself with slipping her counters in her reticule. The night had been profitable. Not overwhelmingly so, but it was a good start.

'Was luck with you, madam?'

She startled and turned, knowing who she would find. 'Luck?' She smiled. 'Yes, luck was with me, Mr Rhysdale.'

'Do you cash in, then?' He stood so close it seemed he stole the air she needed to breathe.

She clutched her reticule, but tilted her head so as to look in his face. 'Frankly, sir, I would like to continue to play. Dare I presume on you to arrange another game for me?'

'My pleasure, madam.' His voice turned low.

Within a few minutes he had rounded up two gentlemen and a lady needing a fourth and Celia played several more games. The gentleman who became her partner was more skilled than Sir Reginald and her counters multiplied.

When the players left the table, Mr Rhysdale appeared again. 'More partners?'

Her heart fluttered. Why was that? 'I am done for the night.'

He took her arm and leaned close. 'Then share some refreshment with me.'

She did not know what to say. 'What time is it?'

He reached into a pocket and pulled out a fine gold watch. 'A quarter to three.'

Her carriage came at three-thirty.

She glanced around the room. There was not enough time to join another whist game, or even find someone willing to play piquet. 'Very well.' She was certain her tone sounded resigned. 'Some refreshment would be welcome.'

He escorted her out of the game room to the door of the supper room behind. His hand remained firmly on her elbow. Her heart raced. Was he about to tell her why he watched her so intently as she played?

If he discovered she was a card sharp, her plans could be ruined. If he presumed she was cheating, it would be even worse. Was not her father's fate proof of that?

She wished Mr Rhysdale would simply leave her alone.

When they crossed the threshold of the supper room, Celia gasped.

The room was lovely! It was decorated in the earlier style of Robert Adam. The pale-green ceiling with its white plasterwork mirrored the pattern and colour of the carpet and walls. The white furniture was adorned with delicate gilt. Servants attending the buffet or carrying trays were dressed in livery that belonged to that earlier time, bright brocades and white wigs.

Rather than appear old-fashioned, the room seemed a fantasy of the elegance of bygone days. With all its lightness, Celia felt conspicuous in her dark red gown and black mask. There were four or five tables occupied, some with men entertaining ladies, some with men in deep conversation. Several of them glanced up as she and Rhysdale passed by.

'Are you hungry?' Rhysdale asked as he led her to a table away from the other diners. 'We can select from the buffet or, if you prefer, order a meal.'

Her nerves still jangled alarmingly. 'The buffet will do nicely.'

'And some wine?' His dark brows rose with his question.

She nodded. 'Thank you.'

At least he displayed some expression. She otherwise could not read his face at all, even though it was the sort of face that set a woman's heart aflutter. His eyes were dark and unfathomable and his nose, strong. But his lips—oh, his lips! The top lip formed a perfect bow. The bottom was full and resolute, like the firm set of his jaw. In this early pre-dawn hour, the dark shadow of his beard tinged his face, lending him the appearance of a dangerous rogue.

It was his position as the proprietor of the Masquerade Club that posed the most peril to her, though. She did not want the attention of the proprietor. She wanted only to play cards and win as much money as she could.

He pulled out a chair and she lowered herself into it, smoothing her skirt. Her chair faced the curtained window, but she wanted to face the room, so she could see what he was doing behind her back.

When he walked to the buffet, she changed seats.

Even as he made his selections at the buffet, he looked completely in charge. There was no hesitation on his part to pick this or that tidbit. His choices were swiftly accomplished. When a servant came near, Rhysdale signalled the man and spoke briefly to him. A moment later, the servant brought two wine glasses and a bottle to the table. He poured wine in both glasses.

Celia sipped hers gratefully. The night's play had given her a thirst and the mellowing effect of the wine was a balm to her nerves.

When Rhysdale turned from the buffet, he paused slightly, noticing, she supposed, that she had moved from the seat in which he had placed her.

He walked towards the table and her nerves fired anew.

Setting a plate in front of her, he lowered himself into the chair directly across from her. She would be unable to avoid those dark eyes while they conversed.

'I hope my selections are to your liking.' His voice rumbled.

She glanced at her plate. 'Indeed.'

He'd provided some slices of cold ham and an assortment of cheeses, fruits and confections, all items she enjoyed, but she would have given her approval no matter what he had selected.

She pushed the food around with her fork.

'I am curious.' His tone was casual. 'Why did you come to the Masquerade Club tonight?'

She glanced up, her heart pounding. 'Why do you ask?'

The corner of his mouth twitched, ever so slightly. 'I am eager to make this place a success. I want to know what entices a woman to attend.' He paused. 'And what would entice you to return.'

Her brows rose. Was this all he wanted from her? She could not believe it.

She chose her words carefully. 'I heard that a woman might play cards here without revealing her identity.'

He nodded. 'I had hoped anonymity would be an appeal.' He took a sip of his wine. 'And where did you hear this of the place?'

Now it was she who must avoid the truth. To answer truthfully would reveal that she moved in society's finest circles and that she could not do.

What could she say that would avoid tipping her hand? 'At the theatre.'

Yes. That ought to suffice. Anyone might attend the theatre.

He stared at her for a moment too long for comfort.

Finally he tasted the food on his plate. 'And what do you think of my establishment now you have seen it?'

She relaxed a little. Perhaps he was being honest with her. It made sense that a proprietor would want to know if his place appealed or not.

'It meets my needs very well.'

He glanced up. 'And your needs are?'

She swallowed a piece of cheese. 'A place to play cards where a woman might feel secure.'

'Secure.' He held her gaze.

She struggled to explain. 'To feel safe from… the stories one hears about gaming establishments.'

He pinned her with his gaze again. 'You have felt safe here?'

'I have,' she admitted.

What she witnessed from behind her mask was not the worst of what she'd heard of gaming hells, where drinking and debauchery might share the night with charges of cheating and, worst of all, challenges to duels. It almost seemed as civilised as a Mayfair drawing room, except for the wild excitement in the eyes of those on a winning streak and the blanch of despair on the faces of losing players. Those highs and lows were part of gambling. Something she must guard against at all costs.

As well as guarding against this special notice from the proprietor. His watchful dark eyes made her tremble inside.

He turned again to his plate. 'And what about the gaming here appeals to you? You played whist. Would you also be interested in the hazard table? Faro?'

She shook her head. 'I do not trust so much in luck.'

Too often in her life luck had totally abandoned her.

His eyes bore into her again. 'You prefer to rely on skill?'

Her gaze faltered. 'One must have some control over one's fate.'

'I quite agree.' To her surprise he smiled and his handsome face turned into something wondrous.

She found it momentarily hard to breathe.

His smile turned wry. 'Although you might say opening a gaming hell cedes too much of one's fate to luck.'

She forced her voice to work. 'Chance favours you at the hazard and faro tables, which is why I do not play them. Nor *rouge et noir.*'

She finished her wine, aware that he continued to stare at her. She fingered her reticule, heavy with counters. 'May—may I ask the time, please?'

He pulled his watch out again. 'Three-twenty.'

She stood. 'I must go. My carriage arrives at three-thirty and I need time to cash out.'

He also rose and walked with her to the ground floor where the cashier sat in a room behind the hall. She felt a thrill watching the coins she'd won stack up in front of her. After scooping them into a leather pouch and placing it in her reticule, she collected her shawl from the dour-faced servant attending the hall.

And Rhysdale remained with her.

He walked her to the door and opened it. 'I trust you will return to us?'

She suddenly was very eager to return. So eager a part of her wanted to re-enter the game room and deal another hand of whist.

She curbed her excitement. 'Perhaps.' Curtsying, she said, 'Thank you for your assistance, Mr Rhysdale. And for the refreshment.'

'You are very welcome.' His voice turned low and seemed to resonate inside her.

She crossed the threshold, relieved to take her leave of him, but he walked out into the dark night with her.

The rush lamp at the door must have revealed her surprise.

'I will see you into your carriage,' he explained.

Her coachman drove up immediately and she was grateful her carriage no longer had a crest on its side.

Rhysdale opened the coach door and pulled down the steps. He held out his hand to assist her. His touch was firm and set her nerves trembling anew.

He closed the door and leaned into the window. 'Goodnight, madam. It has been my pleasure to assist you.'

His pleasure? She took a breath.

'Goodnight,' she managed.

The coach pulled away, and she swivelled around to look out the back window.

He stood in the road, illuminated by the rush light.

Still watching her.

Rhys did not leave the road until her carriage disappeared into the darkness.

Who the devil was she?

He did not need to be captivated by a woman. A woman could become an inconvenient distraction and he needed to keep his wits about him. The gaming house must be his priority.

Rhys had known too many women who made their living by acting pleasing at first, then cutting the man's purse and dashing away. He expected that sort of woman to show up at the gaming hell—women who played at gambling, but who really merely wished to attach themselves to the evening's big winners.

This woman was not a cutpurse, however. Neither did she come to the gaming hell on a lark.

She came to win money.

He'd watched her play, had seen the concentration in her posture, the calculation in her selection of cards. She was here for the card play.

She was a kindred spirit, a gambler like himself.

Would she return? She must. He wanted her in every way a man wanted a woman.

He walked back into the house, nodding to Cummings as he passed him. When he reached the door to the game room, Xavier appeared, leaning against the wall in the hallway, his arms crossed over his chest.

'What was that all about?' his friend asked.

Rhys did not know how much he wished to say about the woman, even to Xavier. 'She intrigues me.' He gave his friend a warning look. 'If she returns, do not aspire to make her one of your conquests.'

Xavier, who attracted female company so easily he never needed to make a conquest, replied, 'I comprehend.'

They walked into the game room together.

'Do you know who she is?' Xavier asked.

Rhys grinned. 'Not yet.'

Chapter Three

Celia sat at the desk in her library in the rooms she'd taken for the Season, rooms she now had more hope she could afford. Her winnings were stacked in piles on the desk, one half set aside to stake her next venture to the Masquerade Club.

What would she have done had she not discovered the new gaming house? Her widow's portion had been stretched to the breaking point and the bills continued to pour in.

Now she could transfer some of the bills from one stack to another—ones to pay now, ones to pay later.

She rolled some of the coins in her hand, almost giddy at their cool texture and the clink of them rubbing against each other.

She stacked them again and leaned back, appalled at herself. To be giddy at winning was to travel a perilous path. She must never succumb to the mania that was gambling. Not like her father—and, by association, her mother. They both died of it.

If she played with her head and not her emotions, she should be able to resist. She planned to visit the place often enough to learn who the high-stakes players were. Think of the money she could win in games with such gamblers!

Stop! she warned herself. No emotions. Playing cards must merely be what she did to earn money, like any tradesman or skilled workman.

Celia turned her face to the window and gazed out into the small garden at the back of the house. At the moment she must depend on Rhysdale to find her partners, but soon she would become known to the regulars. Then she hoped to be sought after as a partner.

At least Rhysdale had set her up with partners skilled enough to bring her a tidy profit.

She riffled the stack of coins. She needed more. Her stepdaughter's Season cost money and her mother-in-law refused to stop spending recklessly.

Her late husband had been another whose gambling and debauchery ruled his life. Her husband had been excessive in everything. Gambling. Spending. Drinking. Mistresses.

He'd even been excessive in his disdain for his young wife.

Not that it mattered now. His death had freed

her from a marriage she'd never wanted and from a husband she'd abhorred. It had left her with a stepdaughter nearly her own age and a mother-in-law who despised her.

'Celia!' Adele, her stepdaughter, called.

Celia's singular joy, the closest Celia would ever come to a daughter of her own. Adele. Bright and starry-eyed, and full of hope that her first Season in London would bring her the love match she pined for. Celia was determined Adele should achieve her dreams, dreams that might have been Celia's own.

If gambling had not robbed her of them.

'I'm in here, Adele,' she responded.

Dreams aside, it was pragmatic for Adele to make a good match. The girl deserved to be settled and happy with a husband wealthy and generous enough to support Adele's grandmother, as well. Celia's modest widow's portion might be enough for her to live in some measure of comfort if she economised very carefully, but it definitely did not stretch so far as to support her stepdaughter and mother-in-law.

Besides, Celia had no wish to be shackled to her mother-in-law forever.

Adele bounced into the room and gave Celia a buss on the cheek. 'Grandmama and I went shopping. We went to the new Burlington Arcade. It was a positive delight!'

'Was it?' Celia would miss Adele. The girl was the delight of her life.

Adele danced in front of her. 'There must have been a hundred shops. We did not see half of them.' She sobered. 'But, I assure you, I did not purchase a thing.'

Celia smiled. 'I hope you enjoyed yourself, none the less.'

'I did. I cannot tell you of all the items I saw for sale.' Adele lowered herself onto a nearby chair. 'Do not tell me those are bills.'

'They are bills, but do not fret. I have funds to pay some of them.' Celia moved the stacks of bills to pay farther away from those that would have to wait. 'Including the modiste. So you may order a new gown or two.'

Adele shook her head. 'I do not need them. I can make do with my old ones.'

Celia rose from her chair and went over to the girl. 'Indeed you may not!' She took Adele's hands. 'It is very important for you to put in a good appearance! Your grandmother and I agree on that score. Besides I've—I've found some funds I did not know we had. We are not so poverty-stricken after all.'

Adele looked sceptical. 'I hope you are telling me the truth and not shielding me as if I were a child.'

Celia squeezed her hands and avoided the issue. 'Of course you are not a child. A child does not have a Season.' Adele was nineteen years old. Celia herself was only twenty-three, but she felt ancient in comparison.

'I am sending Tucker out with the payments today.' Tucker had been one of the footmen who had served the Gales for years. Without overstepping the boundaries between servant and master, he'd been loyal to Celia through her marriage and widowhood. He was now her faithful butler.

'Where did you find the money?' Adele asked.

Celia pointed to the coins. 'The silliest thing. I was looking for something else and I discovered a purse full of coin. Your father must have packed it away and forgotten about it.'

Adele's expression saddened. 'That was a fortunate thing. Had he found it he would have lost it gambling.'

What would Adele think if she knew where the money had really come from?

Only three people knew of Celia's trip to the Masquerade Club—Tucker, her housekeeper, Mrs Bell, and Younie, Celia's lady's maid. Younie was lady's maid to all three women since Lord Gale's death.

What would Adele think if she knew Celia planned to return to the gaming hell tonight?

An image of Rhysdale flew into her mind. Would he watch her again? Her heartbeat accelerated.

The Dowager Lady Gale, Celia's mother-in-law,

entered the room. 'There you are, Adele.' She did not greet Celia. 'We must decide what you are to wear to the musicale tonight. It cannot be the blue gown again. Everyone has seen that gown twice already. It will be remembered.' She finally turned to Celia. 'She absolutely needs new dresses. You are excessively cruel to deny them to her.'

Celia pasted a smile on her face. 'Good afternoon, Lady Gale.'

Like Celia, Lady Gale wanted Adele to have a successful Season, ending in a betrothal. The difference was, Celia wanted Adele to find someone who could make her happy; Lady Gale cared only that Adele marry a man with a good title and good fortune.

Celia adopted a mollifying tone. 'You will be pleased to know Adele and I have been talking of dresses. I have payment for the modiste, so Adele may order two new gowns.'

Her mother-in-law, silver-haired and as slim-figured as she'd been in her own Season, narrowed her eyes. 'Only two? I cannot abide how tight-fisted you are!'

Celia forced herself to hold her tongue. Engaging in a shouting match with the dowager would serve no purpose. 'Only two for now, but I am confident our finances will soon improve and Adele may order more.'

Her conscience niggled. How many times had

her father purchased something, saying he'd win enough to pay for it?

Lady Gale pursed her thin lips. 'And I am to wear my old rags, I suppose.'

Celia's smile froze. 'You may order two gowns for yourself, if you like.'

'Will you come with us tonight, Celia?' Adele looked hopeful. She was too kind to say she did not find her grandmother's company altogether pleasant at such gatherings.

Celia calculated what time the musicale would end. It would still give her time to attend the gaming house for a few hours of play. 'If you wish.'

'I do!' Adele's countenance brightened.

Her grandmother rolled her eyes. 'You will dress properly, I hope.'

'I will, indeed.' Celia always dressed properly. Her most daring gown was the one she'd worn to the Masquerade Club the night before. Its neckline had always seemed too low. She'd only worn it because she thought no one would recognise her in it, as if anyone at these society events noticed what she wore. None the less, she would change into it to wear to the gaming house tonight, as well.

She turned to Adele. 'Why don't you see if Younie has any ideas of how to alter one of your old gowns for tonight? She is very clever at that sort of thing.'

Adele jumped to her feet. 'An excellent idea! I

will do that right away.' She started for the door. 'I beg your leave, Grandmama.'

Lady Gale waved her away. 'Go.' She called after Adele. 'Younie is in my room, Adele. She is mending.'

Adele skipped away and Lady Gale turned to Celia. 'I do not see why my granddaughter and I must share your lady's maid.'

Celia kept her voice even. 'Because we do not have the funds to hire more servants.'

'Money!' the older woman huffed. 'That is all you ever talk of.'

Money had consumed her thoughts, Celia would be the first to admit. Except this day thoughts of money were mixed with combinations of hearts, spades, clubs and diamonds.

Would Rhysdale be pleased at her return? Celia wondered.

She gave herself a good shake. Why was she even thinking of the man? It was not a good thing that she had come to his notice, no matter how attractively masculine he was. She planned to win and win often.

What if he accused her of cheating?

Lady Devine's musicale was a sought-after event and Celia's mother-in-law said more than once how lucky they were to have received an invitation. Celia, Adele and Lady Gale were announced amidst Lady Gale's grumbling that they ought to have had a gentleman escorting them.

They strolled through the rooms where the pink of the *ton* were assembled. Celia recognised some of the men as having been at the gaming house the previous night and she wondered how many more of these people—ladies especially—had been there, as well, but wearing masks as she had done.

Some of the gentlemen's faces at this entertainment had been quite animated at the gaming house, impassioned by the cards or the dice. Here in this Mayfair town house their expressions were bland. It seemed as if the risks of winning or losing made them come alive.

She did not know their names. The *ton* were known to her only from newspaper articles or books on the peerage. When her parents had been alive she'd been too young for London society. By the time she was married, her husband chose to keep her in the country so as not to interfere with his other 'interests.' The arrangement had suited her well enough. She preferred him to be away.

If she had been with him in London, though, she might have had some warning of his profligacy and the condition of his finances. She would have seen in him the telltale signs of gambling lust. Her childhood had honed her for it.

Her mother-in-law ought to have known how debauched her son had become. Lady Gale had spent most of her time in London as part of the social scene. In fact, it was because of Celia's mother-in-law that they received as many invitations as they did. But her mother-in-law would never countenance anything negative being said about her only son.

Except his choice of a second wife.

One of the men who had been at the gaming hell passed close by. Celia had an impulse to ask her mother-in-law who the gentleman was, but Lady Gale gestured to her dismissively before she could speak.

'Get me a glass of wine,' the older woman ordered. 'It is so tedious not to have a man about to perform such niceties.'

'I will get it for you, Grandmama,' Adele said. 'Do not trouble Celia.'

Before either lady could protest, Adele disappeared through the crowd.

Lady Gale pursed her lips at Celia, but something quickly caught her eye. 'Look. There is our cousin Luther.'

Luther was second cousin to Celia's husband. And he was the new Baron Gale.

Needless to say, Luther was none too pleased at the state of his inheritance, mortgaged to the hilt, all reserves depleted. He had not the least inclination to offer any financial assistance to the former baron's mother, daughter or wife, as a result.

'Yoo-hoo! Luther!' Lady Gale waved.

The man tried to ignore her but, with a resigned look upon his face, walked over to where they stood. 'Good evening, ladies.' He bowed. 'I trust you are well.'

'We are exceeding well,' Lady Gale chirped, suddenly as bright and cheerful as she'd previously been sullen. 'And you, sir?'

'Tolerable,' he muttered, his eyes straying to elsewhere in the room.

'My granddaughter is here, Luther, dear,' she went on. 'You will want to greet her, I am sure.'

Luther looked as if he'd desire anything but.

'It is her Season, do you recall?' Lady Gale fluttered her lashes as if she were the girl having her Season. 'We expect many suitors.'

'Do you?' Luther appeared to search for a means of escape.

'Her dowry is respectable, you know.' That was because her father, Celia's husband, had been unable to get his hands on it.

Luther's brows rose in interest. 'Is that so?'

Celia felt a sudden dread. Surely Lady Gale would not try to make a match between Adele and Luther? Luther had already proved to be excessively unkind. After all, he'd taken over Gale House as soon as Celia's year of mourning was completed, removing Celia, Adele and Lady Gale without an offer of another residence. Even now he was rattling around in the London town house by himself when he could very easily have hosted

the three women for the Season. That simple act
would have saved Celia plenty of money and
would have given Adele more prestige.

'Gale!' some gentleman called. 'Are you coming?'

Luther did not hesitate. 'If you will pardon me.'
He bowed again.

'But,' Lady Gale spoke to his retreating back,
'you have not yet greeted Adele!'

'He can see Adele another time,' Celia assured
her. 'In fact, he could call upon us, which would
be the civil thing for him to do.'

Lady Gale flicked her away as if she were an
annoying fly. 'He is much too busy. He is a peer
now, you know.'

A peer who cared nothing for his relations.

Adele returned, carrying two glasses of wine.
'I brought one for you, too, Celia.' She handed a
glass to her grandmother and one to Celia.

Adele was always so considerate. Sometimes
Celia wondered how the girl could share the same
blood as her father and grandmother.

Lady Gale snapped, 'Adele, you missed our
cousin, Luther. He was here but a moment ago.'
She made it sound as if Adele should have known
to come back earlier.

'Oh?' Adele responded brightly. Did Adele simply ignore her grandmother's chiding or did she
not hear it? 'I have wanted to meet him and ask

how all the people are at Gale House. I do miss them!'

One of Lady Gale's friends found her and the two women were quickly engaged in a lively conversation.

Adele leaned close to Celia. 'The kindest gentleman assisted me. I—I do not know if I properly thanked him. I must do so if I see him again.'

Celia smiled at her. 'You will be meeting many gentlemen this Season.' She so wanted Adele to pick a steady, responsible, generous man.

Luther was certainly not generous.

'You grandmother will wish to select your suitors, you know,' Celia added.

Adele frowned. 'I do want her to be pleased with me.'

Celia sipped her wine. 'You must please yourself first of all.'

Adele would not be pushed into a marriage she did not want and should not have to endure— as Celia had been. Celia would make certain of it.

The start of the programme was announced and Lady Gale gestured impatiently for Celia and Adele to follow her while she continued in deep conversation with her friend. They took their chairs and soon the music began.

Lady Devine had hired musicians and singers to perform the one-act French opera, *Le Calife de Bagdad* by Boieldieu. The comic opera was ideal for an audience who were intent on marriage matches. In the opera, the mother of the ingenue Zétulbé, refuses to allow the girl to marry the Caliph of Baghdad, who meets her disguised as an ordinary man. When he tries to impress the family with extravagant gifts, the mother merely thinks he is a brigand.

It should be every family's fear—that the man marrying their daughter is not what he seems. It certainly was Celia's fear for Adele. If only Celia's experience had been more like Zétulbé's, discovering the generous and loving prince disguised as something less. Celia's husband had been the opposite. Presented by her guardians as a fine, upstanding man, but truly a cruel and thoughtless one in disguise.

As the music enveloped Celia she wondered if all men hid their true colours.

Of course, she disguised herself, too. She pretended to be a respectable lady, but she visited a gaming hell at night. Once there, she disguised herself again by wearing a mask and pretending to be a gambler, when gambling and gamblers were what she detested most in the world.

The tenor playing the Caliph's part stepped forwards to sing of his love for Zétulbé. Celia closed her eyes and tried to merely enjoy the music. An image of Rhysdale flashed through her mind. Like the tenor's, Rhysdale's voice had teemed with seduction.

* * *

Rhys watched the door from the moment he opened the gambling house. He watched for her—the woman in the black-and-gold mask.

'Who are you expecting?' Xavier asked him. 'Someone to make our fortunes or to take it all away?'

He shrugged. 'The woman I told you about last night.'

Xavier's brow furrowed. 'This is not the time for a conquest, Rhys. Your future depends upon making this place a success.'

Xavier was not saying anything Rhys had not said multiple times to himself. Still, he flushed with anger. 'I will not neglect my responsibilities.'

Xavier did not back down. 'Women are trouble.'

Rhys laughed. 'That is the pot calling the kettle black, is it not? You are rarely without a female on your arm.'

'Women attach themselves to me, that is true.' Xavier's blue eyes and poetic good looks drew women like magnets. 'But I've yet to meet one who could distract me from what I've set myself to do.'

'I did not say she was a distraction. Or a conquest.' Rhys tried to convince himself as well as his friend. 'I am curious about her. She is a gamester like me and that is what intrigues me.'

Xavier scoffed. 'Is that why you warned me away last night?'

Rhys frowned. 'That prohibition still stands. I do not wish to have *you* distract *her*.' He paused, knowing he was not being entirely truthful. 'I want to see what transpires with this woman gamester.'

Xavier gave him a sceptical look.

Truth was, Rhys did not know what to make of his attraction to the masked lady gamester. Xavier was correct. The woman did tempt him in ways that were more carnal than curious.

But not enough to ignore his commitment to the gaming hell, not when his main objective was to show the Westleighs he could succeed in precisely the same world in which his father failed.

The buzzing of voices hushed momentarily. Rhys glanced to the doorway as she walked in, dressed in the same gown and mask as the night before. Sound muffled and the lamps grew brighter.

His body indeed thought of her in a carnal way. 'There she is.'

He left Xavier and crossed the room to her. 'Madam, you have returned. I am flattered.'

She put a hand on her chest. 'I have indeed returned, Mr Rhysdale. Would you be so kind as to find a whist partner for me once again?'

Xavier appeared at his side. 'It would be my pleasure to partner you, madam.'

Rhys glared at him before turning back to the masked woman. 'May I present Mr Campion, madam. He is a friend and an excellent card player.'

She extended her gloved hand. 'Mr Campion.'

Xavier accepted with a bow. 'I am charmed.' He smiled his most seductive smile at her. 'Do me the honour of calling me Xavier. No one need stand on ceremony in a gaming hell.'

Rhys groaned inwardly.

'Xavier, then,' she responded.

He threaded her hand through his arm. 'Do you wish to play deep, madam?'

She did not answer right away. 'Not too deep, for the moment. But neither do I wish a tame game.'

Xavier nodded in approval. 'Excellent. Let us go in search of players.'

He looked back at Rhys and winked.

Rhys knew Xavier well enough to understand his intent was merely to annoy. Xavier would always honour his wishes in matters such as this. Rhys was less certain about the lady. Most women preferred Xavier to Rhys. Most women preferred Xavier to any man.

Rhys went back to patrolling the room, watching the play, speaking to the croupiers running the tables. He kept a keen eye out for cheating in those winning too conveniently and desperation in those losing. Gamblers could easily burst out in sudden violence when the cards or the dice did not go their way. Rhys's plan was to intervene before tempers grew hot.

His eyes always pulled back to the masked woman. She sat across from Xavier, posture alert, but not tense. Tonight her handling of the cards was smoother than the night before. She arranged her hand swiftly and never belaboured a decision of what card to play. She'd said she preferred games of skill and she was quite skilled at whist.

She was a gamester, for certain. Rhys could wager on that. He'd also bet that she remembered every card played and that she quickly perceived the unique patterns of play in her partners and her opponents.

He strolled over to the table to watch more closely.

'How is the game?' He stood behind the masked woman.

Xavier looked at him with amusement. 'We make good partners.'

Judging from the counters on the table, Xavier and the masked woman made very good partners indeed. Card partners, that was.

Rhys stood where he could see the woman's cards. If it bothered her, she gave no sign. He watched the play for several hands. She was clever. Deal her four trump and she was certain to win with three of them at least. Give her a hand with no trump and she took tricks with other cards when trump was not played.

She was a gamester all right.

He instantly looked on her with respect.

But, as fascinated as he was watching her play, he needed to move on. No gambler wanted such acute attention to his or her play, especially by the house's proprietor.

Rhys sauntered away.

An unmasked Ned Westleigh approached him. 'How are things faring?' Ned asked in a conspiratorial tone.

Rhys lifted his brows and raised his voice. 'Why, good evening, Lord Neddington. Good to see you back here.'

'Well?' Ned persisted.

'We are near to recouping the original investment,' Rhys replied. 'So all is as it should be.'

'Excellent.' Ned rubbed his hands together.

'There is more to our bargain, do not forget,' Rhys added.

He expected these Westleighs to try to renege on the earl's obligation to claim Rhys as a son. More than once Rhys wondered why he'd made that part of the bargain. Another man might wish for the connection to the aristocracy such an acknowledgement might bring, but Rhys cared nothing for that. Neither was the money he'd reap from this enterprise a motivation. He could always make money.

No, all Rhys really wanted was to force his father to do what he ought to have done when Rhys was a child—take responsibility for Rhys's existence. Once that was accomplished, Rhys was content to spurn him and his sons as they had once spurned him.

'Hugh and I do not forget,' Ned said in a low voice. 'Our father…requires some time.'

Rhys lifted a shoulder. 'I will not release the money until that part of the promise is assured.' The Westleighs, in their desperation, had ceded all the power in this matter to him.

Rhys glanced over to the masked woman and caught her looking back. She quickly attended to her cards.

Rhysdale was talking to the gentleman Celia had seen earlier at the musicale, she noticed. It was fortunate she had changed her gown, even though she doubted the gentleman would have noticed her. The widow of a dissolute baron who never brought his wife to town did not capture anyone's attention.

Rhysdale caught her watching and she quickly turned back to the cards and played her last trump. She guessed Xavier still had two trumps remaining. That should ensure they won this hand.

They'd won most of the games and each time Celia felt a surge of triumph. Their opponents, however, grew ever-deepening frowns. Xavier took the next trick and the next and the game was theirs.

Their opponents grumbled.

Celia shuffled the deck and the man on her right cut the cards. She dealt the hand and the play began, but this time Xavier did not play in the manner to which she'd accustomed herself. The opponents took tricks they ought to have lost. Xavier suddenly was playing very sloppily indeed. He was losing *her* money. She gave him a stern glance, but he seemed oblivious.

When the hand was done, the opponents won most of the tricks and won the game, to their great delight. Luckily that game's wagers had been modest, but Celia's blood boiled at losing so senselessly.

'That was capital!' the man on her right said. 'I'm done for now, however. Excellent play.' He stood, collected his small pile of counters and bowed to Celia. 'Well done, madam.' He turned to Xavier. 'You chose a capital partner, sir. We must play again.'

'I'm done, as well,' the other man said.

Both begged their leave and wandered over to the hazard table.

'They must wish to lose more,' Xavier remarked.

Celia gathered her counters. 'You let them win that last game.'

'You noticed?' Xavier laughed. 'Better they

leave happy. Otherwise they might choose other opponents next time.'

Her eyes widened. 'You made certain they would be willing to play us again.'

He nodded. 'Precisely.'

He smiled and his incredibly handsome face grew even more handsome. He'd been an excellent partner, she had to admit. She now possessed even more money than she'd won the night before. Still, she sensed he'd had motives of his own for partnering her, something that had nothing to do with trying to win at cards.

Another man hiding something.

She stood and extended her hand to him. 'It was a pleasure, sir.'

His smile flashed again. 'The pleasure was mine.' He held her hand a moment too long for her liking. 'What's next for you? The hazard table?'

She shrugged. '*Vingt-et-un*, perhaps.'

'Ah, there is a *vingt-et-un* table. Let me take you to it and see if we can get you in that game.'

Vingt-et-un was another game where she could exercise her skill. All she need do was remember the cards played and bet accordingly.

Xavier led her to the large round table with a dealer at one end and players all around. Xavier facilitated her entry into the game and it soon occupied all her concentration.

When the croupier reshuffled the cards, she glanced up.

Mr Rhysdale was again watching her. He nodded, acknowledging that she'd again caught him watching. She nodded in return and refocused on the cards.

Time passed swiftly and Celia's excitement grew. She was winning even more than the night before. Her reticule was heavy with counters. She fished into it and pulled out her watch.

Quarter after three.

In only a few minutes her coach would arrive and she still must cash out.

Mr Rhysdale appeared at her elbow. 'Almost time for your coach, madam?'

Her senses flared with his nearness. 'Yes.'

He touched her elbow. 'I will escort you.'

'That is not necessary, sir.' His attention made it hard for her to think. And to breathe.

He touched her reticule. 'I cannot allow you to walk into the night alone. Especially with a full purse.'

As he had done the night before, he escorted her to the cashier and waited for her while the hall servant collected her wrap. He again walked her out the door and onto the pavement.

It had apparently rained. The street shone from the wet and reflected the rush lights as if in a mirror. From a distance, the rhythmic clopping of horses' hooves and the creaking of coach wheels echoed in the damp air. Celia's coach was not in sight.

Rhysdale stood next to her. 'How did you find the cards tonight, madam?'

She closed her hand around her reticule. 'Quite satisfying.' She glanced down the street again. 'Although I may not spend much time at *vingt-et-un* after this.' She feared he would catch on that she had been counting the cards.

'You did not lose.' He spoke this as a fact, not a question.

She smiled. 'I try not to lose.'

His voice turned low. 'I noticed.'

Her face warmed.

'You have an excellent memory for cards, do you not?' he went on.

Her stomach knotted. He knew. 'Is that a problem?'

'Not for me,' he responded. 'Not as yet.'

Her hands trembled. 'Are you warning me away?'

'Not at all.' His tone remained matter of fact. 'If I saw you make wagers that would jeopardise my establishment, I would certainly warn you away from my tables, but, as long as you play fair, it matters not to me how much you win off of any gentleman brave enough to challenge you.'

'Do you suspect me of cheating?' The very idea filled her with dread.

And reminded her of her father.

He shook his head. 'You are a skilled player.' He paused. 'I admire that.'

She relaxed for a moment, then glanced down the street, looking for Jonah, her coachman.

'Who taught you to play?' Rhysdale continued conversationally.

She averted her gaze, not willing to reveal the pain she knew would show in her face. 'My father.' Her throat grew dry. 'He once was also a skilled player.'

Before he died.

She faced Rhys again, wanting to take the focus off of her. 'And who taught you to play, sir?'

He made a disparaging sound. 'Certainly not *my* father.' He looked reluctant to tell her more. 'I learned in school, but I honed my craft later when it became necessary.'

'Why necessary?' she asked.

It was his turn to glance away, but he soon faced her again. 'I was living on the streets.'

She was shocked. 'On the streets?'

He shrugged. 'When I was fourteen, I had no one and nothing. I came to London and learned to support myself by playing cards.'

No one and nothing?

How well she remembered the desolation of no one and nothing.

She opened her mouth to ask why he'd been alone, what had happened to his parents, but her coach turned the corner and entered the street. She was silent as it pulled up to where they stood.

As he had done the night before, he put down the steps for her and opened the door.

He took her hand and helped her inside, but did not immediately release it. 'Will you come play cards again, madam?' His voice seemed to fill the night.

She wanted to return. She wanted to win more.

And she wanted to see him again.

All seemed equally dangerous.

'I will return, sir.'

He squeezed her hand.

After he released her and closed the coach door, Celia could still feel the pressure of his fingers.

Chapter Four

Ned waited until almost noon for his father to rise and make his appearance in the breakfast room. He'd tried to confront his father on this issue before and knew he must catch him before he went out or he'd lose another day.

Hugh had waited with Ned most of the morning, but stormed out a few minutes ago, swearing about their father's decadent habits.

Not more than a minute later Ned heard his father's distinct footsteps approaching.

Wasn't it always the way? When Ned needed Hugh, his brother disappeared.

The earl entered the room, but paused for a moment, spying his oldest son there.

He gave Ned an annoyed look. 'I thought to have breakfast in peace.'

Ned stood. 'Good morning to you as well, Father.'

His father walked straight to the sideboard and filled his plate with food that had already been replaced three times. The earl detested cold eggs. 'Do you not have something of use to do? Itemising my bills? Recording my debt in a ledger?'

Ned bristled at his father's sarcastic tone. 'You ought to be grateful to me and to Hugh.'

His father sat down at the head of the table. A footman appeared to pour his tea. Ned signalled for the footman to leave.

His father waited until the door closed behind the man. 'I am anything but grateful that you treat me as a doddering fool. Makes me look bad in front of the servants.'

Ned sat adjacent to his father. 'You were the one to speak of bills and debts in front of Higgley.'

His father glared at him and stuffed his mouth full of ham.

Ned went on. 'But I do need to speak to you.'

His father rolled his eyes.

Ned did not waver. 'It has been a month since Rhysdale opened the gaming house and you have yet to fulfil your part of the bargain.'

'You truly do not expect me to speak to that fellow, do you?' He popped a cooked egg into his mouth.

'Speak to him?' Ned felt his face grow hot. 'You gave your word as a gentleman to do more than that. We need to include him socially. You need to acknowledge he is your son.'

His father waved a hand. 'I already did my part. I sent him to school. What more can he want?'

Ned gritted his teeth. 'You agreed to this, Father. Rhysdale has already amassed the amount we invested to get the place started. But he will not release the money until you do what you are honour-bound to do.'

'Honour?' His father's voice rose. 'Do you call it honourable that *he* is holding *my* money? It is more like extortion, I'd say.'

'I'd say it is more like sound business,' Ned countered. 'Rhysdale is no fool. The money is his leverage. You must do as he says.'

'I do not have to do anything I do not wish to do.'

Good God. The man sounded like a petulant schoolboy.

Ned would not put up with it. 'Father. You must do this. We are running out of time. No one will advance you more credit. The fields need tending. The livestock need feed. Our tenants need to eat—'

At that moment Hugh entered the room. 'Your voice is carrying, Ned.'

So much for keeping this private from the servants—not that one could keep anything secret from servants for long.

'Where were you?' he asked Hugh.

Hugh looked apologetic. 'I was going mad waiting for Father. I just took a quick walk outside.'

He sat across from Ned and poured a cup of tea.

'Father is reneging on his word.' Ned inclined his head towards their father.

Hugh took a sip. 'I presumed.' He slid his father a scathing look. 'Your bastard son has more honour than you, you know. He's kept his part of the bargain.'

Their father straightened in his seat. 'I'll brook no disrespect from you, you ungrateful cub.'

Hugh faced the earl directly, his face red with anger. 'Then be a man I can respect, sir! Do what you agreed to do. Introduce Rhys to society as your son. You gave your word.'

'Only to the two of you,' their father prevaricated. 'I never gave my word to him.'

Ned lowered his voice. 'Your word given to your sons means nothing, then?'

Hugh rose from his chair. 'Let him go, Ned! He is not thinking of us. Nor of the Westleigh estates. Nor the Westleigh people. Let him watch his creditors come ransack the house, carrying away our heritage and that of our own sons. He cares nothing for nobody. Only for himself.'

'See here, you cur!' the earl cried, jumping to his feet.

Ned stood and extended his arms, gesturing for them both to sit down. He had one more card to play. 'Let us bring Mother into this conversation.'

'You'll do no such thing!' his father cried.

'Ned's right.' Hugh seized on this idea immediately. 'Mother needs to know what a sorry excuse for a gentleman you've become.'

Ned suspected their mother already knew what a sorry creature her husband was. But she probably did not know the extent of his debt and the dire consequences that were imminent unless they could begin paying the creditors. This information would certainly shock her.

She, of course, knew of Rhys's existence and Ned did feel sorry that she must endure the humiliation of having him welcomed into the family.

'Very well,' the earl snapped. 'I'll go the gaming hell and make nice to Rhysdale. I'll do that much.'

'You'll have to do more,' Ned warned him.

The earl nodded. 'Yes. Yes.' His tone turned resigned. 'But first I want to see this place and ascertain for myself whether he is swindling us or not.'

'He is not swindling us!' Hugh said hotly.

Their father ignored him. 'If all is as it should be, then we may plan how to divulge the rest to your mother.'

Rhys wandered through the tables of the gaming house, watching the gamblers, perusing the croupiers at their work. He wished he had more eyes, more people he could trust to check on the tables. To make certain the croupiers stayed honest and the gamblers refrained from cheating. With so much money changing hands every night, it was a rare man or woman who would not at some time or another become tempted.

Cheating was the great danger of a gaming house. Gentlemen could accept losing huge amounts in honest games, but the whiff of a dishonest house might swiftly destroy everything.

He also had to admit to watching for the masked woman to arrive. She'd been attending almost every night. Whenever she came, Rhys contrived to spend a few minutes alone with her.

The mystery of her sometimes filled his thoughts.

Where had she come from? Who was she? Why had she chosen gambling to make money?

She had a life outside the gaming hell, a life she wished to protect, that much he understood. Was she married and hiding her gambling from her husband? He hoped not. Married women held no appeal for him.

He'd had some opportunity to attend the Royal Opera House and Drury Lane Theatre. He and Xavier had joined Xavier's parents in their theatre box. But Rhys had seen no one who resembled her. He knew he would recognise her without her mask. He'd memorised her eyes, her mouth, the way she moved.

He glanced up at the doorway, for the hundredth time. But it was not she who appeared.

He stiffened. 'Well, well,' he said to himself, looking around to see if Xavier noticed, but his friend was deep in play.

Earl Westleigh sauntered in with one of his cronies.

Rhys had spied the earl from time to time in the two years he'd been back from the war. He and the earl had sometimes gambled at the same establishments. At those times, though, Rhys doubted the earl noticed him. Even if he had, how would he recognise Rhys now from the scrawny fourteen-year-old he'd been when he'd begged the earl for help?

Rhys watched the earl survey the room in his self-important way. He leaned over to say something to his friend and both men laughed.

Rhys flexed his fingers into a fist, feeling as though the men were laughing at his youthful self, near-helpless and so desperately alone. He was not alone here. Not helpless. This was *his* place. Under his control. His to build into a success beyond any of the earl's expectations.

He straightened his spine.

'Where is the owner of this establishment?' Lord Westleigh asked in a booming voice. 'I should like to see him.'

Rhys turned to one of the croupiers and asked the man about the play at his faro table. It was the

sort of surveillance he might do, but this time, of
course, his motive was to avoid responding to the
earl's beck and call.

Out of the corner of his eye he saw someone
point him out to Lord Westleigh. He also saw
Xavier looking up from his play, his gaze going
from the earl to Rhys. Xavier appeared ready to
vault out of his chair, daggers drawn.

Rhys did not need his friend's aid. He could
handle the earl. He knew he was the better man.

He deliberately busied himself with checking
the faro deck, but the hairs on the back of his neck
rose when Westleigh came near.

'Rhysdale!' The earl made his name sound like
an order.

Rhys did not respond right away, but finished
replacing the faro deck in its apparatus.

Slowly he raised his eyes to the earl. 'Lord
Westleigh,' he said in a flat voice.

'I've come to see what people are talking about.
A gaming hell and a masquerade.' He made a
somewhat disparaging laugh.

'What do you wish to play?' Rhys asked, treat-
ing him like any other gentleman—but with a bit
more coldness.

'I fancy some faro,' the earl's companion said.
'Haven't tried my hand at faro in an age.'

It was a game going out of fashion, but still
making enough here to satisfy Rhys.

'I do not know you, sir.' Rhys extended his

hand to the man. 'I am Mr Rhysdale and, as the earl so loudly announced, I am the owner.'

The man clasped his hand. 'Sir Godfrey's the name.'

Rhys made room for Sir Godfrey at the faro table. 'I hope you enjoy yourself, sir.'

He turned to Lord Westleigh. 'And you, sir, what is your fancy?'

Lord Westleigh's attention had turned to the doorway where the masked woman for whom Rhys had been waiting all night entered.

'I'd fancy that,' the earl said under his breath.

Rhys's fingers curled into a fist again.

He stepped in front of the earl, blocking his view of the woman. 'This is an establishment for gambling and nothing more. Do you comprehend?' His voice was low and firm. 'The ladies who play here will be left in peace. Am I speaking clearly enough?'

Lord Westleigh pursed his lips. 'Meant no harm.'

Rhys narrowed his eyes.

Westleigh glanced away. 'My sons tell me this establishment is making money. Is that true?'

'It is true.' Rhys guessed the earl wanted his share. Not a damned chance until he met his part of the bargain.

'But you have not paid my sons a farthing.' Westleigh had the gall to look affronted.

Rhys levelled his gaze at the man. 'It is you who have held up payment, sir. I await you.'

'Yes. Well.' Westleigh looked everywhere but at Rhys. 'It is complicated.'

Rhys laughed dryly. 'And distasteful to you, I might imagine.' He shook his head. 'Matters not to me whether you do this or not. This place is making me rich.' He walked away.

Rhys had begged once from his father, but never again. Let his father beg from him this time.

As soon as she walked in the room, Celia's gaze went directly to Rhysdale. He stood with an older man, a gentleman, to judge by the fit and fabric of his coat. This man had not visited the gaming house before, at least not when she'd been here, and she had not seen him at the few society functions she attended with Adele and Lady Gale.

Whoever this man was, Rhysdale did not seem pleased at his presence. That piqued her curiosity even more.

She detested herself for looking for Rhysdale as soon as she walked through the door, for wondering about who he was with and how he felt about it.

As the days had gone on, she'd come to enjoy his attentions.

It felt almost like having a friend.

She turned away and made her way through the room, returning greetings from players to whom she was now a familiar figure. She no longer needed Rhysdale to find her a game of whist; plenty of men and some ladies were glad to play.

She passed by Xavier Campion. That man's eyes usually followed her, not with the interest of other gentlemen. She swore he watched her with suspicion. Tonight, however, Xavier watched Rhysdale and his brow was furrowed.

Who was that man?

Rhysdale turned away from the gentleman and walked away, his expression one of distaste and suppressed rage.

She lowered her gaze and set about finding a whist partner.

Not too long after, she was seated at a table and arranging a hand of cards into suits. Still, she was acutely aware of whenever Rhysdale passed near.

She no longer feared he was trying to catch her cheating. She liked his attention. It seemed as if the air crackled with energy when he was near, like it might before a summer storm. She liked him.

Even though he made his living from gambling.

To her distress, the cards did not favour her this night. Even when she had partnered with Xavier, she lost hand after hand. Counting in her head, she knew it was not a trifling amount. She kept playing, thinking the next hand would turn her luck around. When that did not happen, she counted on the hand after that.

As the night advanced, her pile of counters grew lower and lower. She'd lost over half the money she staked. Still, the urge was strong to keep playing, to bet more, to keep going so she could change it all back to the way it had been before.

But still she lost.

Celia stared at her counters and came to her senses. *Stop!* she told herself. *Before you return home with nothing.*

She stood up abruptly. 'I am done.'

Before the others at her table could protest, she hurried away and made her way to the cashier. She wanted the counters changed back to coin so she would not be tempted to return to the games.

It was only two in the morning, too early to wait outside for her coachman. Instead, after cashing in her counters, she walked to the supper room, not hungry, but greatly desiring a glass of wine or two to quiet her nerves.

Several of the tables were occupied, but her gaze went instantly to the table where she'd sat before with Rhysdale.

He was there, staring into nothing, a glass in hand.

She approached him, needing at least the illusion of a friend. 'Hello, Rhysdale.'

He glanced at her with a look of surprise that turned into a smile. 'The lady with the mask.' He stood and pulled out a chair. 'Would you care to sit with me?'

She sat.

'What is your pleasure?' he asked. 'Shall I fix a plate for you?'

'Wine.' She sighed. 'Just wine.'

He signalled a servant to bring her wine.

Now that she'd so brazenly approached him, she did not know what to say.

'How was your night?' he asked finally.

'Not good,' she replied.

What more was there to say? Losing called into serious question her whole plan to finance Adele's come-out with winnings. Worse than that, it showed how easily she could slip into a gambling fever where nothing mattered but trying to win back her money.

The wine arrived and she quickly downed half of it.

His brows rose. 'Bring the bottle,' he told the servant and turned back to her. 'I take it you lost.'

Her fingers drummed the tabletop. 'I did.'

He reached across the table and quieted her busy hand. 'Do you need assistance? Are you in distress?'

She glanced into his eyes, which conveyed only concern and earnestness. His hand was warm against hers, even through the thin fabric of her glove.

She slipped her hand away, shaken at how comforting his touch felt and how much she needed comfort.

'I'll come to rights,' she said, although her voice lacked any semblance of confidence.

'I can lend you money,' he went on.

She shook her head. 'I know better than to borrow from moneylenders.'

His eyes flashed. 'I am not a moneylender. I offer as a friend.'

She took in a breath. 'But…you do not even know who I am.'

He traced the edge of her mask with a finger. 'Tell me, then. Who are you?'

She sat very still at his gentle touch while her heart fluttered in her chest.

'I am nobody,' she said, speaking with a truth that had been proved over and over. She had not mattered enough for anyone to care what the impact of their actions would be to her.

She raised her eyes to his.

His promise seemed so genuine, as if he was a man she could believe. Would he truly lend her money if she needed it? And then what? Without gambling she could not repay him. What would she do then? Turn to moneylenders?

She shivered as the memory of her father returned. He had to sell her pony, he'd told her. He had to pay the moneylenders. Life after that had been filled with more times of want than times of plenty.

Until the day her mother told her news even more horrible than losing a pony. Her father was dead. He'd been accused of cheating at cards and a man—an earl—had shot him dead in a duel.

'I do not need a loan,' she said absently, still caught in the memory of her father's senseless death.

At every society entertainment she feared she would encounter her father's killer. What would she do then?

Rhys spoke. 'But you need money.'

'I'll find another way.' Although she knew there was no other way.

She, Adele and Lady Gale would have to find a set of rooms that Celia's widow's pension could afford. She'd have to let the servants go and Adele's chances of making a good marriage would become extremely slim. At least Celia would not have to encounter the earl who killed her father.

She finished her glass of wine as the servant placed the bottle on the table. Rhysdale poured her another.

'Thank you.' She lifted the glass and decided to push the attention off herself. 'What of you, Rhysdale? When I came in you looked as if you were the one who had lost money.'

A corner of his mouth rose. 'The house never loses, you know. We are doing well.'

She smiled. 'I am glad of it. You seem to have more players each time I've come.'

'More women, as well.' Again he touched her mask. 'The Masquerade seems to be working.'

She put her fingers where his had touched. 'It has worked for me.'

He sat back. 'Until now.'

She shrugged. 'I shall have to consider whether to come again and try to recoup.'

He leaned forwards again. 'Do you mean to say you might not return?'

'I might not.' She paused. 'I should not.'

'Do not say so!'

Her heart started pounding faster again. She took another sip of wine. 'Does one gambler matter so much?'

His gaze seemed to pierce into her. He did not answer right away. Finally he said, 'I believe there are men who come merely in hopes of playing with you.'

She scoffed. 'Surely you are not serious.' She supposed the men who'd partnered with her and those who played against her recognised her skill. 'In any event, I doubt any man will want to partner with me after my losing streak tonight.'

She'd not only lost her own money, but her partners' money, as well.

'You place so little value on yourself?' He continued to pin her with his eyes.

No one else had valued her.

She glanced down. 'Who wants to partner with someone who is losing?'

He drummed on the table like she had done earlier, while his steady gaze began to unnerve her.

'I have a proposition,' he said finally. 'Come work for me.'

Rhys did not know why he had not thought of this before.

Hire her.

'What do you mean, work for you?' She looked shocked. 'Doing what?'

'Gambling,' he rushed to assure her. 'Nothing more.' The idea grew in his head as he spoke. 'I would pay you to gamble. And to encourage others to gamble, as well.'

Her eyes through her mask grew wary. 'Am I to cheat?'

He waved a hand. 'Never! It is not cheating to pay you to gamble. You will receive no advantage.'

She glanced away, as if deliberating.

It gave him time to think, as well. Would he compromise the gambling house by paying her to gamble? He only knew he wanted her to come back. He needed her to come back.

She turned back to him. 'How much would you pay?'

He threw out the first number that occurred to him. 'Two pounds a night?'

'Two pounds?' She looked astonished.

Was that not enough? He paid his man only fifty pounds a year. 'That is more than generous, madam.'

She sat very still, but he fancied her mind was calculating.

Finally she spoke. 'I need money, sir, but if my task is to gamble, then, as generous as two pounds a night might be, it does not allow me to play for bigger stakes. What is more, I still stand a chance that I will lose as I have lost tonight. That I cannot risk.'

She had a point. In gambling there was always the possibility of losing it all.

He wanted her to agree, though. He wanted to see her again. If he did not offer enough to entice her, she might never return.

He tapped on the table again. 'Very well. I will stake you.' He thought for a minute. 'Say, for one hundred pounds. At the end of the night, you return my stake to me but keep your winnings. If you lose, you make an accounting to me of the loss.' If she lost too often, he'd reassess this plan, but his gamble was that she would bring in more money than she would lose.

Her eyes showed interest. 'Do I still receive the two pounds a night?'

He was not that big a fool. 'One pound. Plus your winnings.'

She calculated again, her eyes on his. What did she look like under her mask? He imagined lifting it off her face, discovering the treasure underneath.

In the back of his mind he could hear Xavier's voice, questioning his motives, accusing him of succumbing to the first pretty lightskirt who'd caught his eye in a long time.

She was not a lightskirt, but Rhys would wager she belonged on the fringes of society as did he. His money was still on her being an actress.

She opened her lovely mouth and, God help him, all he could think of was tasting her lips. She was about to agree—he could feel it.

Celia was so tempted. He'd handed her a way to gamble without losing her money. What could be better than that? What did it matter, then, if she succumbed to the excitement of the game? Losing would not imperil her.

It was as if he was handing her the future she so desired. To see Adele well settled. To retire to the country and live quietly within her means with no one directing her life but herself.

Rhysdale did not press her. He poured her another glass of wine and waited.

She accepted the glass gratefully and took a long sip, but even the wine did not loosen the knots of panic inside her.

He'd offered her this help as a friend. When had she last had a friend? For that matter, when had she last been able to trust a man? Even her beloved father broke promise after promise.

What if she refused Rhysdale's offer? Her mind spun with what she would have to do to economise. She'd have to try to pay back most of the creditors. She'd have to give up her coachman, her carriage, her servants. She'd have little left for rooms to let and food to eat. Adele did not deserve such a life. Even her mother-in-law did not deserve such a life.

Rhysdale's gaze was patient and, she fancied, sympathetic. 'You are not required to decide this minute. Come to me tomorrow, in the afternoon.' He glanced about the room. 'We can discuss it without anyone around.' His voice deepened. 'If you refuse employment, my offer of a loan still stands.'

She felt tears prick her eyes. 'You are kind, Rhysdale.'

A smile grew slowly across his face. 'Do not say so too loudly or you will ruin my reputation.'

She almost laughed.

Some gentlemen entered the room and she came to her senses. 'What time is it?' She fished into her reticule to check her timepiece. 'I must take my leave.'

He stood and offered his hand to assist her.

As they walked towards the door, they passed the older man she'd seen with Rhysdale when she'd arrived that night.

'Charming supper room!' the man remarked to his companion.

When he spied Rhysdale, his eyes hardened to ice. He walked past them without a word.

Even the air seemed chilled as he passed.

Celia inclined her head to Rhysdale. 'Who is that gentleman?'

Rhysdale's entire manner changed into something dark and bitter.

'No one you need know,' he answered.

It pained her to see him so disturbed. 'Does he come here often?'

'Never before.' Rhysdale's voice rumbled with suppressed emotion. 'But I suspect he will come again.'

He led her out into the hallway and down the stairs to collect her cloak. As had become his custom, he escorted her into the street to wait for her coachman.

Clouds hid the stars and made the night even darker than usual. Celia's own woes receded as she stood waiting with him for her carriage, an overwhelming desire to comfort him taking over.

She touched his arm. 'Rhysdale, it will not do for the both of us to be glum.'

He covered her hand with his and his typically unreadable face momentarily turned pained and vulnerable. 'Come this afternoon. Let us talk more about my offer.' His grip on her hand tightened. 'Do not leave me entirely.'

She blinked and her throat constricted. 'Very well. I'll come.'

He smiled and his gratitude was palpable. He leaned down, his eyes half closing.

Celia's heart thundered in her chest as the night itself wrapped around them and his head dipped lower and lower. She wrestled with an impulse to push him away and a desire to feel his arms around her.

The *clop-clop* of a horse team sounded in her ears and he stepped away. Her carriage approached from the end of the street. When the coach pulled up to where they stood, he put the steps down and reached for her hand to help her into the couch.

When she placed her hand in his, she suddenly turned to face him, her words bursting from her mouth. 'I will do it, Rhysdale. I will come work for you.'

His face broke out in pleasure. 'Indeed?'

She smiled, as well. 'Yes.'

For a moment he looked as if he would pull her into his arms and kiss her. Instead, he gently cupped her cheek. 'We will talk more this afternoon.'

'Until then,' she whispered.

She climbed into the coach and he closed the door. As the carriage pulled away, her heart raced. Had she been afraid he would kiss her or had she yearned to feel his lips on hers?

Chapter Five

A gnarl of nerves amidst a flutter of excitement, Celia donned her hat and gloves. It was half-past twelve, barely afternoon, but she wished to be finished with her interview with Rhysdale before two, when no respectable woman dared walk near St James's Street.

She supposed she was not truly a respectable woman. Not when she spent her nights gambling in a gaming hell. But that did not mean she wished to suffer the taunts and catcalls of dandies who loitered on corners for that very purpose.

Her mother-in-law descended the staircase. 'And where are you going?'

Celia had hoped to slip out before her mother-in-law knew she was gone. 'I have an errand. I shall be back shortly.'

'Do you take Younie with you?' the older woman snapped. 'Because I have need of her.'

Celia kept her tone mild. 'She is at your disposal. My errand is not far. I have no need of company.'

'Hmmph!' her mother-in-law sniffed. 'I expect you will not tell me the nature of this errand of yours.'

'That is correct.' Celia smiled.

Lady Gale continued to talk as she descended the stairs. 'Most likely it is to pay a bill or beg for more credit from shopkeepers who ought to be glad to have our business. Needless to say you are not off to meet a man. My son always said you were frigid as well as barren.'

The barb stung.

The cruelty of this woman was rivalled only by that of her son. Ironic that Lady Gale was blind to her son's faults, but took great enjoyment in cataloguing Celia's.

Primary among Celia's shortcomings, of course, was her inability to conceive a child. Neither Gale nor his mother had forgiven her for not producing sons, but neither had they ever considered how crushing this was for Celia. A baby might have made her marriage bearable.

Knowing she could never have a child hurt more than her mother-in-law would ever know, but today her mother-in-law's abuse merely made her angry.

After all she'd sacrificed for the woman's comfort…

Celia faced her. 'You speak only to wound me, ma'am. It is badly done of you.'

Her mother-in-law stopped on the second stair. She flushed and avoided Celia's eye.

Celia maintained her composure. 'Recall, if you please, that your son left you in more precarious financial circumstances than he did me, but I have not abandoned you.' Much as she would like to. 'Nor have I abandoned Adele. I am doing the best I can for all of us.'

Lady Gale pursed her lips. 'You keep us both under your thumb with your tight-fisted ways. You control us with the purse strings.'

Celia tied the ribbons on her hat. 'Think the worst of me, if you wish, but at least have the good manners to refrain from speaking your thoughts aloud.' She opened the door. 'I should return in an hour or so.'

Younie had sewn a swirl of netting to the crown of Celia's hat. When she stepped onto the pavement, Celia pulled the netting over her face so no one would recognise her if they happened to spy her entering the Masquerade Club.

The afternoon was grey and chilly and Celia walked briskly, needing to work off her anger at the woman.

Lady Gale had well known of her son's debauchery, but still she preferred to blame all

Gale's ills on Celia. In truth, the man had countless vices, many more than mere gambling. He'd treated Celia like a brood mare and then thrust her out to pasture when she didn't produce, all the while taunting her with his flagrant infidelities and profligate ways. As if that were not enough, he neglected his daughter.

And his mother.

Celia had known nothing of men when her aunt and uncle arranged her marriage to Gale. She'd still been reeling from her parents' deaths and barely old enough for a come-out. Her aunt and uncle simply wished to rid themselves of her. She'd never felt comfortable with Gale, but thought she had no choice but to marry him. She never imagined how bad marriage to him would be.

The only thing he'd wanted from Celia was a son and when she could not comply, he disdained her for it. Over and over and over. Life was only tolerable for her when he went off to London or anywhere else. Celia cared nothing about what he did in those places as long as he was gone.

Little did she know he'd squandered his fortune, leaving only what he could not touch: Celia's widow's portion and Adele's dowry.

She'd worn widow's black after Gale died, but she had never mourned him. His death had set her free.

And she would free herself of his mother, as well, when Adele was settled. As long as her husband would be generous enough to take on the responsibility of the Dowager Lady Gale.

It was not until Celia turned off St James's on to Park Place that she remembered her destination. She was indeed meeting a man. Would not Lady Gale suffer palpitations if she knew? She was meeting a man who offered her the best chance of escaping life with her mother-in-law. A man who had almost kissed her.

The gaming hell was only a few short streets away from her rooms. In daylight it looked like any other residence.

But it was an entirely different world.

As she reached for the knocker, her hand shook.

For the first time he would see her face. Was she ready for that?

She sounded the knocker and the door opened almost immediately. The burly man who attended the door at night stood in the doorway.

Celia made herself smile. 'Good afternoon. I have an appointment with Mr Rhysdale.'

The taciturn man nodded and stepped aside for her to enter. He lifted a finger. A signal for her to wait, she supposed. He trudged up the stairs.

Celia took a breath and glanced around to try to calm her nerves.

At night this hall looked somewhat exotic with its deep green walls and chairs and gilded tables. At night the light from a branch of candles made the gold gilt glitter and a scent of brandy and men filled the air. To her right was a drawing room, its door ajar. To anyone peeking in a window this house would appear as respectable as any Mayfair town house.

The doorman descended the dark mahogany stairs and nodded again. Celia assumed that meant he'd announced her to Mr Rhysdale. He then disappeared into the recesses of rooms behind the hall.

A moment later Rhysdale appeared on the stairs. 'Madam?'

She turned towards him and lifted the netting from her face, suddenly fearful he would not approve of her true appearance.

He paused, ever so slightly, but his expression gave away nothing of his thoughts.

He descended to the hall. 'Come. We will talk upstairs.'

Dismayed by his unreadable reaction, Celia followed him to the second floor where sounds of men hammering nails and sawing wood reached her ears.

'Forgive the noise,' he said. 'I'm having this floor remodelled into rooms for my use.' He lifted the latch of a door to her right. 'We can talk in here.'

They entered a small drawing room. Its furnishings appeared fashionable, as well as comfortable. They were stylishly arranged.

He gestured for her to sit on a deep red sofa. He sat on an adjacent chair. 'I've ordered tea.'

She might have been calling upon one of her mother-in-law's society friends. Escorted into a pleasant drawing room. Served tea. The conventions might be identical, but this was no typical morning call.

In daylight Rhysdale was even more imposing. His dress and grooming were as impeccable as the most well-attired lord, even though he managed to wear the pieces as casually as if he'd just walked in from a morning ride. His eyes, dark as midnight in the game room, were a spellbinding mix of umber and amber when illuminated by the sun from the windows.

His gaze seemed to take in her total appearance, but his expression remained impassive. Did she disappoint? She was too tall to be fashionable. Her figure was unremarkable. Her neck was too long; her face too thin; her lips too full; her hair too plain a brown—she could almost hear her husband's voice listing her faults.

But what did Rhysdale think?

And why was it she cared so much for his approval?

He blinked, then averted his compelling eyes. 'I assume you have not changed your mind about my proposition?' His smooth voice made her quiver inside.

She swallowed. 'I would not have kept the appointment otherwise.'

A smile grew across his face. 'Then, perhaps an introduction is in order?'

She was prepared for this, at least. He would be a fool to hire her without knowing her name.

And he was no fool.

She'd already decided to give him her true name. Her maiden name.

She extended her gloved hand. 'I am Celia Allen, sir.'

It pleased her to be Celia Allen again. The surname was common enough and her father minor enough that no one would connect the name to Lord Gale's widow.

He took her hand, but held it rather than shake it. 'Miss Allen or Mrs Allen?'

She pulled her hand away. 'Miss Allen.'

Rhys felt the loss of her hand as if something valuable had slipped through his fingers. With this first glimpse of her face, he wanted her more than ever.

She reminded him of a deer with her long regal neck and alert-but-wary eyes that were the colour of moss at twilight. She seemed wrong for the city. She was meant for the country, for brisk walks in fresh country air. The bloom in her cheeks, the hue of wild raspberry of her lips looked out of place in London.

But he was becoming distracted.

And much too poetic.

He could almost hear Xavier's voice in his head, admonishing him to keep his focus on the gaming house. He would tell his friend later about employing her—not of almost kissing her—both had been too impulsive to meet the approval of his friend.

Not that Rhys cared if his zealously protective friend approved of his employing Miss Allen. Or of wanting her in his bed.

He fixed his gaze on her again. To call her Miss Allen seemed wrong to him. He had no wish to be so formal with her.

'Will you object if I address you as Celia?' he asked. 'You may call me Rhys.'

She coloured.

Her discomfort made him wonder. A woman of the theatre would expect the presumption of intimacy of using given names.

She paused before answering. 'If you wish it.' She met his eyes. 'Not in the gaming house, though.'

Clever of her. 'Of course not. You are exactly right. No one must know you are in my employ. They will suspect us of manipulation.'

'Manipulation?' Her lovely brows knit in anxiety.

'I hire you because your presence in the gaming house encourages patrons—men—to gamble. You are not expected to do anything different from what you were doing before.'

She nodded.

He leaned closer and put his hand on her wrist. 'That is not my only reason for hiring you, however—'

A knock at the door interrupted. She slipped her hand away and Rhys straightened in his chair.

MacEvoy entered with the tea tray, managing to give her an un-servant-like look-over. Undoubtedly Rhys would hear Mac's assessment of the lady later.

'Shall I pour?' She looked rattled. 'How do you take your tea?'

'No milk, no sugar.' He'd accustomed himself to drinking tea that way from times when he could not afford milk and sugar. It pleased him that he did not need those inconsequential trappings of wealth.

He gestured to MacEvoy to leave.

MacEvoy closed the door behind him and Celia handed Rhys his cup of tea.

He lifted the cup and took a sip.

Perhaps it was for the best that Mac had interrupted him. His desire for her was making him move too quickly. When he got close, he sensed her alarm, another clue that his theory about her identity might be wrong.

He changed the subject. 'I should explain something else about your employment here.'

She gave him her attention.

'Some time ago, before I owned this gaming house, a woman came here in disguise to play cards. It is where I got the idea to set up the place as a masquerade.' He waved that tangent away. 'But no matter. About this woman. She created a stir. Men were taking wagers on who would be the first to unmask her.' He paused. 'And who would be first to seduce her. Men came and gambled merely for the chance to win the wager.'

She paled. 'You wish me to offer myself as some sort of prize?'

He shook his head. 'No. No, indeed. I am merely warning you. Some men who come to gamble may ask more of you than merely to partner them in a game of whist.'

Her eyes narrowed in calculation. 'Like that man who so distressed you last night?'

Westleigh, she meant.

His voice hardened. 'Yes. Men like him.' He looked directly into her eyes. 'I will be near if any men ill treat you. Do not hesitate to alert me or Xavier. We will protect you.'

She put her hand on her heart and glanced away.

He took another sip of tea. 'You are a good card player. And that is all that is required of you. None the less, your feminine allure will attract admirers.'

'Feminine allure?' She looked surprised.

How puzzling. Did she not know she was alluring?

'You are a beguiling mystery. A lovely young woman who knows how to play cards. You will—you *do*—attract men. Men will want to partner you, play against you, sit next to you.' He gave her another direct look. 'But they must not cross the line of proper behaviour. If they do, you must let me know.'

She became absorbed in stirring her tea. Finally she answered. 'If such a thing should happen, I will let you know.'

He became even more convinced he'd been wrong about her being an actress. If not someone connected to the theatre, who was she?

'May I know more of you, Celia Allen?'

She turned wary again, like a deer about to bound away. 'There is nothing else I can tell you.'

He must not push her further. He would learn about her in due time, he resolved. Even though he knew solving the mystery of her would not diminish his desire.

She placed her teacup on the table. 'The terms of payment are what we agreed upon last night?'

He nodded, regretting the conversation turning businesslike. The desire to taste her lovely lips grew more difficult to resist. 'One pound per night, plus all your winnings. I stake you one hundred pounds, which you will return if you win. I will forfeit if you lose.'

She stood. 'I will try not to lose.'

'I know you will try not to lose. You are a true gamester.' He rose with her. 'Chance sometimes does not favour us, though, Celia. You will lose. At hazard or faro, at least, but those losses will come directly to me, so I do not credit them. Play all the hazard and faro you like. At whist or *vingt-et-un* I suspect you are skilled enough to win most of the time.'

'I hope I do not disappoint.' Her lips formed a tremulous smile. 'For both our sakes.'

That was another thing. Why did she need money so urgently?

She pulled on her gloves. 'I will try to come to the gaming house as many nights as I am able.'

What might keep her away? She was one mystery after another, even without her mask.

'Good.' He adopted her businesslike tone. 'When you arrive, stop at the cashier. He will be instructed to provide you your stake.'

'Is there anything else?' she asked. 'I must leave now.'

'One thing more.' He extended his hand. 'We must shake on our agreement.'

Slowly she placed her hand in his. He liked the feel of her long graceful fingers and strong grasp.

He drew her closer to him, just short of an embrace. 'I am glad of our partnership, Celia Allen,' he murmured, his lips inches from hers.

Her eyes widened. The deer wished to bolt, he feared.

He released her and she started towards the door.

'Will I see you tonight?' he asked.

She reached the door and turned. 'If I can manage it.'

He let her walk out on her own, but when he heard the front door close, he stepped to the window and held the curtain aside to watch her.

She paused for a moment on the pavement, as if getting her bearings. Seeming to collect herself suddenly, she walked down the street with purpose.

He watched until he could see her no more.

'I'll solve the mystery of you, Miss Celia Allen,' he said aloud. 'And I will see you in my bed.' He dropped the curtain. 'Soon.'

Celia gulped in air and tried to quiet her jangling nerves. Taking one more quick breath, she hurried away.

God help her, being with Rhysdale excited her even more than the prospect of gambling without losing her own money. What was wrong with her?

She'd had no experience with men—other than Gale, that is. Rhysdale looked as if he wanted to try to kiss her again, but she could not be sure. He'd called her *alluring,* but had he meant it?

Gale had poured on pretty compliments at first,

when he'd been courting her. He'd obviously not meant them. How was she to know if Rhysdale spoke the truth?

She paused.

Why was she even *thinking* this way?

Her task was not to become enthralled with the handsome owner of the gaming house. He was blowing her off course, robbing her of the power to think straight. She must never allow another man any power over her. Not emotionally. Certainly not legally. Never would she marry again and become the property of a man, legally bound to his every whim.

Once had been enough.

Rhys represented a different sort of bondage, one that captured her thoughts and senses. She had no idea how to cope with the temptation to allow his kiss, to allow what was simmering below the surface to burst forth and consume her.

All Celia needed to do was return to the gaming house and play cards, but that presented another temptation. Rhys's offer encouraged precisely what she should battle. She should eschew the cards and games, not throw herself into playing them. How did she know she would be able to escape when Rhys's employment ended? Would she be able to stop gambling then, or would she become like her father, compelled to return to the tables against all good sense? Gambling might not be content to have merely killed her father and mother and ruined her young life; it could destroy her future, as well.

She started walking again, though her vision was blurred by the storm of thoughts inside her.

There would be no future at all for Adele unless Celia accepted this risk.

Adele was everything to her. The daughter she could never have, even though only a few years younger.

Rhysdale had given Celia this chance to secure Adele's future and Celia must embrace it.

She quickened her pace.

All she needed to do was remain resolute. Resist temptation. Play cards and nothing else. What did she care what Rhys or any man thought?

He'd suggested that men might become attracted to her while she played cards with them. What utter nonsense. If anything, it was the mask and nothing more. The novelty of a disguised woman who liked to play cards.

Rhysdale, though, had seen her face. He'd still thought her alluring.

A frisson of pleasure raced through her. She closed her eyes and again stopped walking.

She was back to Rhysdale. He could so easily invade her thoughts.

How pitiful she was. The first time a man showed her any kindness she turned as giddy as a girl fancying herself in love with Lord Byron after reading *Childe Harold's Pilgrimage*.

Had Rhysdale been the reason she agreed to his proposition? Was he, not money, the reason she agreed to face the gambling demons again?

Chapter Six

That evening William Westleigh, Viscount Neddington, searched Lady Cowdlin's ballroom as he had done every other entertainment he'd attended this Season.

He'd thought she was a vision when he first gazed upon her. Pale skin flushed with youth. Hair a shimmer of gold, its curls looking as artless as if she'd just stepped in from a breezy day. Lips moist and pink as a summer blossom.

She'd turned him into a romantic in an instant. He'd felt both exhilarated and weak when she'd allowed him to assist her in selecting wine at the musicale, but he'd lost her in the crowd afterwards.

He needed an introduction to her. If she appeared tonight—if he found her again—he'd beg someone to do the honours. He'd try his damnedest to dance with her and share supper with her.

Thinking of her was a welcome respite from worry over the finances, the estates, the welfare of his sister and mother. Those matters were largely out of his hands and under the control of his father at the moment.

Unless his father fulfilled the bargain they'd made with Rhysdale, they were about two weeks from disaster.

He walked the rooms of this ball three times without finding her, but it was early yet and guests continued to arrive.

'The Lord Westleigh and Lady Westleigh,' the butler announced.

Ned twisted away. He was too angry at his father to witness his joviality, as if he had not caused his family the extreme stress that currently plagued them. How his mother could walk at his father's side foxed Ned.

Of course, she did not yet know how severely her husband had squandered their fortune.

If only the beauty he encountered at the musicale would walk in, Ned could momentarily free himself from thoughts of their troubles. He glanced around the room once again, looking everywhere but in the direction of his father.

The butler's voice rang out again. 'Lady Gale, Dowager Lady Gale and Miss Gale.'

Ned turned to the door.

It was she!

She stood a little behind two other ladies, one

tall and as young as herself and the other certainly the dowager. This family was unknown to him, but the name *Miss Gale* now pressed into his mind like a hot iron brand.

She was as lovely as he remembered, this night donned in a pale pink gown that had some sort of sheer skirt over it that floated about her as she moved. Her lovely blonde hair was a mass of curls on top of her head and was crowned with pink roses.

As she and the other two ladies made their way to greet the host and hostess, she paused to scan the ballroom and caught him staring at her. He bowed to her and she smiled, ever so slightly, but enough for his hopes to soar.

Hope that he could find someone to present him to her. Hope that she was unattached. Hope that her smile meant she felt the same strong attraction to him that he felt towards her.

Ned kept her in view and occasionally he caught her eye again. But he'd seen no one of his acquaintance talking or dancing with her. The time neared for the supper dance and he was determined to partner her.

He marched over to the hostess. 'Lady Cowdlin, may I beg a favour?'

'A favour?' She patted his hand. 'Tell me what I might do for you.'

'There is a young lady here…' He paused. 'I need an introduction.'

'Who is it, my dear?' She smiled.

'I believe she is Miss Gale.' He inclined his head in her direction.

'Ah, I knew her mother. A lovely lady.' Lady Cowdlin gave him a knowing look. 'I understand, Neddington, that Miss Gale is worth five thousand at least—'

As if he cared a fig about that.

'But she is not very grand. Her father was only a baron, you know. This is her first time in town and Edna—her grandmother—wants her to marry her cousin who inherited the title.'

That was not welcome news. 'Who is her cousin? Do I know him?'

'Luther Parminter. He is the son of her father's cousin. I am certain you have seen him around London. Of course, now he is the new Baron Gale. He inherited, you see.'

Ned knew who the man was, but could not even count him an acquaintance. Now must he think of him as a rival?

Lady Cowdlin took his arm. 'Come with me. Let us make this introduction forthwith.'

She brought him directly to where Miss Gale stood next to her grandmother's chair. Lady Gale stood nearby.

Lady Cowdlin spoke to the dowager. 'Ma'am, may I present this young man to you and the other ladies.'

The dowager looked up.

'This is Lord Neddington.' She turned to the younger Lady Gale, who looked upon him with a quizzical expression. 'Lady Gale and Miss Gale.' She nodded towards Ned. 'Lord Neddington.'

Ned bowed. 'Madams.' He looked into the eyes he'd longed to see up close again. 'Miss Gale.'

She lowered her long thick lashes and curtsied. 'Lord Neddington.'

'May I perform any service for you ladies?' He glanced at Miss Gale. 'Bring you some wine, perhaps?'

She coloured and looked even more lovely.

'That is kind of you, young man.' The Dowager Lady Gale smiled.

'None for me, thank you,' the younger Lady Gale said.

'I will return directly.' He hated to leave Miss Gale's presence.

Ned quickly found a servant toting a tray of wine glasses. He took two and returned to the ladies.

When he handed a glass to Miss Gale, their fingers touched and his senses heightened.

'Thank you, sir,' she murmured.

He took a breath. 'Are you engaged for the supper dance, Miss Gale?'

She lowered her lashes. 'I am not.'

'Adele,' the Dowager Lady Gale broke in. 'I have asked your cousin to claim you for that dance.'

'But, Grandmama…' she murmured.

The younger Lady Gale spoke up. 'He did not ask Adele, though, Lady Gale. Let her decide.' She turned to Miss Gale. 'You do not want to sit out at a ball when you could dance, do you?'

Miss Gale smiled. 'Indeed not.'

Lady Gale faced him. 'Then it is settled.'

Ned peered at this woman who had just helped him engage the dance. He had the oddest notion that he'd seen her before.

Ned bowed. 'I will return for the pleasure of dancing with you, Miss Gale.' He walked away, hoping the supper dance would be announced very soon.

Celia noticed the change in Adele as she danced with Lord Neddington. The girl gave evidence of enjoying every dance and every partner, but never had such a dreamy look crossed her face as when she glanced at this man.

'He is likely a fortune hunter,' Celia's mother-in-law commented.

'Her dowry is respectable, nothing more,' Celia responded. 'Perhaps he just fancies her.' That he visited gaming hells was Celia's prime worry. She'd recognised him immediately.

'Hmmph.' The dowager frowned. 'You ought not to have encouraged that young man, in any event. You know I am determined she should marry her cousin.'

Celia probably should not have encouraged Neddington. She'd done so only to oppose her mother-in-law. And because she'd seen the look in Adele's eye, how much she wanted to dance with the man.

'Luther shows very little interest in Adele, Lady Gale,' Celia said.

Luther was the more likely fortune hunter.

Celia would not see Adele forced into a marriage, but could she allow Adele to marry a gambler? She had seen Lord Neddington at the gaming hell more than once. She could never recall seeing him play more than once or twice at hazard. He spoke to Rhysdale on occasion.

Rhysdale.

Rhys, he'd asked her to call him, although could she really think of him in such intimate terms? Her heart skipped at the mere thought of speaking his name aloud. Her name on his lips came back to her, as well as his smile and the way those lips touched the edge of his teacup.

And had almost touched hers.

She placed her hand over her heart.

She would see him tonight after the ball. And once again yield to the temptations of the gambling den, with no need to wager her own money. She felt a dangerous excitement at the prospect of playing cards with a hundred pounds to wager. Think how much she could win!

The Dowager Lady Gale's voice broke through

Celia's thoughts. 'You should have refused Ned-dington the supper dance. Now he will spend supper with her. That is entirely too much time.'

Her mother-in-law had a point.

Celia gazed in Adele's direction. Adele was glowing with pleasure each time the figures joined her with Neddington. His face was filled with admiration.

Was this how young love appeared?

Celia had been given no chance to experience a youthful romance. She could not bear to take such joy away from Adele.

She turned to her mother-in-law. 'Do not interfere, Lady Gale. Allow your granddaughter the pleasure of supper with an admirer.'

Lady Gale's nostrils flared. 'I've half a mind to fetch her to me for supper.'

Celia seized her arm with just enough pressure to make her point. 'You will do no such thing. Do you hear me clearly?'

Lady Gale shrugged. 'You are indeed a wretch, are you not?'

'Interfere with Adele's life and you will see what a wretch I can be.'

Celia's conflicting wishes for Adele waged inside her. Let the girl choose her suitors. Let her fall in love with whom she wished. But not a man who would be cruel or thoughtless or more enamoured of gaming than of a wife and children. Celia had endured all of those.

* * *

Later that night Celia's lady's maid helped her get out of her ballgown and prepare to dress for the Masquerade Club. Celia sat at her dressing table, pulling pins from her hair so that they could fix it to fit under the new turban Younie had fashioned, to go with a new mask of white silk adorned with tiny seed pearls taken from one of her mother-in-law's discarded gowns.

There was a knock on the door and Adele entered. 'Celia, I saw the light under your door.'

Celia grabbed the new mask and hid it under her table. 'I am still awake.'

Younie, new gown in hand, quickly retreated to the dressing room.

Adele flopped onto Celia's bed. 'I cannot sleep!'

Celia brushed out her hair. 'What is the matter?'

Adele stretched and sighed. 'Nothing is the matter! Everything is wonderful!'

'What is so wonderful that you cannot sleep?' Celia asked, although she was certain she knew.

'I had such a lovely time at the ball. The best ever!' Adele sat cross-legged. In her nightdress with her hair in a plait, she looked as young as when Celia first met her six years ago.

Celia smiled. 'And to what do you attribute this pleasure?'

Adele wrapped her arms around herself. 'I—I think I met someone I really like.'

Celia turned back to the mirror. 'Lord Neddington?'

Adele's reflection showed surprise. 'How did you know?'

Celia kept brushing her hair. 'A lucky guess, I suppose.'

'He is so wonderful!' She flopped back onto the bed. 'And so handsome.' She sat up again. 'Do you not think he is handsome?'

'I do,' Celia agreed. 'Very handsome.'

'And very gentlemanly,' Adele continued. 'It was he who helped me procure the wine for you and Grandmama at the musicale. And tonight he fixed me the nicest plate at supper and gave me the choice of sitting with my friends. He was so agreeable, do you not think?'

'Indeed.' Celia had watched Neddington carefully and had seen nothing to object to in his manner towards Adele. It was his activity after the society events that concerned her.

Adele bounded off the bed and paced. 'I do not know how I can sleep. Do you think he will call? I hope he will call. But I'm afraid Grandmama does not like him. Do you think she will send him away if he calls?'

Celia rose and hugged the girl. 'She would not be so impolite.' Celia would see to it.

Adele clung to her. 'But she wants me to marry Cousin Luther and I do not even know him!'

'Leave your grandmother to me. She will not interfere in your wishes.' She loosened her hold on Adele and made the girl look into her eyes. 'But know that neither your grandmother nor I would let you marry a man who was unsuitable.'

'Lord Neddington is very suitable!' Adele cried.

Celia hugged her again. 'Indeed he seems to be, but you must not put your hopes beyond tomorrow. Merely hope he calls and, if he does, see if you still like him so well.'

'I will like him tomorrow and the next day and the next,' Adele cried. 'But will he like me?'

Celia kissed her on the cheek. 'Any man would be a fool not to fall heels over ears in love with you. But you should go to sleep now so you will not have dark shadows under your eyes tomorrow.'

Adele's hands went to her cheeks. 'Oh, my goodness, yes! I must look my very best.' She kissed Celia and hugged her tightly. 'Goodnight, Celia. I hope you sleep well.'

'Sweet dreams,' Celia murmured as Adele rushed out of the room.

Celia breathed a relieved sigh and looked towards her dressing room door. 'It is safe to come out, Younie.'

Her maid appeared in the doorway. 'That was a near go, wasn't it?'

'Indeed.' Celia retrieved the mask from beneath her dressing table. 'We'd best wait until we are certain she is sleeping.'

Celia arrived at the Masquerade Club later than she'd ever done before. Would Rhysdale—Rhys—be angry at her for being late?

She rushed inside, undeterred by the doorman, who seemed to recognise her even with the new gown and mask.

Rhys stood in the hall, as if waiting for her. Her breath caught. He wore an impeccably tailored but conservative black coat and trousers. With his dark hair and glowering expression he looked as dangerous as a highwayman.

'You are late,' he said.

'I had difficulty getting away.' She handed her shawl to the footman and tried not to sound defensive.

Rhys walked her out of the hall and she prepared to hear him ring a peal over her head as soon as they were out of earshot.

But he said nothing. When they stepped up to the cashier's desk, Rhys withdrew. The cashier was the same man who had served the tea in Rhys's drawing room and the only other person connected to the gaming house who had seen her face. He obviously knew precisely who she was, even masked, because he counted out the exact number of counters Rhys had promised her.

As she turned to make her way to the game

room, she caught Rhys still standing in the door-way. She forced herself to lift her chin and meet his gaze head-on.

His eyes shone with admiration, much like Neddington's had done when looking upon Adele. 'The new gown is effective.'

Celia felt an unfamiliar rush of feminine plea-sure and immediately forced herself to sober. She would not melt at mere compliments.

Her smile was stiff as she clutched her reticule, the counters safe inside. He stepped back for her to pass, but he followed her into the game room.

The room was crowded and she recognised many gentlemen who a couple of hours before had been dancing in Lady Cowdlin's ballroom.

Xavier Campion approached her with his dis-arming smile. She sensed something unpleasant beneath it.

'Madam.' He bowed. 'Do you fancy a game of whist?'

She glanced at Rhys, who frowned.

'I came to play,' she answered, unsure if she should accept Xavier's invitation or not.

'I will partner you if you wish,' he said.

She glanced back to Rhys, but his back was to her and he was conversing with a group of gen-tlemen.

'Yes, Mr Campion. Do you have some oppo-nents in mind?'

He smiled again as he took her arm. 'It is

Xavier, remember. Let us go in search of some worthy opponents.' His grip was firmer than was necessary. He leaned towards her and murmured in a tone that seemed falsely convivial. 'I understand you are in Rhys's employ. How did you manage that, I wonder?'

She did not miss a beat. 'He made me the offer and I accepted. How else might it have been accomplished?'

'He is my friend,' Xavier said through gritted teeth. 'I will not have him trifled with.'

Celia lifted her chin. 'Rhysdale seems capable of selecting his own employees. Ought I to tell him you think otherwise?' His concern was ridiculous. 'Or perhaps he has asked you to protect him from me?'

Xavier's eyes flashed. 'He does not need to ask. I protect all my friends. Do you tell tales on all of yours?'

'I do not.' Celia paused. 'But, then, you are not my friend, are you?' She shrugged from his grip. 'I have changed my mind, *Mr Campion*. I believe I will try my luck at hazard.'

She left him and did not look back.

It made her feel wonderfully strong. A man had tried to intimidate her and she'd held her own against him.

The hazard table was crowded with mostly men. Celia faltered a bit, then remembered Rhys said she was equally as alluring as his mysterious masked woman who had played here before.

She'd just stood up to a man; perhaps she could also be a little bit alluring.

'Pardon me.' She made herself smile in what she hoped was a flirtatious manner. 'Might a lady play?'

The gentlemen parted. One was the man who had so disturbed Rhys the previous night. Her skin turned to gooseflesh. He, too, had been at Lady Cowdlin's ball.

What did such a gentlemen say to his wife to explain going out again after a ball? Did the wife pace with worry as Celia's mother had done?

'You are welcome to play, my dear.' The gentleman flicked his eyes quickly over her person. 'Have you played before?'

Disgust roiled through her. She remembered Rhys's warning.

She dropped any flirtatious affectations. 'I am accustomed to card games like whist and piquet and *vingt-et-un*. I've not tried a game of dice before.' But tonight she had money she could afford to lose.

The croupier at the hazard table was a pretty young woman with curly red hair. 'Do you play, miss?'

The gentleman rose on his heels in self-importance. 'I will assist the lady, if she so desires.' He scooped up the dice. 'I will stake you for this first round.' He put a pound counter on the table and placed the dice in her hand. 'Call a number between five and nine.'

'Nine,' she called, the date her father died.

'Nine,' he repeated.

Around the table there was a flurry of side-betting accompanying her call.

'They are betting on your chances to win,' he explained. 'If you roll a nine, you will win. If you throw a two or a three, or an eleven or a twelve, you will lose. Now shake the dice in your hand and roll them on the table.'

She shook the dice and threw them down. They landed in the middle of the green baize, one landing on three, the other, on five.'

'Eight!' the croupier called.

'That is a called a *chance*,' the gentleman explained. 'You did not win, but neither did you lose.' The croupier handed him the dice. 'Roll again.'

He dropped the dice into her palm.

'I want a nine, correct?' She shook the dice in her hand.

'No, this time you want a two or a three to win. Or anything but the *main*—your nine—to continue to roll.'

She dropped the dice onto the table, this time rolling one pip on one die and two on the other.

'Three!' called the croupier. 'A winner.'

Westleigh handed the winnings to her.

A man next to her pushed the dice back to Celia. 'Let the lady keep playing. She has the luck.'

Celia continued to play and to win. The rules of winning and losing changed depending upon what number she chose as chance and she quickly calculated that choosing the numbers five or nine reduced the odds of winning. The crowd around the hazard table grew, most betting with her.

Each time she won she jumped for joy and could not wait to throw the dice again. Her heart was beating fast and her breath as rapid as if she'd run all the way to Oxford Street. Even knowing this gentleman was having a grand time as her host did not dampen her excitement. The impact of his presence faded with each roll of the dice, each possibility that her pile of counters would increase.

As the gentlemen betting with her gathered their winnings, she caught sight of Rhys. He stood at the edge of the crowd, his face a dark cloud.

No wonder he was upset. Every time she—and those who bet with her—won, Rhysdale lost. It woke her from her reverie.

When the dice were again handed to her, she held up her hands. 'I am done, gentlemen.' She made herself smile. 'I wish to keep all these lovely counters.' She'd won at least forty-five pounds.

She gathered her counters and backed away

from the table, shocked at herself. She'd lost all sense of time, all reason.

Rationally she should continue to play until losing again and lead her followers to do the same.

She blinked.

Like a swarm of bees around a hive, the other players filled her space at the table and resumed the play.

To her dismay the gentleman who had assisted her was not among them. Instead he remained at her side.

'Allow me to introduce myself.' He bowed. 'I am Lord Westleigh.'

She felt the blood drain from her face. 'Lord Westleigh.'

Lord Westleigh was the man who'd accused her father of cheating at cards, who'd accepted her father's challenge of a duel, who'd fired the pistol ball that pierced her father's heart.

Because he was an earl with friends and influence, he'd walked away from killing her father with impunity, broke her mother's heart, destroyed her health and, in effect, killed her, as well.

Celia tried to remain upright, even though her legs trembled. She tried to keep her face expressionless.

Westleigh waited, as if expecting she would reveal her name.

He finally smiled. 'You will not tell me who you are?'

She took a breath. 'I have chosen to wear a mask. That means I do not wish to reveal myself.'

He laughed. 'I thought you might make me an exception.'

Never for him.

Undaunted by her obvious reserve, he glanced around the room. 'Shall we find some partners for whist?'

'No!' she snapped.

She scanned the crowd for Rhys, needing him. He'd said she should find him if this man bothered her. He was bothering her greatly. He was making her ill.

She caught herself and moderated her tone of alarm. 'I—I am looking for someone.'

Rhys stood some distance away and he did not glance her way.

She found another familiar face. Sir Reginald. 'There he is. I must speak with him.' She inclined her head. 'Thank you for teaching me hazard.'

Before he could protest, she started to cross the room to where Sir Reginald stood, but someone stepped in her way.

Rhys.

Tears of relief pricked her eyes.

He touched her arm. 'I saw you with Westleigh. Was he uncivil to you?'

'Yes,' she blurted out. 'No. Not really. He wanted me to play cards with him.' She took a deep breath. 'I did not know that man was Westleigh. It—it surprised me.'

His brows lowered. 'What do you know of Westleigh?'

'I cannot tell you here.' Her knees weakened.

He must have noticed because he offered her his arm. 'Come with me.'

He walked them to a back staircase, one used by the servants, perhaps. They climbed to the second floor. They passed dark rooms that smelled of sawed wood and linseed and entered the drawing room where he had received her earlier.

He led her directly to the sofa. 'Sit here.'

She removed her mask and rubbed her eyes, trying to calm herself from the shock of learning she'd spent the greater part of her night in the company of her father's killer.

Rhys handed her a glass. 'Have some brandy.'

She took the glass gratefully and drank, the liquid warming her chest. She sipped more. And finished it.

Rhys sat in an adjacent chair and poured her some more. He asked nothing. Just sat with her.

She finally calmed enough to look up at him. 'Thank you, Rhys.' The brandy was helping. 'I am afraid it was a shock to learn that gentleman was Westleigh.'

He did not press her to tell him more.

Since her mother's death she had spoken to no one about Westleigh, but suddenly it seem too great a burden to carry alone. 'You must wonder why I became so upset.'

He shrugged. 'With Westleigh, nothing would surprise me.'

She stared into his eyes. 'Would it surprise you to learn he killed my father?'

His brows rose, but his gaze did not waver.

She glanced away. 'My father enjoyed gambling…too much. He sometimes played unwisely. He played cards with Lord Westleigh and apparently was winning when Westleigh accused him of cheating.' She looked back to see his reaction to that information. Would he think her father a cheat? 'My father would never cheat. He was outraged and challenged Westleigh to a duel.' She blinked away tears. 'The duel was fought and Westleigh killed my father.' She choked on her words and quickly took another sip of brandy. 'He walked away with impunity.'

The sound of her mother's voice telling her of her father's death returned to her and the horror and grief struck her anew. Dear God, she was about to lose control of her emotions.

He moved from the chair to the sofa and took her into his arms.

Celia collapsed against his chest, heaving with sobs, and he held her and murmured to her. She could not even tell what he said, she just felt his voice, low and rumbling.

It had been so long since she'd been held, so

long since anyone had comforted her. The years of loneliness and loss overwhelmed her and his arms were so warm and strong.

She had to pull herself together, though. She could not do this.

Rhys held her close, relishing the feel of her in his arms, but, even more, feeling her pain and wanting to do anything he could to ease it.

Damned Westleigh! The man had killed her father? It was more than even Rhys would have suspected. Fighting a duel over a game of cards was foolish beyond belief. Killing a man over cards was a million times worse.

'There, there,' he murmured, realising he sounded like his mother. His own throat tightened with the memory of her loss. Another deed he could throw at Westleigh's feet. His mother might have lived a long happy life if not for that cursed man.

She pulled away, wiping her eyes with her fingers. 'I am so sorry.'

He handed her his handkerchief. 'Do not say so.'

'It is the surprise of seeing him.' She blew her nose. 'I wondered how it would be. I did not know I would turn into a watering pot.'

He suspected that weeping was not something she often allowed of herself. 'What would you like me to do about Westleigh?'

She gaped at him in surprise. '*Do* about him?'

'It cannot be comfortable for you that he comes here. I can prevent him, if you like.' Rhys disliked seeing the man here anyway.

She finished her second glass of brandy. 'I do not know what to say. I do not know what to think. I do not want him to know who I am.'

Rhys did not know who she was.

Her face hardened. 'I would like to make him pay in some way.'

'Revenge?' He well knew the need for revenge.

'Yes!' She covered her mouth with her hand. 'I suppose that is wrong of me.'

A corner of his mouth turned up. 'Quite natural, I would say. You are probably one of many who would like revenge on Lord Westleigh.'

She peered into his eyes. 'You detest him, as well.'

He could explain to her that Westleigh was his father, but, at the moment, the idea that the blood of such a man flowed in his veins filled him with disgust. He did not wish to take the chance she would feel the same.

They could each keep their secrets from the other, could they not?

He held her gaze. 'I detest him. It will give me pleasure to throw him out for you.'

She stared for a moment, as if thinking, then shook her head. 'It would not do to ban an earl from your gaming house, would it? Especially one who likes to gamble. I would never ask this of you.'

'Nonetheless,' he responded. 'It would be my pleasure to do so, if it will ease your mind.'

She reached over and touched his hand. 'It is enough to know I have an ally.' She withdrew her hand almost as quickly and turned away. When she turned back, she smiled the ghost of a smile. 'Perhaps there is some restitution I can force on him. Engage him in a card game and win all his money…'

As if he had any sum of money to lose, Rhys thought.

She straightened. 'At least that would be something, would it not?'

He would have preferred an excuse to toss Westleigh out on his ear, although her course was undoubtedly the wiser for both of them. He preferred a more subtle revenge, one that would cause Westleigh even greater pain.

'It will be as you wish.'

She dabbed at her face again and folded his handkerchief. 'I will launder and return this.'

He waved that away. 'It is of no consequence.'

She picked up her mask. 'I have taken up enough of your time. We should return to the game room, do you not think?'

Leaving her was the last thing on his mind, but she was correct. He should get back. 'You may stay here, if you wish. Stay until it is time for your coachman.'

She shook her head. 'I think it is like falling from one's pony. One must remount immediately.'

She'd ridden a pony? Riding a pony seemed unlikely for an actress.

He'd pursue that thought another time. 'Then I will go down first. You may follow a moment later. It will not seem as if we have been together.'

She gave him a grateful smile.

They both rose. She lifted the mask to her face and fussed with its ribbons. He stepped behind her and tied the mask in place.

She stood very still as he did so.

When he finished, his hands hovered over her shoulders, wanting to explore more of her.

Instead, he stepped away and walked out of the room.

Down in the game room, he found Westleigh almost immediately, laughing at something his companion had said. Westleigh caught his gaze and froze for a moment, an icy expression on his face. Rhys returned the unfriendly glare and resumed his patrol of the room.

In a few moments Celia appeared, searching the room, her reaction to finding Rhys as warm as Westleigh's had been cold. She appeared perfectly composed, strolling to where Sir Reginald stood.

Sir Reginald greeted her like a long-lost friend.

This man was a member of the aristocracy who Rhys could like. Sir Reginald was kind and friendly to everyone.

Westleigh also noticed Celia's entrance. Rhys watched him leave his friend and make a beeline to where Celia stood.

Xavier appeared beside Rhys. 'Would you mind telling me what all this is about?'

'All what?' Rhys countered.

Xavier inclined his head towards Celia and Westleigh.

Rhys waved a dismissive hand. 'Nothing of consequence, I am certain.'

Xavier frowned. 'Between Westleigh and the woman who captivates you? Do not take me for a fool.'

Celia watched Westleigh make his way across the room and knew he was coming after her. She cast a glance towards Rhys. He stood close by.

She turned to Sir Reginald. 'Do you need a whist partner tonight, sir?'

Sir Reginald smiled in a jolly way. 'Is that an invitation, madam? If so, I would be honoured.'

Westleigh came up to her side. 'There you are, my dear. I feared I had lost you forever.'

She inclined her head slightly and spoke without expression. 'Lord Westleigh.'

He bowed. 'Are you ready for our game of whist?'

He presumed she would play cards with him? 'I fear you are too late.' She managed to sound civil. 'Sir Reginald and I will be playing.'

That did not daunt him. 'Whist? You will need partners, certainly. Allow me and my companion to challenge you to a game.'

Whist had been the game that Westleigh had played with her father that fateful night.

Her eyes narrowed.

Sir Reginald broke in. 'Madam, I am completely at your disposal. We do need partners, but I leave it to you to say who that should be.'

She glanced over to Rhys, who had stepped away from his friend, but looked her way.

He was still near.

It emboldened her. 'Very well. Sir Reginald and I will play whist with you.'

Westleigh fetched his companion. Celia wondered if his companion had been his partner when Westleigh engaged her father in play. If so, why had the man not intervened? Someone should have stopped such folly.

They took their places at a card table and the cards were dealt.

Soon Celia focused on the play instead of the detested player who sat at her right, too often brushing his arm against hers or fussing over her counters as if it were his job to tend to her.

The play was tame. Westleigh and his partner were particularly predictable in which cards they put down and when. Even Sir Reginald's limited skills more than outmatched them. Westleigh could not have been a challenge to her father, who was very good at whist. Her father would have had no reason to cheat.

That knowledge was like a burden lifted from her shoulders. She now had no doubts that the charge of cheating against her father had been unfounded.

It also made Westleigh's actions that night all the more reprehensible.

Perhaps the revenge she could enact against him was to play cards with him as often as she could. To take as much of his money as she could. It would probably not put a dent in an earl's fortune, but it would be some restitution—the sort of restitution her father might admire.

While Sir Reginald shuffled the cards for the next hand, Celia glanced around the room, as she often did, looking for Rhys. Instead, her gaze caught upon Lord Neddington.

It did not please her that this young man was so frequent a visitor to this place. She had no wish for Adele to be enamoured of a gambler.

Celia watched Neddington walk through the room aimlessly. He turned towards her table and she quickly averted her eyes, but Neddington was not concerned with her. He was scowling at Lord Westleigh.

At least that was in the young man's favour.

Between hands Celia kept tabs on Neddington who walked around, but never seemed to gamble. How odd. It did make her a bit less concerned about his character, though.

After several games Westleigh's partner threw up his hands. 'No more!' He turned to Celia. 'You have emptied my pockets, madam.'

He was even worse a player than Westleigh.

She smiled good-naturedly. 'Perhaps you would like a rematch another night, sir.'

He laughed. 'A night when luck is with me.' He winked. 'At least I won when you played hazard. We must coax you back to the hazard table, must we not, Westleigh?' He turned to the earl.

'It would be my pleasure to play whatever game the lady wishes.' Westleigh eyed her in the same manner her husband had done before they were married.

It made her cheeks burn.

Sir Reginald, so harmless and friendly, said, 'Well, madam, you may count on me to partner you any time.'

'You are an excellent partner, Sir Reginald.' She dropped her counters into her reticule and stole a glance at her watch. It was nearly time for her coach to arrive.

She stood.

Westleigh took her elbow. 'Shall we play more hazard, my dear?'

'Thank you, no.' She drew her arm away. 'I bid you gentlemen goodnight.'

She looked for Rhys, but he was not in the game room, so she made her way to the cashier and repaid the hundred pounds she'd not touched in her play. At the end, she carried away over seventy pounds. The huge sum filled her with guilt. Winning at hazard would cost Rhys directly. It was a poor way to repay his generosity.

Celia wanted to see Rhys before she left. After cashing out, she glanced in the supper room, but he was not there. She asked the hall servant where Rhys was.

'Drawing room,' the man told her.

Celia climbed the stairs. As she neared the doorway to the drawing room, she heard Rhys's voice and held back.

'Your concern is unfounded, Xavier,' Rhys said. 'And insulting, as well.'

'Insulting?' His friend's voice rose.

'I am well able to make my own decisions about business and about women.' Rhys spoke with heat. 'I do not caution you against dallying with any of the several women who vie for your attention, you know.'

'There would be no need.' Xavier's tone was just as angry. 'I know how to handle women.'

'And I do not?' Rhys countered.

'Come now.' Xavier turned placating. 'This infatuation with the masked woman is something else. You do not know who she is. Or what she wants.'

'She wants what I want. Money,' Rhys answered. 'And she has given me her name. That is enough for me.'

'Rhys—' Xavier began.

'Enough,' Rhysdale broke in. 'I need you as a friend, not a nursemaid. Do not press me further on this matter.'

Celia stepped away from the doorway as Xavier strode out of the room. Seeing her, he hesitated only briefly, long enough to look half-apologetic, half-provoked. He continued on his way down the stairs.

She knocked on the door.

Chapter Seven

'May I speak to you, Rhys?'

Rhys turned in surprise at the sound of her voice. 'Celia! Come in. Close the door.'

She looked wounded, as well she might. He'd been about to pour himself some brandy. Now he needed it even more.

He lifted the decanter. 'Would you like a glass?'

She nodded.

'How much of that did you hear?' he asked as he poured.

She took the glass from his hand. 'Enough to know that Mr Campion does not like that you hired me.'

He'd been afraid of that.

'It is none of his affair,' he assured her. 'He thinks he is acting out of friendship.'

'If my employment causes you a problem—' she began.

'You cause me no problem.' He reached over and gently removed her mask. 'That is better.' He brushed a lock of hair off her face and gestured to the sofa. 'Please sit, Celia.'

By God, she looked lovely this night. The white of her gown was embroidered with a cascade of flowers created from shimmering silver thread. In the game room amongst the sea of black-coated men, she'd glowed like moonlight.

She lowered herself onto the sofa where she'd sat before. Where he'd held her before.

'I did not mean to overhear,' she said. 'I only came upstairs to thank you again. And to let you know that I managed being in Westleigh's company without too much distress.'

'I was watching.' He sat in the nearby chair. 'I also noticed that you won.'

'I did.' She shook her head. 'He is a terrible player.'

Their conversation was stilted and devoid of the intimacy they had so recently shared in this room. That she'd overheard Xavier did not help.

'Terrible?' That knowledge pleased him. Rhys was a master of cards. He took a sip of brandy. 'A competent card player would have no need to cheat against him, then.'

Her face shone with pleasure. 'You have guessed my thoughts.'

She looked even more lovely.

He took another sip. 'How much did you win?'

'From Westleigh and his partner? About twenty-five pounds.'

His brows rose. 'So much?'

She waved a hand. 'They were reckless in their betting, as well. I decided to play him as much as I can. Take as much of his money as I can.' Her voice cracked. 'For my father.'

He understood her need for revenge, but it puzzled him. How did Westleigh have that much to lose? He was supposed to be on a tight leash regarding his spending.

She lowered her gaze. 'I must confess that I won much more than the twenty-five pounds from Westleigh. I won even more from hazard.'

He'd noticed. 'You had a winning streak. How much did you win finally?'

She looked apologetic. 'Fifty pounds.' She quickly added. 'I know it was not well done of me. It is a great deal of money out of your pocket.' She opened her reticule. 'I wanted to see you so I could pay it back. I only regret I cannot repay all that the patrons betting with me must have won.'

He pushed the reticule away. 'I'll not take your winnings. And do not concern yourself about the gentlemen betting with you. Those who stayed at the hazard table will have lost it all again. Or will another night.' He gazed at her. 'Not everyone is so wise as to stop when ahead.'

'I was not wise….' She made a nervous gesture with her hand. 'To own the truth, I was terrified. The excitement made me lose all sense.'

'Not all sense, or you would have played until your reticule was empty.' He finished his brandy. 'That excitement is all part of the game. I have been a gambler too long not to have felt that same exhilaration.'

'It makes a person foolish,' she rasped. 'I cannot afford to be foolish. It will hurt me, but tonight my foolishness hurt you.'

'Gambling is always a risk, but remember that this was a risk I agreed to take. This night you won and I lost. Tomorrow it may be different. We will keep an eye on it.' He reached over again and touched her cheek. 'Do not fear. I will not let you be harmed by it.'

Her eyes grew wider and her fair skin glowed like an angel's.

Xavier was right when accusing him of wanting to make her a conquest. He wanted her as intensely as a man could desire a woman. But Rhys also genuinely liked her. He felt a kinship with her.

It was rare for him to feel kinship with anyone. He'd long ago accepted that he was alone in the world. He even expected to lose Xavier's friendship eventually, when the man finally found a woman he wished to marry. Xavier's allegiance would shift, as it should, to a wife and family of his own making.

Or perhaps his friendship with Xavier was ending over Celia.

Rhys dared not hope for anything more than temporary with Celia. No doubt her secrets would eventually separate them.

As his secrets might from her.

But for the moment he relished her company. When had a woman ever made him feel such sympathy as he felt towards her? He wished he could make Westleigh pay for killing her father, for bringing her such pain.

He wanted to enfold her in his arms and take all her pain away.

He looked into her eyes. 'I like you, Celia Allen.'

Her eyes darted around the room. He'd frightened her.

She smiled nervously at him. 'You have been… like a friend. I cannot tell you how grateful I am to you for paying me to gamble. For enduring my fit of tears over Westleigh.'

He held up a hand.

She twisted the laces of her reticule. 'I should go. My coachman will be here soon.'

He stood and offered her his hand. She hesitated a moment before placing her hand in his. He pulled her to her feet, but did not stop there. He pulled her into an embrace.

He could not tell if she was alarmed or pleased.

'I suspect we are two of a kind, Celia,' he said.

'I am glad you are in my employ. I am glad I will see you night after night.'

Her eyes grew huge and her voice trembled. 'You are holding me. Are—are you going to kiss me?'

'Is it what you wish?' He could feel the rise and fall of her breast against his chest.

It fired his senses, but he waited. She must want this, too.

She rose, no more than an inch, but it was all the invitation he needed.

He lowered his mouth to hers.

Her lips were warm, soft and tasting of brandy and he wanted more, much more. She melted into him and her lips pressed upon his, as if she, too, could not get enough. He lost himself in the pleasure of her, his hands eager to explore her, undress her, pleasure her—

She broke away. 'This is not wise, Rhys,' she cried.

His body was still humming with need, but he forced himself to give her the space she needed.

'You are sounding like Xavier.' He smiled. 'It probably was not wise to hire you in the afternoon and kiss you in the night, but I do not feel like being wise with you, Celia. I want more from you.'

Her eyes grew big. 'More from me?'

Did she not understand?

He would be clear. 'I want you in my bed.'

She stepped away. 'I—I do not know.'

He honoured her distance. 'It is your choice, Celia. No matter what you decide, our employment agreement still stands.'

Her expression turned puzzled. 'My choice,' she said to herself.

The clock on his mantel chimed four bells, causing them both to jump.

She rubbed her forehead. 'I must go. I am already late. My driver will be concerned.'

He reached out and took her hand. 'Tomorrow, give your driver a later time.'

She looked like a frightened deer.

He did not wish her to bolt. 'Do not distress yourself,' he spoke in a soothing voice. 'You know what I want, but do not let that keep you from coming back and gambling. You need not answer me now. I am a patient man.'

She stared at him, but finally said, 'I will think about it.'

It was not the answer he had hoped for, but he contented himself that it was not a definite no.

'Do not think.' He touched her cheek. 'Feel.'

She made a sound deep in her throat, before turning away from him and hurrying towards the door.

'Celia,' he called to her.

She stopped and looked over her shoulder at him.

'You forgot your mask.' He picked up the piece

of white silk and crossed the room to her. 'Stay still. I will put it on you,' he said.

Her breath accelerated as he affixed the mask to her face and tied the ribbons that held it in place.

'There you go,' he murmured.

She stepped away, but turned and gave him a long glance.

He opened the door. 'I will walk you to your coach.'

As they left the room he kept his distance, but walked at her side down the stairs to the hall where Cummings quickly retrieved her shawl. She put it on herself carelessly, but as soon as they were out the door, he wrapped her in it to protect her from the misty night's chill. Almost immediately the sound of her coach reached their ears even before it became visible.

She stepped forwards so her coachman could see her. He stopped the horses and Rhys lowered the steps. He squeezed her hand as he helped her into the coach.

He watched her face in the window as the coach started off, disappearing into the mist as if only a dream.

The next day Rhys sounded the knocker at the Westleigh town house. It was time to confront Westleigh. He'd had enough of the man, especially after what he'd learned from Celia.

He was ready to drop the whole bargain with

the Westleighs, but Celia wished her revenge and Rhys would not deny her it. He would, however, push along his own dealings with the Westleighs and be done with them.

A footman opened the door.

'Mr Rhysdale to see Lord Westleigh.' Rhys handed the footman his card.

The footman stepped aside and gestured for him to enter the hall. 'Wait here a moment.'

The last time Rhys called at this house, he'd been escorted into the drawing room. Why not now?

Likely Westleigh had left instructions to treat him like a tradesman.

The footman disappeared towards the back of the house.

Rhys gazed at the marble-tiled floors and swirling staircase. Such grandeur in contrast to the set of rooms in which he and his mother had lived. Or how he had lived after her death.

Gazing at it all, Rhys realised this was not what he wanted in life. Yes, he wanted comfort, but comfort would be enough. More than anything, he wanted to build something. A business. A factory. Something useful. He wanted not to be like his father, who had wasted his life and squandered his fortune.

He did not give a fig about being acknowledged as Westleigh's bastard son. In fact, he'd just as soon not be known to have the connection. He'd go through with it, though, only because it was *his* revenge against Westleigh. He would make the man do what he would detest the most, what he ought to have done when Rhys was born—to declare openly that Rhys was his son.

This bargain with the Westleighs had become like a game of cards. Westleigh behaved as if he held all the trumps, but he was bluffing. It was time to up the ante and win the hand.

It was a gamble. Everything in life was a gamble. Westleigh could choose poverty over admitting Rhys was his son, but how likely was that? Rhys knew a good bet when he saw one.

A servant who could only have been the butler entered the hall. He lifted his nose at Rhys. 'Do you have an appointment with his lordship?'

Rhys glared at the man and used the voice he'd once used to command men in his regiment. 'I do not need an appointment. Announce me to Lord Westleigh.'

The butler shrank back and quickly ascended the stairs. Rhys's eyes followed him. Westleigh would show himself promptly or Rhys would go in search of him.

A huge allegorical painting hung in the hall. Rhys turned to examine it. The painting depicted Minerva, representing wisdom, pushing Mars, the god of war, away from the goddess of peace. He chuckled to himself. Would Minerva prevail

with Westleigh? Or would he and Westleigh engage in battle?

A woman's voice said, 'Ned! I thought you had
gone.'

He turned to see a finely dressed woman de-
scending the stairs.

She looked startled. 'I beg your pardon. I
thought you were my son.'

He recognised her from the times he'd glimpsed
her in his old village, an older but still beautiful
Lady Westleigh.

He bowed. 'Allow me to present myself, my
lady. I am Mr Rhysdale, here to speak with your
husband.'

Her eyes flickered at the mention of his name.
Did she know of him? Did she remember that poor
woman who'd once been in her service so many
years ago?

'Mr Rhysdale.' Her voice tightened. 'Perhaps
you can tell me why you call upon my husband.'

'I have no objection to doing so, ma'am, although perhaps Lord Westleigh ought to be present.' He inclined his head. 'As a courtesy.'

She swept across the hall. 'Come into the drawing room. I will ring for tea.'

It was the same room where he had spoken
to Ned and Hugh. She pulled a bell cord and the
butler appeared.

'Some tea, Mason,' Lady Westleigh ordered.
'Do sit, Mr Rhysdale.'

He waited for her to lower herself into a chair and chose one a distance from her that she might consider comfortable.

She could not look at him.

Rhys took pity on her. She was merely one more person who had been ill-used by Lord Westleigh. 'I surmise you know who I am, my lady.'

She glanced at him and gathered some pluck. 'Why would you show your face here, after all this time?'

He spoke gently. 'Your sons involved me…' he paused, trying to think how to say it '…in a business matter.'

Her mouth opened in surprise. 'Ned and Hugh?'

'Yes.'

Lord Westleigh thundered in. 'See here, Rhysdale. You were told to wait in the hall.' He came to a sudden halt. 'Honoria!'

'Charles.' Her lips thinned.

Rhys rose. 'Lady Westleigh happened upon me and was gracious enough to invite me into the drawing room.'

'Yes, well.' Westleigh wiped his brow. 'Thank you, Honoria. You may leave. This does not concern you.'

She remained in her seat. 'Mr Rhysdale has no objection to my presence.'

Westleigh tossed him a scathing look. 'It is a matter of business, Honoria. You would find it tedious.'

She smiled at him. 'Oh, since it also involves Ned and Hugh, as I understand, I doubt I should find it tedious. You know that nothing about my sons is trivial to me.'

'Did you think you could conceal the whole from Lady Westleigh?' Rhys asked him. 'I do not see how, unless you decided to go back on your word. Which is why I am here. To determine once and for all if you intend to keep to the bargain your sons made on your behalf.'

The butler brought in the tea tray, halting the conversation at that point. He placed the tray on the table in front of Lady Westleigh. 'Thank you, Mason,' she said.

The butler bowed and turned to leave, but she called him back. 'Mason? If Hugh is about, tell him to join us, please.'

The man bowed again. 'As you wish, my lady.'

When he left the room and closed the door behind him, Lord Westleigh spoke again. 'We do not need Hugh here.'

'I would not talk behind his back,' his wife countered. 'I would invite Ned, as well, but he went out a little while ago.'

Rhys realised his revenge upon his father was certainly going to hurt his wife, which suddenly gave Rhys no pleasure. Still, it was better than the complete financial ruin of the family.

'Shall we wait for Hugh?' Rhys asked the lady.

'I would prefer it,' she said. 'Do sit, Mr Rhysdale. How do you take your tea?'

'No cream. No sugar.'

Ned was surprised at the modest accommodations Miss Gale had on Half Moon Street. He'd expected something grander—not that it mattered to him. She just looked as if she belonged in luxury, protected from any discomfort or stress.

Not that he could provide her such a setting at the moment. He really had no business courting her, except that he could not bear it if her heart went to another.

He sounded the knocker and was admitted by the butler who announced him.

He entered the drawing room where Miss Gale sat with her stepmother and grandmother.

Also present was Luther Parminter, the new Baron Gale.

He bowed to the ladies.

The grandmother frowned in an unwelcoming manner, but Lady Gale extended her hand. 'How nice of you to call, Neddington.'

He glanced to where Miss Gale was seated with the baron. 'Am I interrupting a family visit? Do forgive me.'

'Nonsense,' the young Lady Gale said. 'You are welcome here. Join us.' She gestured to a chair near Miss Gale. 'Shall I pour you some tea?'

'I'll not trouble you.' He bowed to Miss Gale.

She sat in a pool of sunlight from the window, her hair shining like spun gold. Her skin was flawless and her eyes sparkling and clear as a cloudless sky.

She robbed him of speech.

He glanced from her to Luther, whom he'd known in school. 'Gale.'

'Neddington,' Luther said without expression.

Ned was distressed to see him here. Was he courting Miss Gale? Most people liked to keep their wealth and property in the family. Lady Cowdlin said Miss Gale's dowry was a generous one. Was that why Luther was here?

Still, if she had a large dowry, why did she live in such economy?

'I hope you are well today, sir,' she murmured to him.

'Very well, miss,' he responded.

'Hmmph,' the Dowager Lady Gale broke in. 'Our cousin Luther was telling us about Gale House and its people. And the news from the village. We have always made it a point to concern ourselves with the needs of the people, you know.'

Ned turned to Gale. 'I hope you found the people at Gale House in a good situation.'

'Of course,' Luther snapped.

The man was as happy to see Ned here as Ned was to see him. It depressed Ned that he might have a rival. Ned had so little to offer, how could he compete?

His family's partnership with Rhysdale must reap its hoped-for benefits. It all depended upon his father.

Ned could hardly abide the presence of his father these days; he was so angry with the man. His father was being stubborn about Rhysdale and could ruin everything. They'd be worse off than before.

Then there would be no use in pursuing Miss Gale at all.

They chatted about the ball the night before. At one point Luther pulled out his timepiece and examined it.

A few minutes later, Luther stood. 'I must take my leave.' He bowed to Miss Gale, her stepmother and grandmother. 'Ladies, it has been a pleasure.' He tossed an unhappy glare at Ned.

After he left, Miss Gale asked Ned about the weather.

It gave him courage. 'I wonder if you would like to take a turn in the park this afternoon, Miss Gale. I would consider it an honour to drive you in my curricle.' He turned to her stepmother. 'With your permission, ma'am.'

Lady Gale smiled. 'If Adele wishes.'

'Oh, I do!' she cried. 'I mean, I would like that very much, my lord.'

Miss Gale's grandmother frowned.

He rose. 'Then I shall return at four.' A good three hours. How would he be able to pass that much time knowing he would have her company all to himself?

And with everyone else crowding Hyde Park during the fashionable hour.

Ned took his leave, his heart soaring.

'What is this?' Hugh entered the Westleigh town house drawing room. 'Rhysdale, what are you doing here?'

Rhys was accustomed to Hugh's brashness. He had always been so.

Rhys straightened and glanced at each of them. 'I will not prevaricate. I came to get what is due me. I fulfilled my part of our bargain and—' he turned to Lord Westleigh '—you, sir, have not fulfilled yours. I am done being trifled with.'

'See here, Rhysdale—' Lord Westleigh snapped.

'What bargain?' Lady Westleigh asked.

Rhys gestured to Westleigh and Hugh to explain.

Hugh glared at his father. 'You explain it to her, Father.'

Lord Westleigh, still standing, wrung his hands.

'Well.' He looked at his wife. 'Your sons made the plan. Just because finances have become a little strained these days—'

'A little strained!' Hugh broke in. 'It is more serious than that.' He turned to his mother. 'We are a hair's breadth from complete ruin. We owe everybody and Father has not kept up with payments to the bank, for money he borrowed to cover his gambling debts.'

Her gaze flew to her husband, who did not deny this. 'What has this to do with Mr Rhysdale?'

Hugh answered her. 'Ned and I went to him with a proposition.' He explained the scheme to run a gaming house. 'But Father will not do what he gave his word he would do.'

'What is that?' Lady Westleigh asked.

Her husband made a sound of disgust.

Rhys spoke up. 'My lady, I fear what I've asked may cause you some distress. For that, I am sorry.' He riveted his gaze on his father and spoke only to him. 'I once came to you with one request—to support me after my mother died until I had a means of supporting myself. You refused. Now I have no need of your money, so I ask more.' He turned back to Lady Westleigh. 'Your husband must acknowledge me publicly as his natural son. It must seem to society that I am welcomed into the family. I do not ask for a true welcome,' he assured her. 'This is more a matter of recompense. But I insist upon a plan for this to be done and done soon. If it is not accomplished in a reasonable length of time, I will not release any of the money from the gaming hell to your sons.'

Hugh swung around to his mother. 'We need the money, Mother. We need it *now*. Matters are desperate.' His eyes shot daggers at his father. 'If you had behaved with any decency, with any thought to our mother and sister, you would have done the right thing in the first place and you certainly would not have gambled and caroused until money for their food and clothing would be in jeopardy!'

Lady Westleigh's eyes grew huge. 'Is it as bad as that?'

'It is desperate, Mother. Desperate.' Hugh dropped into a chair.

The lady closed her eyes and pressed her fingers to her temples as she took in all this information. Finally she spoke. 'We shall give a ball and introduce you, Mr Rhysdale. I'll arrange the date with you, but it might take a few weeks. The social calendar is full. You will, I presume, wish to have good attendance.' She lifted her chin. 'I will give you my word that it will happen. Will that be enough to release some of the money?'

Rhys stood. '*Your* word will be enough, my lady. I will release the money to Ned today. Have him call upon me this afternoon.' He turned to Lord Westleigh. 'If you prevent this ball in any way, no further profits will be forthcoming.'

'I have no other choice, do I?' Westleigh said.

'As my mother had no choice when you forced her into your bed. As I had no choice but to survive on my own when I was fourteen.' He bowed to Lady Westleigh. 'I will act in a manner that will not embarrass you, my lady. It will suffice that the truth become known.'

She nodded.

'Hugh.' He nodded to his half-brother. 'I'll bid you all good day.'

As he left the house and walked out to the street, he lacked the feeling of triumph that he'd expected. Instead he thought of Lady Westleigh. Her pained expression. Her evident distress.

He'd succeeded in putting his father in a helpless position, but in so doing he'd hurt someone even more helpless. Lady Westleigh.

Another casualty of his father's selfish behaviour.

But it was done.

Rhys would make arrangements with his bank and get the money to Ned this day.

Sun peeked through the buildings and Rhys was reminded of his youth in the village. It had not all been unhappy. He remembered running over hills, fishing in the river, climbing the highest tree he could find to look down on a world where he ordinarily felt quite small. The seeds of his ambition were sowed in that childhood—to succeed. To build something lasting.

The world was changing. The gaming hell belonged to a past where a few had so much money they could throw it away on dice and cards. The future belonged to men with brains and courage, no matter who parented them. Rhys had brains and courage and, with the help of the gaming hell, he'd soon have enough capital to build anything he liked.

His thoughts turned to Celia Allen as the sun warmed the air and lit the buildings in a golden light. Which world did she belong to? He no longer knew. He only knew that in the gaming hell, they were one of a kind.

Would she share his bed this night?

Would she approve of his actions this day?

Not that he would ever tell her, but, somehow his visit to the Westleighs, the family to which he would never truly belong, had left him feeling abandoned.

He wanted the comfort of her arms, her kiss.

He looked up to cross the street and saw Ned approaching from the other side. He stopped and waited. He might as well inform Ned about the afternoon's events.

Ned walked right past him, not pointedly cutting him, as was typical of him, but apparently utterly oblivious.

Rhys called after him, 'Ned!'

Ned stopped then and shook his head as if in a daze. He finally turned around. 'Oh, Rhys. I did not see you there.'

He must be dazed. He called him Rhys, not Rhysdale.

He peered at Ned. 'Are you unwell?'

Ned laughed. 'Not at all. Merely thinking.'

The man looked like a sapskull. 'What is so engrossing?'

Ned grinned. 'Nothing.'

Oh. A woman.

A man only acted in such a manner when he was a besotted fool. 'May I pull your head from the clouds?'

Ned sobered. 'What is it?'

'I've come from your father.' Their father, he meant. 'I have forced the issue with him and I am satisfied that my introduction to society will happen soon. I am prepared to transfer the money back to you. Your original investment and some modest profits.'

Ned brightened. 'My father came through? I feared he would not.' He grasped Rhys's arm. 'This means… This means… We may retrench. We may actually pull out of this!'

Rhys recoiled from this unexpected camaraderie. 'Do not be so hasty. It is not all song and celebration. I am afraid this matter has caused your mother some distress. For that, I am regretful.'

'My mother?' Ned's demeanour blackened. 'Did Father tell her?'

'I did,' Rhys said. 'Although not by design. She encountered me in the hall.'

Ned lowered his head, his euphoria gone.

Rhys felt badly for him. 'Think, Ned. She would have to know of this.'

'I realise that,' Ned responded. 'I just hate what this does to her.'

Rhys actually felt sympathetic to Ned. 'If it is any consolation, she knew who I was as soon as I told her my name.'

Ned nodded. 'That does not surprise me. I am certain, though, that she did not know the state of our finances.'

'Yes, I do think that shocked her,' Rhys admitted. 'I admired her. She handled the whole situation with exceptional grace.'

Ned glanced up at him. 'She is an exceptional woman.'

Rhys clapped Ned on the soldier, surprising himself that their conversation was devoid of hostility. 'Come with me to Coutts Bank. I'll transfer the money to you right now.'

'Excellent!' Ned's mood improved. 'But I must be done by four o'clock.'

'We'll be done,' Rhys assured him.

Celia excused herself after two of her mother-in-law's friends came to call. Adele had already begged to be excused so that she might ready herself for her ride in Hyde Park.

It was endearing to see Adele so excited and happy. This past year of mourning had been so difficult. First the shock of their financial situation, then what amounted to an eviction from the only home Adele had ever known.

And now Luther thought he could court Adele?

Not if Celia could help it.

Although Celia was unsure about Neddington, as well.

But she was getting ahead of herself. Adele was engaged only for a ride in Hyde Park, not marriage.

Celia retreated to her bedchamber.

Her lady's maid emerged from her dressing room. 'Good afternoon, ma'am.' She lifted a gown she carried in her arms. 'I came in for this. Needs some mending.'

'Thank you, Younie.' Celia smiled. 'I am surprised to see you here, though. I thought Adele would be running you in circles to get ready for Hyde Park.'

'Oh, I am to go to her in one half hour,' Younie said. 'After she has rested so the dark circles under her eyes disappear.'

'What dark circles?' Adele looked as fresh-faced as ever.

Younie chuckled. 'The ones in her imagination, I expect. It is best to go along with these notions, though. You cannot convince a girl that age of anything.'

'I am certain you are right.' Celia had never had an opportunity to be so young and infatuated. She'd been married two years by the time she was Adele's age. Love seemed impossible.

An image of Rhys flew into her mind.

'And what of you, ma'am?' Younie asked. 'Do you go out tonight?'

Celia knew what she meant. 'After the theatre? Yes.'

Her insides fluttered.

She could hardly think of anything else but going to the Masquerade Club tonight. Or that Rhys wanted to bed her.

Her body roused as if he'd again been near. Could Younie tell? she wondered.

'Which gown do you wear tonight?' Younie asked, appearing not to notice anything amiss.

Celia wished she had something new and even more fashionable to wear tonight. She wanted him to look on her with admiration.

Which made her not much unlike Adele, she supposed.

Celia sat at the dressing table and peered at her reflection. 'Do you think I have dark circles?'

Her maid clucked. 'You ought to have, with the amount of sleep you are getting.'

She looked closer, pulling the skin under her eye taut to examine it better. 'Oh, dear, is it taking a toll?'

Younie put her fists on her waist. 'Does it look like you only sleep four or five hours? No. No one would know.'

'That is good,' Celia murmured.

Younie picked up the dress again and walked

over to her. 'You ought to rest, ma'am. You need it more than the young miss.'

'Excellent advice.' Celia touched the woman's hand. 'Perhaps I will lie down a little. Will you make certain I am up before Adele leaves?'

'That I can do! Shall I untie your laces?' Younie asked.

'Yes. I'll take off the dress only, though. I can lie down in my shift and corset.'

After Younie helped her from her gown, the maid left. Celia climbed into the bed.

And thought about Rhys.

His invitation was scandalous.

And exciting.

He *liked* her, he'd said. And he had been kind to her. And protective, all of which was extremely novel to her. Besides, he was young and vital and strong. What would it be like to lie with such a man?

She was inexperienced, but not naive. One could not be naive having been married to a wastrel like Gale. She well knew that men and women engaged in affairs without being married.

What would she discover if she allowed herself to accept Rhys's proposition? Would she feel pleasure?

His kiss had promised pleasure. It made her yearn for more.

That was what shocked her.

She hugged herself and imagined his arms around her again.

Would there be any harm in having an affair with him? Plenty of widows had affairs and society turned their eyes away from it. She would never marry again, so this might be her only chance to see what the sexual act would feel like with a man other than her husband.

It might even erase the memory of what it had been like with her husband.

That was something she very much desired.

Her time with Rhys was limited. As soon as Adele was settled, Celia would move away and live the quiet, independent life she craved.

She was in no danger of losing her heart to Rhys. He was a gambler. Her mother had shown her that loving a gambler was a very bad risk. The only person she intended to place her bets on was herself. She could trust herself to pay the bills, to live within her means, to do whatever she chose to do.

She sat up and climbed off the bed.

There was the one thing she wished most to do that she could not choose. She could not choose to have a baby.

She paced the room, finally coming to the window. She gazed into the street below, but saw nothing of the carriages passing by or people walking to and fro. Her arms still ached to hold a child of her own, and nothing would replace that void in her life—not even the babies Adele would have.

Those babies would never be hers.

She swung away from the window and sat at her dressing table, staring at her reflection.

Rhys had said she was alluring.

She could not see it, but his words did thrill her.

He admired her, liked her, comforted her, protected her. Why not let him make love to her, as well?

Why not accept what Rhys offered her?

Chapter Eight

Rhys strolled through the game room, keeping his eye on what he'd laboured to create. The hazard and faro tables were the most crowded, but several patrons also played *vingt-et-un* and *rouge et noir*. The occasional gentleman wore a mask, but all of the women came disguised. More and more of them came each night.

Xavier glanced up at him from a game of whist and gave him a look that showed Xavier was still at outs with him. Rhys could forgive it. Xavier's concerns came from friendship, a friendship Rhys valued. Xavier, and perhaps MacEvoy, were the only people in the world who cared a fig about whether Rhys lived or died.

Rhys nodded to Xavier and continued his rounds.

He turned towards the doorway and saw Celia enter.

She wore the same gown and mask as the night before, but her hair was simply dressed with only a ribbon threaded through it. She paused just inside the room and turned in his direction.

Their gazes caught and held.

He smiled. Her mouth moved ever so slightly. Was that a yes?

It surprised him how much his spirits were heightened. He'd not quite allowed himself to think about whether she would come this night. And whether she would agree to his invitation.

Some gentlemen approached her and, amidst her protests, led her to the hazard table. She finally nodded her head and took the dice in her hand.

'Rhys?' A voice at his elbow caused him to turn away from the sight of her.

Both Hugh and Ned stood there. They rarely came to the Masquerade Club on the same night.

'Gentlemen.' He nodded to them. 'Did you make your appointment in time?' he asked Ned.

'My appointment?' Ned looked puzzled.

'At four?'

Ned coloured. 'Ah, that appointment. I did indeed.'

Hugh's brows rose.

Rhys asked, 'How is your mother?'

Hugh glowered. 'Quite upset.'

Rhys said, 'I regret that.'

Hugh turned away.

Ned broke in, 'We came to say again how grateful we are that you paid the money today.'

'Your mother gave her word,' he responded. 'It was enough for me.'

Hugh glanced back at him, his expression quizzical.

Ned surveyed the room. 'It looks like a good crowd.'

Rhys agreed. 'The numbers grow every day.'

Ned paused, but finally said, 'We will not stay long. We came only to thank you again.'

If their situation were different, Rhys might find Ned a comfortable acquaintance. He was sober and earnest, a decent sort. Rhys had known boys like him at school. They'd always treated him fairly. Hugh, though, was a different story. Rhys suspected they were too much alike to ever co-exist without battling each other.

The same blood flowed in their veins, so it should be no surprise that their personalities were similar. Of course, Rhys had learned to hide his emotions. Hugh's emotions were always on display.

'I bid you goodnight, then,' Rhys said, extending his hand.

Ned shook hands with him. Hugh did not.

Rhys turned back to the hazard table. Westleigh had joined the crowd and handed Celia the dice.

'Pass them on, sir,' Rhys heard her say. 'I've lost enough.'

'One more roll,' Westleigh urged. 'Your luck could change.'

She hesitated, but finally accepted the dice and threw them on the table. 'Six!' she called out.

She nicked the roll with a twelve.

A cheer went up from the men crowding around the table. At their urging the young woman croupier scooped up the dice and handed them back to Celia.

She called out a seven this time, but rolled a four and a two. The croupier handed her the dice again and she won this toss with another roll of six.

Another cheer rose from the table.

It looked like she was on another winning streak tonight. Last night's tally showed they had indeed lost at the hazard table, but nothing alarming. The profits at faro and *rouge et noir* more than made up for it. Rhys liked that her winning drew a bigger crowd to the hazard table. In the long run hazard would turn a profit.

Rhys moved through the room again, still keeping an eye on the hazard table. Celia won a third time, and, egged on by the patrons betting with her, she more eagerly accepted the dice from the croupier to try again.

He'd seen winning streaks like this before. He did not mind if she had some big wins, since money was important to her. Better she win than lose.

He wanted her to be happy.

He also wanted her to come to him this night. He felt the twinges of arousal merely thinking of it.

When Celia had entered the game room, she'd immediately caught of glimpse of Rhys. She'd also seen Neddington and another young man approach him, so she avoided speaking to him right away. Before his conversation ended, two gentlemen whisked her over to the hazard table.

'Come give us the luck, madam,' they'd said to her.

'As you wish,' she responded.

She played hazard again because she expected to lose. If she could encourage men to bet with her like the night before, they would also lose and maybe she could return to Rhys some of the money she'd cost him.

It worked, too. An occasional roll was successful, but most were not. She'd set her limit at fifty pounds, which she would then try to recoup by playing card games that gave her better odds.

As she tossed the dice on to the green baize table, a man's hand touched her back.

Westleigh.

Her skin shuddered where he touched.

'Greetings, my dear. Allow me to assist you.'

He scooped up the dice, put his closed hand up to his lips and blew. 'For luck.' He smiled.

It made her sick.

She tossed the dice and won. And won again. And again.

Soon she'd lost all sense of time. All she knew was the feel of the dice in her hand, the sound of dice hitting the table, the cheers when the right numbers turned up. Her heart pumped wildly and she became dizzy with excitement. The fever had returned.

This night she woke from her reverie at the sight of Xavier Campion scowling at her.

She came to her senses and threw up her hands. 'I am done!'

She hurried away from the table. Pausing to check the timepiece in her reticule, she realised she'd not even thought about Rhys while in the fever. The dice had been too important.

It was two-fifteen! She'd spent all her time at the hazard table.

Someone touched her back again.

'Would you care for some supper, my dear?' Westleigh had followed her.

She'd even forgotten he'd stood next to her all that time. 'No. Not at all. Forgive me. I must speak with Mr Rhysdale.'

'Rhysdale?' Westleigh sniffed with contempt.

'Yes.' She could not be bothered with this man.

She searched instead for Rhys and found him

leaning against the door jamb, his arms folded across his chest.

He saw her, nodded and walked out of the room.

Surely he knew of her new winning streak.

'I must go,' she said to Westleigh.

As she made her way to the door, she suddenly felt unable to breathe. She'd not decided about his proposition, but now she feared he would withdraw it. She walked briskly through the room.

A gentleman stopped her. 'Some whist, Madame Fortune?'

'Madame Fortune?' She did not comprehend.

The man smiled. 'That is what we call you now.'

She groaned inwardly. Her good fortune was Rhys's loss. 'I see.'

'It would honour me if you would partner me in whist,' he persisted.

She glanced toward the door. 'I—I cannot tonight, but perhaps next time?'

He bowed. 'I shall count on it.'

She hurried to the door and made her way to the room where the cashier sat.

'Cashing in early, ma'am?' he asked.

She nodded.

When her accounts were settled she thanked him and made as if she were leaving, but instead of entering the hall, she turned towards the servants' stairway and climbed those stairs to Rhys's private rooms, not knowing what reception she would find.

The drawing-room door was ajar and she could see him in the centre of the room. He'd removed his coat and waistcoat and stood only in his shirt-sleeves, his back towards her. Her hands flew to her suddenly flaming cheeks.

She took a breath. 'Rhys?'

He turned, but his expression was impassive. 'I was uncertain you would come.'

'Of course I would come.' She spoke the words without thought. 'I needed to.'

His brows rose.

She entered the room and closed the door behind her, her heart pounding. 'I—I mean I must speak with you.'

He did not move, but she felt him withdraw as she came closer.

'I must explain.' A wave of guilt washed through her. 'I won tonight, Rhys.' Had this been how her father had felt when he lost? Ironic she should feel it for winning. 'I must have cost you over a hundred pounds between my winning and those who bet with me.'

The experience was now a blur of dice hitting the table, people cheering and the intoxication of win after win.

She took a breath. 'Surely you noticed.'

'Is that why you are here?' His posture was stiff and his shirt so white it seemed to light the room.

She gripped her reticule to keep her hands from shaking. 'I expected you to be angry.' Her husband had become angry at so much less.

He stared at her. 'I told you it is of no consequence. You and the others will lose eventually.'

His tone was still so stiff she feared he'd meant the opposite of what he said.

He gestured to her. 'At least take off your mask, Celia.'

Her hand flew to her face. She'd even forgotten her mask. She wearily lowered herself onto the sofa, setting her reticule down beside her. She untied her mask and dropped it next to the reticule.

He crossed his arms over his chest. 'You have not answered my question.'

She searched back, but could not remember what it was. 'I've forgotten it.'

He remained standing, but sipped his drink. 'Did you come here merely to tell me you won tonight?'

She gazed at him, so tall, so taut in his stance that it felt he was coiled like a spring. A flutter of nerves—or excitement—made her press her hand against her stomach. It did not help that his shirtsleeves accentuated his broad shoulders and narrow waist. She was robbed of breath.

'Not only for that,' she answered. No matter her fear or her nerves, her decision was made.

He met her gaze, but remained grim. 'For what, then?'

She blinked. 'Are you going to make me say it?'

One corner of his mouth turned up. 'Indeed.'

Courage was failing her. 'What you asked of me—I might say yes.'

He tilted his head. '*Might* say yes?'

She gathered her resolve and stood. 'Will say yes.'

He took her hand and raised it to his lips, which were warm and firm and sent a thrill deep within her.

'When does your driver return?' he asked.

'Five-thirty,' she said. Three hours away.

Her coachman had raised his brows at the request for a later hour. She herself was surprised she'd asked for it.

Perhaps she'd always known what she would decide.

He raised a hand and touched her cheek. 'You are certain?'

No. She was not certain at all. But she could not make herself refuse.

She did not *want* to refuse.

'Come.' He took her by the hand. 'I will show you my bedchamber.'

He led her to another room on that floor. Candle flames fluttered when they entered, illuminating a chest of drawers, a table, side chairs…and a bed. He'd prepared for her.

She had not thought beyond her impulsive yes.

Once inside the bedchamber, she was as unsure as a new bride.

He led her to a table where two glasses of wine stood. 'A toast to you.' He handed her one of the glasses and lifted the other. 'And to pleasure.'

'To pleasure,' she whispered in return, her heart racing in her chest.

The wine was a strong and sweet sack. She drank it quickly and he poured her another. When she finished that glass she felt as if she were floating.

'Come to the bed,' he said.

Acting precisely like an experienced lady's maid, he unbuttoned the row of buttons decorating the back of her gown. She let it fall to the floor. Next he untied the laces of her corset. Each motion of his fingers made her tremble, more and more unsure of herself. Still, she slipped off her corset, leaving only her shift.

His eyes raked over her, dark as the night and full of desire.

He made quick work of removing his shirt, tossing it aside in a flash of white that tumbled to the floor. Dark hair peppered his chest and his muscles were as defined as those of a Greek statue. He moved slightly and the lamplight caught a webwork of scars on his side.

Her hand reached out to touch them, but he picked her up by her waist and sat her upon the bed. 'Next your shoes and stockings.'

She could not move. Never had a man touched her feet, nor slipped his hands up her legs to remove her stockings. An ache grew inside her, an ache of want.

Her legs still tingled when he stepped back, removed his trousers and stood before her naked.

She stared transfixed. No mere Greek statue could appear as magnificent.

He climbed on the bed, cupped her face and kissed her.

At first his kiss was gentle, a mere touch, but he pressed harder, moving his lips as if needing to devour her. Such a kiss was not one to be endured, but one that made her want to return such ardour. She kissed him back, daring even to touch her tongue to his. His lips parted and the kiss became something wondrous.

Sensation shot through her and his hands moved to explore her body through the thin fabric of her shift. She could do no more than rest her hands on his shoulders, but even that contact gave a thrill. His skin was warm and slightly damp to the touch.

Not cold. Not clammy.

He bunched the fabric of her shift in his hands, pulled it over her head and tossed it aside. Leaning back, he gazed at her, his eyes darkening, his breathing deepening.

Her husband's gaze always made her wish to cover herself. Rhys's felt like a caress.

'You please me,' he said.

Filled with a delight she'd never known before, she lay back on the pillows.

And he rose over her.

All at once it seemed as if the room grew dark.

Her heart raced so hard that it hurt. Her limbs trembled.

He covered her with his body and she gasped for air.

His male member pressed against her skin—

Panic engulfed her. She cried out and flailed at him, struggling to free herself.

He lifted himself off her immediately, shock on his face. 'What?'

She was still trapped by his body. She pushed at his chest, but he seized her arms and held her down.

'What is it?' he demanded. 'Have I hurt you?'

'Get off!' she begged. 'Please get off!'

He released her and moved off her. She scooted away from him, curling up into a ball, trying to hide from her panic and her shame.

'Celia!' He sounded as if he'd run a great distance. 'Tell me. What. Happened.'

She sat up, hugging her knees to her chest. 'I—I remembered.'

'Remembered what?'

For the second time that night she expected anger from him. Not anger. Rage. Her husband always raged at her if she'd dared push him away.

Rhysdale merely sat up. She braced herself for a blow.

But he did not strike her. He tucked her in front of him, wrapped his arms around her and held her close like her mother used to do when she woke from a nightmare.

'What did you remember, Celia, that frightened you so?' His voice was low. Soothing. Comforting.

It calmed her. 'I—I remembered. The only other man I was with…' She paused, searching for the right words. 'He was not gentle.'

The muscles of his arms bunched. 'He hurt you?'

She nodded. 'It came back. I thought it was happening again.'

'Who is this man?' His voice turned hard. 'I will pay him a call.'

She did not even think of inventing a story. 'My husband,' she answered.

He tensed. 'You have a husband, *Miss* Allen?'

She'd misled him on purpose. Now she regretted it. 'I once had a husband. Not any more. He is dead.'

'How fortunate for him. And me.' He laughed as if in relief. 'Tell me of this husband of yours.'

She owed him an explanation. 'I was very young when I married him. Younger than—' She stopped herself. She'd almost said she was younger than Adele, but giving him a clue to who her husband was—who she was—still felt too exposing. She took a breath. 'It all came back. I am sorry.'

He nuzzled her and rocked her. 'Do not be distressed, Celia. Lovemaking is not supposed to bring pain. It is supposed to bring pleasure. I will not hurt you, I promise.' He paused. 'I will stop now, if you wish it.'

She twisted around to face him. 'No. I—I want to know what it is like without me being so—so afraid.'

She rose to her knees, as did he. He pulled the pins from her hair and released the ribbon threaded through. When her hair fell about her shoulders, he combed it with his fingers.

'I will be gentle, Celia.'

Slowly her panic dissolved. He stroked her, like one might pet a cat. Like a cat, she relaxed under his fingers. She lay down again and urged him down beside her. 'Your touch is gentle.'

He kissed her neck and murmured, 'Say my name, Celia.'

'Rhys.' It was a name to be whispered beneath sheets.

'See? I am not the man who hurt you,' he soothed. 'I will never hurt you.'

He remained beside her, keeping his promise so well her limbs turned to warm butter under his touch. His fingers traced around her nipples and she writhed at the pleasure of it. His hand slipped down her body and rested on her belly.

Aching with need, she pushed it further and still his touch was excruciatingly gentle as he explored her most private of places. Her hips rose to meet his hand, urging him to take greater access.

'You must tell me when you want me,' he whispered.

She wanted him at that very moment, but she held back. The fear hovered near, ready to flood her again. He waited and eventually his touch pushed away the fear and replaced it with more need.

'Now,' she rasped.

He rose over her again and she opened her legs to him even as she braced herself for the event that inevitably brought her pain.

To her surprise his entry was as tender as his touch. He eased inside her and new, unimaginable sensations flooded her. He moved softly as if she might break beneath him. The rhythm lulled her and slowly a sensation akin to bliss arose inside her, growing more urgent with each thrust.

Suddenly his restraint became torture, albeit an exquisite one. Her hands grasped his backside and a frustrated sound escaped her lips.

He moved faster and she gladly kept up with him. This wonderful new sensation grew. The stronger it became, the more she wanted to rush towards it.

Suddenly pleasure exploded within her. She cried out and, at the same time, he convulsed inside her, spilling his seed, slaking his desire a moment after fulfilling hers.

He did not collapse atop her, as her husband had done, crushing her with his weight. He eased himself off her, settling at her side again. She could feel the rise and fall of his chest against her bare skin.

'Rhys,' she managed to whisper as tears formed in her eyes. She blinked them away.

'We have made love, Celia,' he murmured, his voice rumbling. 'Whatever your husband did to you, it was not making love.'

She curled up against him. 'I did not know of that—that pleasure. It was a surprise. I thought the pleasure was going to be only in how you touched me.'

'You are built for such pleasure, Celia. Settle for nothing less.' He cradled her under his arm.

She placed her hand on his chest, relishing the feel of him.

'Tell me about why you married this husband of yours.' He placed his hand over hers.

At this moment she wanted to pretend Gale had never existed, but she acquiesced. 'I was only seventeen.'

'Seventeen?' He rose on an elbow to look down on her.

'My guardians demanded I marry him,' she explained. 'I had no other choice. To be fair to them, they thought it a good thing for me. He was quite a bit older and—and of good reputation, at least of what they knew. He wanted a young wife.'

He frowned. 'How old are you now?'

'Three and twenty.'

'And he is dead?' His voice turned gruff.

'Over a year,' she said. 'He left me little money. That is why I must gamble. So that I have enough to support…myself.' She'd almost said *us*. 'I want to take care of myself, so that I do not have to do what any one else wants me to do. I do not require much. Not a large fortune. Just enough for comfort and security.' It was not the whole truth, but enough of it.

He kissed her temple. 'I am glad you came here.'

She looked into his eyes. 'I am glad of it, too.' And for more than just the chance to win at cards.

He grinned. 'It seems to me that you may need many lessons in lovemaking, though. To catch up.'

She smiled in return. 'I expect I do.' She feigned innocence. 'I do not suppose you know of a man who might be willing to teach me?'

'Only one.' He lowered his lips to hers for a long, lingering, arousing kiss. 'It would be my pleasure to teach you.'

He made love to her again, every bit as tenderly. The pleasure of her climax was equally as intense and she was left wanting more.

When they were finished he asked, 'Do you need to take care of yourself?'

'Take care of myself?' Her brows knitted.

'Do what women do after. To prevent a baby,' he explained.

Her eyes widened. Women could *prevent* a baby? She'd had no idea.

'I do not need to do anything.' That familiar empty feeling returned. 'I am barren.'

He peered at her, saying nothing, but gathered her in his arms again and kissed her. 'We should check the time.'

He climbed off the bed and searched the clothing on the floor. 'Drat. I left my coat in the drawing room.' He pulled on his trousers.

She wrapped herself in the bed linens. 'There is a timepiece in my reticule.' She scrambled from the bed. 'Oh, my goodness! I left my reticule in the drawing room. It has all my money.'

He lifted a hand. 'I will bring it to you.'

He put on his shirt and walked from the room in his bare feet.

By the time he returned she'd donned her shift.

He lifted the reticule before placing it on a table. 'It feels like you did win a great deal tonight.'

She picked up her corset. 'What time is it?'

'Ten minutes after five.'

'I must hurry.' She turned her back to him. 'Would you help me with my corset?'

She held it in place while he tightened the laces.

In a reverse of the more sensual undressing, they quickly put on all their clothes.

She felt the floor for her hairpins and quickly twisted her hair into some sort of order. She stuffed the ribbon in her reticule.

As they rushed down the stairs, she covered her face with her hand. 'My mask.'

'I'll get it.' He bounded back up the stairs.

She waited on the stairs, covering her face.

Xavier Compier entered the hall. He did not speak to her, merely leaned against the wall and watched her. When Rhys's footfall sounded on the steps, Xavier retreated into the shadows.

'Here it is.'

She turned away and held the mask in place while he tied its ribbons.

They made it outside and he blew out a breath. 'I think we made it.'

There was the faintest glimmer of dawn peeking through the darkness. She smiled at him. 'Thank you for a lovely time, Rhys.'

He put an arm around her. 'Come to me again tonight.'

She looked up at him. 'For more lessons?'

His eyes darkened. 'Yes indeed.'

After Celia's coach turned the corner, Rhys re-entered the house and saw Xavier standing in the hall.

'You are still here?' He was not particularly

pleased. No doubt his friend had known he'd been with Celia.

'I waited for you,' Xavier said.

Rhys gestured for Xavier to come up the stairs with him. 'Well, come upstairs. You might as well have a brandy with me.'

They sat together in the drawing room, a bottle of brandy between them on the table.

'Do you want to stay?' Rhys asked. 'You can use one of the beds upstairs.'

Some of the rooms remained unchanged from when the house's girls once entertained gentlemen in them.

Xavier shook his head. 'I'll go back to the hotel.' He'd kept his rooms at Stephen's.

'Any problems in the game room after I left?' Rhys asked.

Xavier frowned. 'We lost at hazard again.'

Here it comes, Rhys thought. Xavier would have noticed Celia's winning streak. 'I heard about it. We didn't recoup later?'

'Not enough.' Xavier inclined his head towards the cashier's room. 'I asked MacEvoy to count the money right away.'

Rhys tapped his fingers on his brandy glass. 'It happens sometimes. Luck occasionally turns bad, even for the house. You know that.'

Xavier gave him a direct look. 'The only time we lost at hazard was when she was winning.'

Rhys met his eye. 'I know. I watched her, too.'

'I have a bad feeling about this,' Xavier persisted. 'You do not know who she is. What she is about. You don't know what she wants from coming here.'

'We've been through this already, Xavier,' Rhys shot back. 'She wants to win money, like everyone else.'

Xavier's voice rose. 'I know you've taken her to your bed. Your judgement is clouded.'

Rhys levelled a gaze at him. 'Stay out of it, Xavier. I mean this.'

But Xavier went on. 'All I'm saying is, do not close your mind too tightly. Watch her.'

Rhys glared at him. 'Enough. Say no more.'

Xavier opened his mouth, but wisely closed it again.

He stood. 'I ought to be going.' He glanced towards the windows where slivers of light appeared through the gaps in the curtains. 'It's morning already.'

Rhys stood, too, and clapped him on the shoulder. 'Do not worry over me, Xavier. You are like a mother hen sometimes.'

Xavier merely nodded. 'I'll see you tonight.'

Xavier would not let this go, Rhys feared. He'd consider it his duty to look out for Rhys, even if Rhys demanded he stop. It was ingrained in Xavier's character.

Rhys knew precisely what he was doing and had no need of Xavier's caution. Rhys intended to enjoy this affair with Celia for as long as it lasted, and if Xavier did not like it, it would stand like a wall between them.

Chapter Nine

Celia hugged herself during her short ride back to her rooms. Her body felt languorous, at peace with itself for the first time in her memory.

How could she have ever guessed lovemaking could be like this?

The carriage turned a corner.

She'd turned a corner, too. She felt free of her husband at last. There was no reason ever again to think of what it had been like being married to him. That part of her life was over and nothing like it would ever again happen to her.

A new door had opened. A door to new experiences and new delights. Celia planned to enjoy every minute of them.

Her heart was as light as gossamer when the carriage stopped. She gathered her mask and her reticule, opened the door and climbed out.

'Thank you, Jonah,' she called to her coachman. 'Get some rest.'

He touched his hat in acknowledgement and flicked the reins. The coach pulled away.

Celia walked to the door and turned the latch. Tucker knew what time to unlock the door for her. He would have risen from his bed and be waiting to attend her in the hall.

How good her servants were to her.

She opened the door and stepped inside. Her butler indeed stood before her, but with an anxious expression and wringing hands.

She tensed. 'What is it, Tucker?'

He inclined his head towards the staircase. 'The dowager.'

Was Lady Gale ill? 'What about her?'

His face turned grim. 'She awaits you in your bedchamber.'

Celia froze. She was discovered.

She lifted her chin, though. This would change nothing. Her mother-in-law had no control over her life. The woman was dependent upon Celia, not the other way around.

She gave Tucker a rueful, but reassuring smile. 'Well, this will be unpleasant, will it not?'

'Quite, ma'am.' He relaxed a bit at her calm manner.

Celia climbed the stairs, feeling weary and in a great need of sleep.

Her maid stood outside her bedchamber door. 'She's in there,' Younie whispered. 'Fit to be tied.'

'So I would expect.' Celia opened the door.

Lady Gale had positioned one of Celia's chairs to face the door. She sat on the chair as if it were a throne and wore an outraged expression.

Celia did not give her mother-in-law time to speak. 'You have not been invited into my private room, Lady Gale. Nor were you given permission to rearrange my chairs.' When holding a weak hand, it was always best to make a bold move. Celia's father had taught her that. 'Leave now and never trespass here again.'

The dowager's mouth dropped open and it took time for her to find her voice. She rose out of the chair. 'How dare you speak to me like that, you little wretch! Especially when you have been out all night. Where have you been?'

'I do not owe you an explanation, Lady Gale.' Celia stood at the open door.

The dowager grabbed her cane and pounded it across the floor. She stopped inches from Celia. 'You have been with a man. I'd wager a fortune on it. Who did you find willing to bed you? Surely someone you had to pay.'

Celia recoiled from the insult and fought the impulse to strike her mother-in-law across the cheek.

Instead she leaned down into her face. 'Remember your place, ma'am.' Her voice trembled.

'It is only because of my affection for Adele that you are here.'

The older woman shook a finger at Celia. 'You need me, girl! You are known to nobody. Without my connections, you would be invited nowhere.'

'I care nothing for your connections, ma'am.' Celia wanted nothing to do with society. 'The invitations are for Adele's sake, not mine.'

'You have obviously found some opportunity through my connections or you would not be out all night.' Lady Gale sneered. 'Unless you merely walk the streets like a common strumpet.'

Adele appeared in the doorway, rubbing her eyes. 'I heard shouting. You said my name. Are you arguing about me? Because I do not want you to argue about me.'

Lady Gale jabbed her finger at Celia. 'This woman is trying to ruin your reputation. She is gallivanting on the streets of London all night. If anyone discovers this, we'll all be ruined. Even your cousin will not wish to court you.'

She was still pushing Luther on poor Adele.

'That would be a good thing,' Celia snapped.

Adele clapped her hands over her ears. 'Stop! Stop!'

Celia caught herself and lowered her voice. 'Lady Gale, please leave now. Say no more.'

Younie stepped forwards. 'Come along, ma'am.' The maid spoke soothingly. 'Let me have Cook fix you a nice posset, so you can have a rest. All this fuss does you no good.'

Lady Gale allowed Younie to put her arm around her and coax her out of the room. 'She has given me palpitations!' she wailed.

'There, there, my lady,' Younie murmured. 'Let me fix you up.'

The maid got her into the hall and halfway to her own bedchamber before Lady Gale turned around. 'Ask her whose bed she's been warming, Adele. She's trying to ruin us all!'

When Lady Gale disappeared into her bedchamber with Younie, Adele turned to Celia, with her lip trembling. 'Is it true?'

'Come in my room.' Celia took the girl's hand and led her to the chair her grandmother had so recently vacated.

She moved another chair closer and sat. 'I will tell you the truth.' Or rather part of the truth, Celia thought. Enough of it, she hoped. 'It is true that I have been out all night, but I have not been walking the streets as your grandmother suggests.'

'Have you been with a man, though?' Adele asked, her voice wobbling.

Celia sidestepped that question. 'I have been at a place called the Masquerade Club.' That was truth enough. She lifted her arm where her mask dangled. 'It is a place where ladies may dress in disguise and gamble.'

Adele's eyes widened. 'Gamble?'

Celia nodded. 'Play cards. Hazard. Faro. It is where I go almost every night.'

'You go to a gambling house?' Adele's voice rose in alarm.

'That is how I have funded your new gowns and paid our bills.' Celia opened her reticule and removed the leather purse, heavy with coin. 'See? These are my winnings. They will pay the servants' wages. And pay for another ballgown for you. And more.'

'You pay for my gowns with money from *gambling?*' Adele looked horrified.

'Adele.' It was time to acquaint her stepdaughter with the realities of their situation. 'I have never had enough money to fund this Season for you. I had to do something.'

'But to *gamble?*' She said the words with disgust. 'Is not gambling what ruined my father?'

Not merely gambling. Debauchery, gluttony and carousing greatly contributed.

'Your father gambled rashly.' As did Celia's own father when he was on a losing streak. 'I am not rash.' At least she would not be rash again. She lifted the purse. 'This is proof.'

Adele jumped to her feet. 'Oh, Celia! What if you are found out? What if Lord Neddington learns you *gamble?*'

Celia did not have the heart to tell the girl that her dear Neddington was a frequent visitor at the same gambling house. 'No one will find out. That is the beauty of this establishment. Because ladies may come in disguise, no one knows who they are.'

'You do not understand, Celia,' Adele cried. 'He comes from an *important* family. He will never look at me again if it is discovered you gamble every night.'

Before Celia could respond, Adele ran out of the room. Her sobs could be heard in the hallway.

Celia rubbed her eyes. Wearily she rose and sat down at her dressing table, taking her hair down and putting it in a plait.

Younie entered. 'Her ladyship has settled a bit.'

'Thank goodness.' She stood and Younie undid her buttons. 'I fear I handled that badly.'

Younie did not disagree. 'No sense in weeping over shed milk.'

'I am so tired I feel like weeping. I need to sleep. Perhaps I can think better when I am rested.'

She slipped out of her dress and Younie helped her off with her corset. She climbed into her bed in just her shift.

Once under the bed linens she closed her eyes.

She pushed her mother-in-law and Adele out of her thoughts and let her mind wander. It went immediately to Rhys. How it felt lying next to him. How his arms had comforted her and his touch had thrilled her.

Did she not deserve some happiness after all she'd been through? All she needed was to avoid the intoxication of the hazard game and confine herself to whist. She wanted to gamble at the Masquerade Club and share Rhys's bed for as long as she wished, for as long as she needed to stay in London.

When the Season was over, when Adele was settled, it would be over.

That afternoon Ned again called upon Adele for a drive in the park. While he waited for her in the drawing room, he could not even sit, he was so filled with excitement. Rhys had opened the door to restoring his future. Ned could dare to anticipate better fortune from now on.

She walked in and he knew immediately that something was amiss.

'Miss Gale.' He moved towards her.

'I am so sorry to keep you waiting, sir.' She glanced at him and her eyes looked red as if she'd been weeping.

What had upset her? Ned vowed to fix whatever it was, if it was at all in his power.

He did not press her to speak until he turned his curricle in to the park. It was early for the heaviest traffic and he was able to keep some distance from other carriages.

'What is distressing you, Miss Gale?' he began. 'I dislike seeing you so unhappy.'

'Oh.' She sighed. 'Nothing.' She tried to paste on a smile, but he could see it was false.

'Do not say it is nothing,' he pressed. 'I am your friend. Whatever troubles you, I will help.'

She looked away and wiped her eyes with her fingers. 'I ought not to be such a watering pot.'

He wanted to gather her in his arms, but he settled with covering her hand with his. 'Let me share your burden.'

She glanced up into his eyes and it took his breath away. 'It will seem nonsensical to you.'

He squeezed her hand, trying his hardest not to kiss her. 'Nothing you do or say will ever seem nonsensical to me.'

She blinked and one tear slid down her flawless cheek. 'It is just...just that my grandmother and my stepmother are quarrelling and there is nothing I can do about it.'

'What are they quarrelling about?' he asked.

She glanced away. 'I cannot tell you!'

He felt his face grow hot. 'Forgive me. I do not want to pry into your family's business. I only wish to help if I can.'

She sighed. 'Oh, you did not pry. I—I just cannot tell you.'

'I know what it means to keep family matters private.' His whole family situation was a carefully guarded secret. No one—except Rhys, that is—knew how near they were to financial ruin. 'But I want to help you in any way possible. All you need do is ask.'

She gazed at him again, her blue eyes glittering like sapphires through her tears. 'You are the kindest of men.'

He took a deep breath. 'There is…perhaps… something I wish to ask of you. If you feel able to listen to it.'

Her expression softened. 'You may ask anything of me. I am your friend as you are mine.'

He made himself attend to the horses and the path. 'It is an impertinence, I know, but I cannot resist.' He dared glance back to her. 'May I have permission to court you? I desire it above all things.'

She gasped and covered her mouth with her hand. 'Oh, my! Oh, yes. Yes!' She laughed, but quickly sobered. 'You should speak with my stepmother. She will tell you about my dowry and about—about my family. You should know our situation before committing yourself so.'

'If you wish it, I shall do so,' he said. 'This afternoon, if possible. But you must know that your dowry, your family, will make no difference to me. I want you to be my wife.'

'Oh, Neddington,' she whispered.

He glanced around quickly. They did not seem to be in view of any other carriage. Holding the reins in one hand, he cupped her cheek with the other and touched his lips to hers.

Celia did not wish to receive callers. All she wanted was to remain in her bedchamber and sleep.

And avoid her mother-in-law.

And wait for night and time to return to Rhys.

But Adele knocked on her door. 'Lord Neddington is in the drawing room. Will you see him, Celia?'

At least she was dressed. 'Of course I will.'

Adele walked with her down the stairs, whispering instructions the whole way. 'Please listen to him, Celia. Do not tell him about Grandmama's plan for me to marry Cousin Luther. Tell him the truth about my dowry and about Father. I do not wish to hold anything back from him.' She paused for a moment. 'But, do, please, refrain from telling him about your gambling. I fear he will disapprove greatly and I so want him to like me. And you. And Grandmama, too.'

Adele walked with her all the way to the drawing-room door. 'I cannot go in with you, but do treat him well, Celia. My entire life and happiness depends upon it!'

'I will treat him well, I promise.' Celia reached for the latch.

Adele seized her arm and pulled her back. 'Come find me as soon as you are finished. Will you?'

Celia suppressed a smile. 'I will. The moment I am finished.'

She opened the door and walked in the room.

Lord Neddington stood at the window. He turned quickly and bowed. 'Lady Gale.'

She hated being called that. In her mind her mother-in-law was Lady Gale and she was Celia Allen.

'Good afternoon.' He gestured to the window. 'I was just checking my curricle. Your man was good enough to hold the horses for me.'

She walked over and peeked out. 'A lovely pair of horses.'

'Thank you, ma'am.'

She gestured to the sofa. 'Do sit, sir, and tell me why you wished to speak to me.' She might be standing in the role of Adele's father, but, ironically, Neddington was probably older than she. She guessed him to be at least thirty.

He waited for her to sit first. 'I will speak plainly. I wish to court your daughter—your step-daughter, I mean. She wished me to seek your permission. I know you are not her guardian, but she said you were the one I should speak to first.'

Adele's guardian was an old friend of her husband's, a man who was in ill health and had retired to Bath. He did not care enough about Adele to oppose anything Celia decided.

'I am very inclined to comply with Adele's wishes.' Celia wanted Adele to be free to make her own choices. 'Whatever makes her happy.'

He frowned. 'I, too, desire her happiness.'

'You have only just met each other.' Adele should not make too hasty a decision. More importantly, she should not marry a gambler.

'I realise this,' Neddington said. 'That is why I request a courtship. Adele must be sure of me. To be frank, there is one matter that may cause you to decide against me.'

Celia's brows rose. 'Oh?'

He rubbed his face. 'I have tried to behave as a gentleman ought, but, at the moment my family finances are strained. I have taken steps to resolve the problem and in a matter of a year, I expect to be on solid ground again.' He paused. 'But it is not a given. It is…a sort of gamble.'

'A gamble?' She tapped on the arm of her chair with a finger. 'Are you fond of gambling, sir?'

He looked surprised. 'Me? Not at all.' Comprehension dawned. 'I do not gamble at cards and such, if that is what you mean.'

As she had noticed at the gaming house. She longed to ask him why he showed up there.

He went on. 'In any event, my family's finances are not yet quite what they ought to be, so I need time before I can in good conscience commit to marriage. I wanted you both to know that.'

She narrowed her eyes. 'Do you know of Adele's dowry?'

He waved a hand. 'I care nothing for her dowry. Whatever the amount, it will satisfy me.'

He certainly sounded genuinely like he was not in pursuit of her fortune. 'It is ten thousand pounds,' she told him.

His brows rose, but he turned thoughtful. 'It

will be designated for any children we might have, of course. I'll not touch a penny.'

'Adele also wishes you to know that her father was a gambler and carouser, which was why I asked about your gambling habits. Besides her dowry, she inherits nothing. Her grandmother has only a pittance, as well.'

'And you?' he asked.

'I have enough.' She bit her lip, but decided to speak further. 'It would be desirable for Adele's husband to support her grandmother. It would be, shall we say, a great deal for her grandmother to bear to live with me.'

He bowed. 'It shall be my honour to do whatever is required of me.' His expression turned imploring. 'I would not have presumed to ask permission to court Miss Gale but for my fear of another suitor.'

Cousin Luther, he meant.

'I see,' Celia responded. 'I can assure you that no other man has secured Adele's affections.'

Neddington expelled a relieved breath, but he turned earnest again. 'Miss Gale does, of course, have every right to cry off.' His expression turned miserable. 'If she should ever prefer another gentleman to me.'

She reached over to touch his hand. 'As I said, Adele's happiness is of great importance to me. I think you prudent to request a courtship. Take your time to become acquainted, to see if marriage is truly what you desire. Perhaps by the time your finances are in order, you will know for certain if you are suited.'

And Celia would have time to find out why Neddington regularly attended the Masquerade Club.

He clasped her hand. 'I am grateful, my lady. Truly grateful.'

She stood. 'Shall I send Adele in so you might apprise her of our conversation?'

He rose, looking as if the sun had come out after a month of rain. 'Yes. Yes. I would greatly desire to tell her.'

Celia walked to the door and called for Adele, who, she suspected, was waiting in the hall. Adele came running. Celia gestured for Adele to enter and the girl rushed in. Instead of joining them, Celia retreated to allow the besotted young couple some privacy.

Celia had already decided not to attend the evening's social event with Adele and her grandmother. It was to be another musicale, and this time the attendees would be providing the entertainment. She did not think she had the patience to sit through such an event.

She'd been able to remain in the background at the few other parties she'd attended. That suited her very well. The less she was noticed, the less chance anyone would guess who she was when she wore her masks.

She rather hoped Neddington's finances would be quickly restored; that is, assuming he told the truth about not gambling. If that were the case, though, she would have no reason to continue her double life and she was suddenly in no hurry to leave London, to leave Rhys.

She would see him tonight.

Avoiding the musicale also meant she could go to the Masquerade Club early…and avoid her mother-in-law's company a little longer.

Celia had pleaded a headache and confined herself to her room, asking that her dinner be brought to her. It would be assumed she was asleep when Adele and her grandmother returned from the musicale.

There was a knock on her door—Adele, probably, needing her opinion on her gown. 'Come in.'

Her mother-in-law appeared in the doorway. 'Did I behave properly this time?'

It was not worth keeping up the feud, not if it upset Adele so much.

Celia returned a civil smile. 'I do appreciate your knocking. It is very courteous.'

Lady Gale did not look in a conciliatory mood. 'I have something to discuss with you.'

Celia kept her tone mild. 'Certainly.'

The older woman took a deep breath before

glaring at Celia. 'Did you allow Adele to make an arrangement with that Lord Neddington?'

Celia stiffened. 'I gave her permission to decide for herself.'

Lady Gale stood with elbows akimbo. 'How dare you! You knew I meant her for Cousin Luther. You must undo this hasty decision.'

Celia met the woman's eye. 'If you can present me with some reason to object to Adele's choice, I will discuss the matter with her. But it is her decision.'

'What can she know of it?' Lady Gale snapped. 'She is but nineteen.'

'She has time to decide,' Celia assured her. 'Neddington is not pressuring her.'

'What do you know of his family? I have heard gossip about his father—'

Celia put up a hand. 'I am certain there was plenty of gossip about Adele's father, as well. If there is anything to cause undue concern, we will discuss it with Adele. She is a sensible young woman.'

'She is too young—' Lady Gale began again.

Celia levelled a gaze at her mother-in-law. 'Lady Gale, I was younger than Adele and I assure you I knew my own mind.'

The woman's eyes flashed. 'Hmmph! My son should never have married you.'

'Indeed.' Celia did not miss a beat. 'He was a

great deal older than Adele's nineteen years and look what an unwise choice he made.'

'That was your fault,' Lady Gale countered. 'You bewitched him.'

Celia stared at her. 'Do not be absurd. I was seventeen. I did not choose him. I was not even given a choice. Adele will have a choice. Do not interfere or you will have to answer to me.'

Lady Gale spun around and made her way to the door. Before she crossed the threshold she turned back in a dramatic flourish. 'You have not heard the last of this from me.'

After she stormed out and closed the door behind her, Celia whispered, 'I agree. I have not heard the last, because you will never leave it alone.'

Chapter Ten

The next three weeks settled into a predictable routine for Celia, encompassing her greatest happiness, but also her greatest risk. Each night she entered the gaming house she risked losing control over her gambling, but when her night was finished she found unspeakable pleasure in Rhys's arms.

She stayed away from the hazard table as often as she could, but sometimes the gentlemen gambling there, Lord Westleigh especially, insisted she play.

'Madame Fortune,' they implored. 'We need you at hazard. We need your magic touch.'

She continued to win more than she lost, but she thought this was because she forced herself to stop as soon as the euphoria of the game bubbled inside her. It was always a struggle, but the other gamblers began to respect her skill at card playing as well as her luck at the dice, and their pressure to play hazard eased somewhat.

They also quickly learned that Madame Fortune had become Rhysdale's lover, preventing any attempts at flirtation. None wanted to offend the gaming-house owner. It suited Celia very well that she did not become an object of seduction like the woman Rhys had told her about, the one who inspired his idea for the Masquerade Club.

Neddington often came to the Masquerade Club, but Celia never saw him play. He talked to other patrons and watched others gamble, but never did so himself. She was relieved for Adele's sake, especially because the two were becoming more and more attached.

Life was splendid at the moment, even if the Season demanded ever more expenditures and the coach required an expensive repair. Other bills were paid. Adele was in raptures over Neddington and even Lady Gale's taunting could not spoil Celia's optimism.

Celia indulged Lady Gale in as many new gowns as she wished, as she did Adele and even herself, although at times she reminded herself too much of her father on a spending binge. She rationalised that looking prosperous for society was still an investment in Adele's future. Celia herself wanted to look presentable to society, but even more she wanted the gowns designed specifically for the night to look alluring. For Rhys. She delighted in night-time costumes in fabrics of vibrant red, blue or green, with matching masks that grew more elaborate as Younie came up with new ideas for how to make them.

It pleased her when her appearance caused Rhys's eyes to darken with desire as it had this night, when she'd walked in wearing a midnight-blue silk dress embroidered at the hem and bodice with pink roses. Her mask matched the pink and was bordered with tiny green embroidered leaves. It thrilled Celia when Rhys later removed her dress and gazed upon her with reverence.

He constantly surprised her in his ability to delight her and be delighted by her. Celia's old fears about lovemaking had vanished completely. Rhys would never hurt her. Never.

This night brought on yet another new experience.

He was not gentle.

And she did not care.

Their lovemaking took on an urgency, a frenzy that had been entirely new to her. It was she who pushed him, almost violent in her need. She rushed them towards their release as if time was running out, even though the night was young. The pleasure that burst forth from her came with a new intensity. No sooner had they finished than she wanted more.

It felt to Celia that her body had changed into one that always wanted more, more, more.

This night her lovemaking with Rhys was wild with sensuality. The violence of it all was evident in the tangled bed linens and the aching of her womanly parts. She did not feel pain, precisely—nothing like it had been with Gale. But it seemed as if Rhys could not make love to her fast enough or hard enough or often enough.

She'd just propelled them towards another frenzied release when he collapsed atop her and slid to her side. 'I never thought I would say it, but I am worn out.'

She lay back, still throbbing, still needing. 'I do not know what has happened. It feels different. More—more intense. I cannot explain it.' It reminded her disturbingly of when she lost control of her gambling.

He rolled towards her and caressed her face. 'I do not complain of it. You are magnificent.'

She smiled. 'You have heard me say this before. I never imagined lovemaking could feel like this.'

He kissed her lips. 'You have mentioned it. Almost every night.'

She pushed on his chest. 'But this is different.'

He kissed her again. 'It certainly is different.'

If he continued she would start all over again.

The clock struck four. She sat up and the room swam. 'I must go.'

He pulled on his trousers. 'Will you come this night?' he asked.

She nodded.

Unexpectedly her stomach roiled.

Oh, no, please! She did not wish to be ill. She pressed her hand on her abdomen, hoping he did not notice.

'Although I may be later than usual,' she answered aloud.

She never explained why and he never asked.

He kissed her. 'I will wait for you.'

She dressed with his help, always an intimate experience. He tied her mask on last. It came off only when she was in his private rooms.

When he walked her down the stairs, she gripped the rail to keep herself steady.

He noticed. 'Are you feeling unwell?'

'Just tired, I expect.' She smiled. 'Worn out.'

He grinned. 'I know precisely how you feel.'

When they reached the hall Xavier was just leaving with Belinda, the croupier at the hazard table. Celia still felt tension from Xavier, but at least he'd stopped watching her so closely.

When Rhys walked her out into the night air, Celia felt much better. Her carriage came quickly and her kiss goodbye was hurried.

The carriage ride did nothing to help her stomach feel any better, though. She could not be ill! Tonight was a ball Neddington's family was giving and Adele would simply perish if Celia were unable to attend.

That evening Ned invited himself to dine with Adele and her family. He'd hinted very strongly to Adele that it would be a good idea for him to dine with her and her family before the ball.

He wanted plenty of time to talk with them.

At the dinner table, the subject of the ball that night inevitably came up.

He took it as his opening. 'I need to warn you about something.'

Adele's grandmother rolled her eyes. 'I knew all was not well,' she said not quietly enough to prevent his hearing.

He swallowed. 'I—I told you my father was not the best of men—'

'Indeed,' commented Adele's grandmother.

It pained Ned that the Dowager Lady Gale still did not like him, although Ned had tried every way he knew to get in her good graces. What he was about to tell them was not going to help.

He took a breath. Might as well come out and say it straight off. 'I must inform you that my father had a natural child.'

The dowager shrugged. 'He is a reprobate. Everyone knows this.'

'Grandmama!' Adele cried. 'Do not speak so!'

'Neddington is our guest,' warned Adele's stepmother.

Ned turned to Adele's grandmother. 'I must agree with you, ma'am. My father is a reprobate. I do not blame you for holding it against me. I can only say that I am not like him.'

'I am sure great numbers of gentlemen have natural children,' Adele said.

He faced Adele. 'You may meet my father's natural son tonight.' There. He had said it. 'He is to be introduced. At the ball.'

Adele's grandmother pursed her lips in disapproval. 'Hmmph!'

He turned back to her. 'I will not present him to you if you do not wish it, ma'am.'

'I certainly do not wish it!'

'I do not mind,' Adele piped up. 'If you wish to present him to me, I do not object. And neither does Celia. Is that not correct, Celia?'

'Whatever you wish, Adele,' Adele's stepmother responded.

She looked ill to Ned, although she denied it. She merely picked at her food.

'I, for one, am eager to meet your family at last.' Adele gazed at him with eyes full of affection.

How was he to wait to wed her? Perhaps he could ask Rhys if the profits of the gaming house would increase soon. Perhaps it would be enough.

'I am particularly eager to meet your sister,' Adele added.

'You have a sister?' her stepmother asked.

'Phillipa,' Ned responded. 'She is not much in society, but my mother wishes her to attend the ball.'

'I suppose something is wrong with her,' Adele's grandmother said sarcastically.

Ned was determined to tell them all. 'She suffered a terrible…accident when she was a child.' It had been an attack, a mysterious one. His family never spoke of it. 'She has a scar that disfigures her face.'

'Oh, how terribly sad!' exclaimed Adele. 'I am sure I will love her all the same.'

When she said things like this, Ned could only adore Adele more.

He disliked that this shameful family event—introducing Rhys—had to take place the same night he was to present Adele to his parents. He was sorry he had to tell her grandmother all about Rhys and his sister, not that Phillipa was to blame for what happened to her. The grandmother would certainly use this information to try to influence Adele to marry her cousin instead of him. Ned could not bear that.

Worse, even her cousin was invited to the ball. So, Luther, too, would learn that the proprietor of the new gaming house was Ned's illegitimate brother.

At least the women would not know about the gaming house. Unless they were among the masked women who attended the club to gamble.

He chuckled inwardly at that impossibility.

* * *

Rhys and Xavier waited in the drawing room, which had been transformed into a ballroom. The folding doors between it and the formal dining room had been opened, creating a space double the size. The carpets had been rolled up and removed, as had the larger pieces of furniture. All the small tables, chairs and sofas had been pushed to the walls.

Standing in the space, at the moment empty, made their presence stand out all the more.

'I hope you know what you are doing with this,' Xavier remarked. 'You've always disdained society.'

Xavier, whose pedigree entitled him to be included in the highest of social circles, had not mixed much in society since the war. He attended this event only because of Rhys.

'Acceptance in society is not the objective, as you know.' At this point, the event was merely something to get through, the next step in a road he'd set upon the evening Ned and Hugh asked him to run the gaming house.

Xavier shook his head. 'Reaching an objective can sometimes involve unintended consequences.'

Rhys was losing patience with his friend. 'Xavier, I need you as a friend, not a nursemaid.'

'I am not so certain,' Xavier muttered, turning away and pretending to look at some inconsequential piece of chinoiserie.

Someone approached the door and both men turned to see who it was.

A young woman in a ballgown of pale blue silk. Her presence was lovely, but for a crooked scar that started below her eye and ended near her mouth. Rhys knew immediately who this was.

'Oh!' she exclaimed, taking a step back and staring directly at Xavier. 'I thought my parents were already here.'

'Phillipa.' His half-sister.

She glanced at Rhys and her eyes widened. 'You must be—'

He stepped forwards. 'I am Rhys.' He surveyed her. 'But I remember you as a little girl I sometimes saw in the village.'

'I do not remember you at all.' Her gaze slipped to Xavier. 'But I know who you are now.'

Xavier returned her gaze and became unusually silent.

Rhys spoke to her again. 'I hope my presence does not cause you undue discomfort, Phillipa. If so, I am sorry for it.'

She lifted one shoulder. 'It is I who usually cause discomfort. That is why I rarely attend events such as this.'

He extended his arm towards Xavier. 'Allow me to present my friend, Mr Campion.'

'We are acquainted,' Xavier said, stepping forwards. He'd never mentioned that fact to Rhys. 'Miss Westleigh. It is a pleasure.'

Her eyes narrowed. 'How do you do, Mr Campion.'

It was not the sort of reception Xavier usually received from ladies.

'You are known to each other?' Rhys gave Xavier a glance. 'How interesting.'

'Since we were children,' Xavier explained. 'Our families often summered at Brighton at the same time.'

'And most recently in 1814,' Phillipa added. 'Perhaps you do not recall, though.'

Xavier met her gaze. 'I recall. I was briefly in London.'

Rhys looked from one to the other. This was fascinating. Would Xavier tell him what happened between these two? It was obvious something had. To Rhys's surprise he felt a protective brotherly impulse. Had Xavier ill-used her? He'd certainly done something to cause this chilly treatment.

At that moment, Hugh entered the room and after him the Westleigh butler and several musicians.

Hugh walked directly to his sister. 'I did not know you were here, Phillipa.'

'I thought I was late, but no one was here… except…'

Hugh turned to Rhys and inclined his head. 'Rhys.'

Rhys returned the gesture.

Hugh looked discomfited. Once Rhys would

have relished putting Hugh out of ease, in repayment for all the fights Hugh had picked with him when they were boys. But Hugh had restrained himself lately.

Hugh shook hands with Xavier. 'Campion. Good of you to come.' He looked back at his sister. 'Papa is stalling and Mama is dealing with him.'

'Ned?' she asked.

'He rushed in a little while ago. I expect he is getting dressed.'

The musicians set up their instruments and began tuning them. Other servants came in, carrying trays of wine glasses.

Hugh stopped one of them. 'We might as well have a glass while we wait.'

Xavier handed a glass to Phillipa, but she waved it away. Rhys welcomed the refreshment. He was not plagued by nerves, but seemed to be catching the discomfort of all three of his companions. Frankly, Xavier had been more correct than Rhys wanted to admit. This had been a foolish idea.

Lady Westleigh swept in, followed by a dour-looking Lord Westleigh.

He bowed to his hostess. 'Ma'am.'

She extended her hand to him. 'Rhys. Your night has come. I hope it is to your satisfaction.'

He clasped her hand. 'Thank you, my lady.'

Xavier stepped forwards to greet her.

'I expect your parents to attend tonight,' Lady Westleigh told Xavier.

'As they told me, ma'am,' Xavier responded.

Rhys and Xavier had dined with them only a week ago.

She turned to her daughter. 'Phillipa, you forgot your headpiece. After the milliner worked so carefully on it.'

'The feather irritated my face,' Phillipa retorted, her hand touching her scar. 'Besides, everyone knows of my scar. Why should I hide it?'

Rhys looked at his half-sister with new admiration. The young woman had pluck.

Lord Westleigh, Rhys noticed, did not greet him, but instead contented himself with glowering.

Lady Westleigh turned away from her daughter. 'Rhys, I thought we would have you stand in the receiving line with the rest of us. We will greet our guests as a family and Charles will introduce you to each guest in turn. Will that do?'

He preferred that to a general announcement. For one thing, it forced his father to do the right thing over and over and over. 'It seems an excellent idea, ma'am.'

Of all the Westleighs, it was Lady Westleigh who seemed the least affected by this uncomfortable situation. Rhys liked her, he realised. She faced the occasion like a soldier.

'Where is Ned?' She glanced around impatiently. 'I can hear the carriages pulling up to the door.'

'I am here, Mama.' Ned rushed in, still pulling at his sleeves and straightening his coat.

Xavier gave Rhys one more sceptical glance before wandering away from the family.

Lady Westleigh positioned them all in order. She stood first, then her husband. She placed Rhys next to Lord Westleigh, then Ned, even though etiquette would have put Rhys lowest. After Ned came Hugh and Phillipa.

As the guests arrived, Lady Westleigh made certain her husband did not skip a single introduction, although he tried. Some of the gentlemen and a few of the ladies reacted with recognition. A few even said, 'Ah, the proprietor of the Masquerade Club!'

The entire process became tedious as it went on. Ned, for one, fidgeted and spent a great deal of the time leaning over to see who next approached the door.

'Lord and Lady Piermont,' the butler announced.

Xavier's parents.

When they were introduced to Rhys, they reacted with pleasure.

'But we know Rhys!' Lady Piermont exclaimed. 'He is like one of our own.'

Lord Piermont pumped Rhys's hand. 'Good to see you here, my boy.' He looked around to anyone who was in earshot. 'This man saved our son's life on the battlefield.'

'Good to see you both.' He bowed to Lady Piermont. 'Ma'am. Your son is here. He is about somewhere.'

'Is he?' She immediately began scouring the room. 'Oh, do let us find him straight away.'

They quickly moved through the rest of the receiving line and hurried off in search of their son. Xavier was fortunate in his parents, Rhys had always thought.

More names began to blur as other guests arrived. Suddenly Ned seized Rhys's arm. 'She is here!'

'Who?' he asked.

But Ned leaned across him to speak to his parents. 'She is here. The young lady I told you about.'

Lady Westleigh looked interested. Lord Westleigh looked as bored as Rhys felt.

'Lady Gale. The Dowager Lady Gale. Miss Gale,' the butler announced.

'She looks like an angel,' Ned murmured.

Rhys glanced over and froze.

The first woman approaching the reception line stopped suddenly. She was not looking at Rhys, but at Lord Westleigh. Shock and dismay filled her expression.

He glanced at Westleigh, who showed not the slightest sign of recognition.

Lady Gale greeted Lady Westleigh cordially. She moved on to Westleigh, who appeared as uninterested as she was cold.

Westleigh gave his desultory introduction. 'May I present my natural son, Mr Rhysdale.'

She turned to him.

'Rhys,' she mouthed.

Rhys took her hand and applied more pressure than would have been polite. 'Lady Gale.'

She fixed her gaze somewhere in the vicinity of his neckcloth. 'Mr Rhysdale.'

'Hurry up, Celia,' the older woman with her snapped. 'You are blocking everyone.'

The older woman passed by Rhys without a word, as she did Ned and his brother and sister. Ned had already left the line to go directly to the young woman announced as Miss Gale. She was already speaking to Lady Westleigh.

'Mama. Papa,' Ned said. 'May I present Miss Gale to you. You have heard me speak of her, I am sure—'

While they spoke with Miss Gale, Rhys turned back to Celia. She met his glance, but there was no pleasure on her face. She, instead, looked horrified.

His attention was called back to Miss Gale, as Ned presented him to the young lady. Her attention to the family, including to Rhys, was more pointed than any other person going through the line.

Once the young woman had finished exuding her pleasure at meeting Phillipa and moved away from the line, Ned said to none of them in particular, 'There is the lady I wish to marry.'

Who was she to Celia? A stepdaughter? A sister-in-law?

A few minutes later a Lord Gale went through the line.

Celia's husband? Had she lied to him?

As the man offered Rhys a limp hand, Rhys said, 'Your family precedes you. They went through the line a few minutes ago.'

Lord Gale did not look him in the eye. 'My cousins?' he said. 'Yes, they would be here, would they not?' He shot a scathing glance towards Ned, who was too happy to notice.

Rhys was relieved.

One thing was for certain. As soon as this receiving line was finished, he would speak to *Lady Gale.*

Celia pressed her hand against her stomach. It felt as if someone had knocked the wind out of her. Twice. She could not even think about Rhys at the moment.

She stopped her mother-in-law. 'Lady Gale, did you know that Neddington was Lord Westleigh's son?'

'Certainly.' Lady Gale sniffed. 'Everyone knows that.'

Everyone except Celia, of course. She'd merely accepted the young man's title without thinking what title his father carried.

She was never meant for London. In that her husband had been entirely correct.

Adele caught up with them. 'I hope they liked me. Do you think they liked me, Celia?'

'I think they liked you,' Celia answered by rote.

'The natural brother seemed respectable enough, did he not?' Adele went on.

Rhys had looked incredibly handsome in his formal clothes. Pristine white breeches and linen. Impeccably tailored coat. How she'd missed seeing him as soon as she was in the doorway was a mystery. Except she'd caught sight of Westleigh and could see no one else.

They were all connected. Adele. Westleigh. Rhys.

'And I adored Phillipa.' Adele was oblivious to Celia's distress. 'I thought her scar was not very evident at all.'

Goodness. Celia had not even noticed.

Lady Gale ignored Celia completely and latched on to one of her cronies. Adele begged to join her friends, obviously eager to pour over each minute detail of her introduction to Ned's family. Celia retreated to the wall. At least her malaise had left her, but now her stomach ached with a different sort of pain.

She glanced back to Rhys at the same moment

his eyes found her. Her skin heated and she could feel the tension that fairly raced across the room between them. Matters had changed between them.

Xavier Campion crossed in front of her. She held her breath. He paused for a moment and his eyes widened ever so slightly.

He bowed and walked on.

Her heart pounded. Had he recognised her? He had never seen her without her mask, but she would wager his had been a look of recognition.

Finally the reception line broke up. Ned made immediately for Adele.

And Rhys came directly to her.

'Lady Gale.' His eyes seemed to bore into her.

'Rhys.'

The music started and Lady Westleigh announced the first dance, taking Lord Westleigh as her partner.

Celia could not even look at Westleigh. It was difficult enough to disguise her abhorrence of him beneath her mask at the gaming house—how was she to do so as a possible family connection? How could she bear being around any of them, knowing he was behind them in the shadows?

How could she again be with Rhys, knowing Westleigh was his father?

'You never told me Westleigh was your father,' she said in a low voice. 'You knew what he did to my father.'

'You never told me you were Lady Gale.' He gazed out to the dance floor as if engrossed in the couples forming for the dance. 'I did warn you about Westleigh.'

She smiled as if they were merely passing pleasantries. 'You acted as if you disdained Westleigh. That does not fit with this family camaraderie.'

He turned to her. In spite of herself her breath caught at how handsome he looked. 'You make an excellent point and I agree with you. I do disdain Westleigh, but I cannot explain here and now why his bastard is suddenly introduced as a son.' He extended his hand. 'Would you do me the honour of this dance? I suspect these people think me deficient in all the social graces.'

'I usually do not dance,' she said.

He held his hand in place. 'Help me, Celia.'

She glanced into his eyes and put her hand in his.

They joined the line and faced each other.

The music began—'Miss Moore's Rant,' a country dance.

Rhys and the other gentlemen bowed to the ladies, who curtsied in return. Then they joined right hands, forming a star with the couple next to them and turning. They completed the figures, changing sides and moving one place down the line.

When she'd been a mere spectator to this dance,

Celia appreciated the symmetry. The dancing couples moved like petals falling from a flower.

Inside the dance was an entirely different experience. She was aware only of Rhys. How he turned. How effortlessly he moved. How he gazed at her when the figures brought them together again. He did not look as if he gave any of the steps a single thought, but performed them as if it were as natural as walking down a country path.

His lovemaking was like that, she realised. Confident, natural and so very excellently done. Her senses came alive at the memory of it. When their hands touched, even gloved, she could feel his bare fingers on her flesh. When his gaze caught hers, she remembered how his eyes darkened at the height of their passion.

They reached the bottom of the set and had to stand out one sequence. Celia's body still felt alive to him. She fanned herself with her hand. It was too bizarre to feel so aroused by him after learning who he was, whose blood flowed through his veins.

She glanced away from him.

To her surprise she glimpsed Xavier dancing with Lady Phillipa. Adele, of course, was Neddington's partner and looked the very picture of delight. How could Celia spoil that for the girl even though it now connected Adele to Westleigh?

Lord Westleigh also danced, but she turned cold at the sight of him.

Rhys leaned towards her. 'Do not allow him to dampen your enjoyment.'

It was time for them to move up the line.

Any further pleasure she might feel from dancing with Rhys was spoiled by glimpsing Westleigh, who was like mould spreading through a bowl of fruit, spoiling everything she loved.

The dance moved her apart from Rhys.

When they came together again, he said, 'Is Miss Gale your sister-in-law?'

It was the sort of question a dance partner might ask to further an acquaintance, but everything they said to each other was now replete with hidden meaning and more questions. 'She is my stepdaughter.'

The dance ended and the couples scattered off the floor.

Rhys escorted her back to where they had been standing. He bowed to her. 'There is much more to say, is there not? You will come to the gaming house later?'

Before she could answer, Hugh Westleigh, whom she had so briefly met in the receiving line, approached them.

'Lady Gale.' He bowed perfunctorily to Celia before turning to Rhys. 'Father wants you in the card room. Apparently several gentlemen are eager to have you play.'

Celia recognised Hugh as another frequent visitor to Rhys's gaming house. The family certainly supported Rhys's enterprise, did they not? At least the family connection explained why Neddington attended the gaming house even though he did not gamble.

Rhys nodded and turned to Celia. 'Thank you again, Lady Gale.'

Rhys followed Hugh through the dancers gathering for the next set. They walked out of the ballroom.

Hugh turned to him. 'Smart of you to dance.'

'Was it?'

Hugh was probably surprised he knew the steps.

'And to ask Lady Gale,' Hugh added as they walked back to the hallway.

'Oh?' Rhys had been certain asking Celia had been unwise. 'And why is that?'

'Surely you noticed Ned is besotted with her stepdaughter.' Hugh spoke with sarcasm. 'Lady Gale would certainly not want to offend the family by refusing you.'

Rhys took hold of Hugh's arm and pulled Hugh back to face him. 'I am accustomed to your insults, Hugh, but Lady Gale does not deserve them.'

He expected Hugh to flare up in anger. Hugh's face turned red, but he averted his gaze. 'By God. I did not realise...' He looked back to Rhys. 'Accept my apology, Rhys. You behaved decently.'

Rhys could not help but smile. 'Almost like a gentleman, I suppose?'

Hugh's mouth twitched as if he'd contemplated smiling. 'Precisely like a gentleman.'

'Did you think I meant to embarrass all of you?' Rhys asked.

Hugh faced him. 'That is exactly what I thought.'

'Then you do not know me.' Rhys released him.

'None of us know you, do we?' Hugh responded in a low voice.

Rhys did not see Celia again until the night grew late. Half the gentlemen at the ball were frequent patrons of the Masquerade Club and were eager to engage its proprietor in play.

The aristocracy foxed him. Ned and Hugh were certain they would be ruined if the *ton* knew they owned a gaming hell, but he, their bastard brother, somehow earned cachet for the role.

Although he'd bet none of these gentlemen would want him to marry their daughters.

As if a gambler should marry at all.

He returned to the ballroom and immediately found Celia. She stood against the wall near her mother-in-law who was chatting to another lady. He watched her.

He'd never guessed that she belonged to the world he scorned, the world he wanted to join merely so he could turn away from it.

Xavier came to stand beside him. 'Did you win?'

'Enough to impress.' He had learned long ago the benefits of not winning every hand. 'I want them to come back to the gaming house.'

'Wise man.'

'How have you been occupying yourself while I was in the card room?' Rhys asked.

Xavier shrugged. 'Dancing, of course.'

'Careful,' Rhys warned. 'These young ladies will think you are looking for a wife.'

Xavier looked completely serious. 'Perhaps I am.'

Rhys was taken aback. 'Are you serious?'

He shrugged. 'I am merely humouring my parents, who would so like to see me settled.'

Rhys said, 'They were more than gracious to me, as they always are.'

Xavier nodded. 'They are excellent parents, I would say.' Which made it all the more mysterious to Rhys why Xavier rarely saw them and rarely attended events that would include him in their circle. Xavier had come to this ball at Rhys's request, not his parents'.

Xavier glanced around the room. 'It has been a much more interesting ball than I had imagined, has it not?'

Rhys's eyes narrowed. 'What is your meaning?'

Xavier gave him an intent look. 'I recognise her, Rhys.'

Xavier knew? Had any others recognised her?

A waltz was announced.

Xavier cocked his head. 'I am engaged for this dance.'

He walked quickly away to where Lady Phillipa stood alone.

Rhys hesitated only a moment more before striding directly to Celia.

He bowed to her. 'Another set, Lady Gale?'

She hesitated and her mother-in-law's face flushed with disapproval.

She suddenly said, 'I'd be delighted, sir.'

He took her by the hand and together they joined the circle of couples forming for the dance. The music began and, facing each other, Rhys bowed and Celia curtsied.

Rhys put his hands on her waist and Celia rested hers on his shoulders. He remembered their first lovemaking when she'd rested her hands in just this way. Their gazes caught and he swirled her into the dance.

No wonder many thought this dance scandalous. The intimacy of moving as one, touching with hands and eyes, left the illusion of being alone on the dance floor, even as the circle of dancers rotated like a wheel.

He was reminded of their lovemaking, of watching her face as pleasure built inside her, her skin flushing, her lips parting. He wished they were this moment in his bed rather than in this ballroom. He did not know how a respectable widow justified an affair with the proprietor of a gaming hell. The secrecy enabled it, he suspected.

They did not speak during the dance; nor did they change position, even though there were several different holds that could be used in the waltz. Rhys saw only Celia. At the same time he fancied he was losing her, that this was their goodbye.

He wanted to hold her tighter, closer, and never release her.

But the music concluded and he blinked as if waking from sleep.

He reluctantly released her. 'Come to me tonight.'

She stepped back. 'I—I do not know.'

He stiffened. Perhaps he'd been correct about the goodbye. 'We need to talk…about who you are, who I am. Will you come?'

She averted her gaze. 'Yes.'

He walked her back to where her mother-in-law stood. 'I bid you goodnight, then.' He leaned to her ear and whispered. 'Until later.'

Chapter Eleven

When Celia walked in to the game room that night, Rhys caught Xavier. 'Watch the room, will you?'

Xavier, for once, did not lecture. He merely nodded.

Celia had transformed herself from the very proper aristocratic widow to the slightly scandalous, mysterious and masked Madame Fortune. Not only by her costume, its deep red more theatrical than the pale green gown she wore to the ball, but by the way she carried herself with a seductive confidence. At the ball she made herself fade into the background, unnoticed apparently, although to him, there had been no other women present.

It was like that in the gaming house, as well. Other women attended, some masked, some not, and he was not blind to the fact that some left with gentlemen patrons. For Rhys, though, Celia was the only one worth a second glance.

He moved through the game room to where she was chatting with other gamblers. Her gaze flicked to him and back to the others.

He touched her arm. 'Madame? May I have a moment of your time?'

She stiffened. 'Certainly.'

He escorted her out of the game room and together they climbed the servants' stairs to his private drawing room.

He closed the door behind them.

She pulled off mask, no longer looking like Madame Fortune or the Lady Gale of the ballroom, but a woman ready to fend off an attack. 'It is good you approached me. Better we discuss this right away. Do we start with who you are or who I am?'

'I think it more to the purpose to talk of who you are.' He lifted a decanter. 'Some port?'

'Please,' she responded.

He poured them each a glass.

She took the glass of port and he noticed her hand trembled. 'Why is it more to the purpose to discuss who I am? Why is that more important than discovering that my lover is Westleigh's natural son and my stepdaughter is being courted by his heir?'

He took a gulp of his drink and set down his glass. 'Because it makes your being here more of a risk.' He moved closer to her and grasped her arms. 'Xavier recognised you. What if others do, too? Your reputation—'

Her eyes widened, but she quickly recovered. 'If your friend wishes to expose me, there is little I can do now, is there?'

He tightened his grip on her. 'He will not expose you, Celia. But if anyone else guesses who you are...it is already known we are lovers. A lady cannot take the owner of a gaming hell as a lover without tarnishing her reputation.'

Her eyes gleamed like the coldest emeralds, but behind them he could see her pain. 'My reputation? I assure you, no one cares enough about Lady Gale to even think she has a reputation.' Beneath her bravado he could see her pain. 'Except you, perhaps. You clearly would prefer not to be a lady's lover.'

'Of course I would not.' Could she not see? 'I would not put a respectable woman in such a position. And I certainly would never have offered you employment, had I known you were Lady Gale.'

She lifted her chin. 'You regret bedding me.'

'Never.' He released her. 'You regret bedding me.'

She turned away and walked towards the window. 'Because of Westleigh. I cannot bear your connection to him and this change of heart towards him—'

'There has been no change of heart,' he broke in. 'I detest Westleigh.'

Now more than ever. Once again Westleigh stood in the way of something Rhys wanted. Needed. He could lose Celia.

In this moment Rhys knew, as strongly as he had ever known anything, that he did not want his affair with Celia to end.

She gave him a sceptical glance. 'Do not take me for a fool, Rhys. You just attended a ball which, for all I could see, had the purpose of welcoming you into Westleigh's family.'

'It was not how it appeared.' Rhys could almost hear Xavier's voice: *I warned you...*

'Then why did you do it?' she asked.

He averted his gaze. 'For restitution.'

'Restitution?' She shook her head. 'Your restitution was to *join* his family? I wish to escape him.' She walked towards the door. 'I need to return to the game room.' She turned. 'That is, if I am still in your employ.'

He frowned. 'Celia, it is not worth the risk.'

She straightened her spine. 'My situation is unchanged. I need the money. Does our bargain still hold?'

Celia kept her posture stiff as she waited for his answer. Inside she felt as bleak as she'd ever felt.

Rhys looked ashen. 'If you wish it, our bargain remains.'

'Thank you.' She donned her mask and walked out, deliberately not looking back at him.

Nothing was settled between them. They'd said nothing to any purpose at all. And nothing made sense.

Her emotions were raw, as raw as if she'd just heard that Westleigh had killed her father. As if she'd just witnessed her mother's last laboured breath. As if she once again heard her own voice speak the marriage vows shackling her to Gale.

She wanted to forget it all, to escape this new pain.

Instead she adjusted her mask and descended the stairs to the game room.

'There she is!' cried one gentleman when she entered.

'Come play hazard, Madame Fortune,' said another. 'We need your luck.'

She straightened and made herself smile. If ever there was a night to lose herself in a game, this was it. 'I hope to be lucky tonight.'

She played hazard, losing more than she won, but still recklessly playing on. The men still cheered her on and bet with her, but one by one they left the table. When she realised they had stopped betting, she woke from the reverie and rid herself of the game quickly.

'Enough,' she said to the croupier.

'Surely one more game will not hurt.'

She looked to see who had spoken. It was Lord Westleigh. She felt a wave of nausea, but forced herself to greet him congenially. 'You are later than usual, are you not?'

He bowed. 'I am flattered you noticed, madam.' His words were slurred as if he'd imbibed too much wine. He picked up the dice. 'One more roll?'

She waved him away. 'No more hazard.'

He placed the dice back on the table. 'How about *vingt-et-un?*'

She glanced around the room, but did not see any likely partners for whist. At least at *vingt-et-un* she would not have to face him across a table. 'Very well. *Vingt-et-un.*'

She allowed him to escort her to the *vingt-et-un* table. He walked unsteadily. Another gentleman and a masked lady were playing against the dealer. Celia and Lord Westleigh joined them.

Celia ignored Westleigh as best she could and concentrated on each turn of the cards, remembering which had been played and calculating the odds of her being dealt what she needed. It worked. She recouped some of her losses and almost forgot her pain.

Then she would glance up and her eyes would inevitably turn to wherever Rhys stood. Her pain would return.

At least she won as often as Westleigh lost. She suspected his vanity was wounded that a mere woman was more skilled than he.

The dealer dealt them each one card down,

one up. Westleigh peeked at his hidden card and tapped the table. The dealer placed another card on his pile and his face fell. Celia requested another card and won.

Westleigh glanced around the room as if looking for someone. 'I fear I must leave you, my dear. Unless you desire more of my company?'

She did not look at him. 'I'm winning. I want to play.'

He grunted and staggered off, unsteady on his feet. She had no time to feel relief at his absence.

Xavier joined the table.

'It seems your luck holds here, as well, Madame Fortune,' he remarked.

'Indeed!' she said with false cheer.

He distrusted her, she knew. And now he was a threat.

He was also as skilled as she at the game, and, ironically, she suspected it was her skill that made Xavier distrust her.

Could he not accept that she was good at cards? And now, after nearly a month of playing several nights a week, she was even better than before. She made money nearly every night, and, so far, she'd been able to stay mostly in control.

She suspected Xavier had noticed every single time the gaming fever overtook her. He watched her that closely.

The dealer reshuffled for a new game and

Xavier leaned towards her, speaking low. 'So we meet twice in one night, do we not, my lady?'

She nodded. 'You recognised me.'

'Yes.'

She glanced around. 'Please say no more.'

He merely smiled his charming smile at her.

The dealer asked Celia to cut the cards and she tried to turn her attention to the game, but her concentration failed her.

After losing three hands in a row, she gathered her smaller pile of counters and told the dealer, 'That is all for me.'

Xavier left the table at the same time. Without being too obvious she followed him to a corner of the room where a servant served wine and other spirits.

When she was certain no one else could hear, she said to him, 'I beg you, sir. Tell no one who I am.'

He did not smile this time. 'I will not.'

She nodded. 'Thank you.'

The scent of the wine made her stomach feel queasy and she was so exhausted she could not stand on her feet. She excused herself to Xavier and made her way to the supper room. Westleigh was there, sitting with a group of gentlemen. She stayed clear of him and made her way to the sideboard where she chose the blandest food she could find.

She chose a table alone and one far from

Westleigh, but, to her dismay, he left his table and joined her. 'Would you like some company, madam?'

She did not feel friendly. 'No. I will not stay long. I just needed something in my stomach.'

He lifted his wine glass. 'As did I.'

She glanced down at her plate, thinking he would leave, but he lowered himself into the chair adjacent to hers.

He took a big gulp from the wine glass in his hand. 'Perhaps you wonder why I mostly play only the table games.'

She bit into her biscuit and swallowed lest she retch in front of him. 'I had not.'

She had noticed that he played whist infrequently; thus she'd had few opportunities to revenge her father by winning Westleigh's money.

He leaned towards her. 'It is a secret.' His breath smelled of the wine.

She waved her hand in front of her nose. 'I see.'

He wagged a finger at her. 'You must tell no one.'

She broke off another piece of biscuit. 'Do not tell me.' She did not want to share confidences with this man.

'I am certain I can trust you,' he slurred.

He steadied himself by gripping the back of her chair. It was nearly an embrace. Or a trap within his arms.

He again leaned towards her ear. 'I mostly play

games where the losses go directly to the house, not to the other players. Do you wonder why?'

She shrank back, but could not escape him. 'No, I do not.'

He leaned away and gestured expansively. 'I own this place. It is mine.'

Ridiculous. 'Rhysdale owns this place.'

He lifted a finger. 'Rhysdale is my natural son, you see. Everything is in his name, but only to protect my reputation. It was my money that bought this place.'

She did not want to believe him. She did not want to believe that Rhys kept this information from her. She did not want to believe that Rhys was merely Westleigh's figurehead.

She swallowed her piece of biscuit.

Westleigh went on. 'So, you see, if I lose at the tables, the money goes right back into my pockets.'

She pressed her fingers to her now-aching head. 'How very clever of you, my lord.'

He seized her hand. 'I can be clever at other things, if you will allow me to show you. There are rooms upstairs, you know.'

She gaped at him, horrified, and pulled her hand away. 'How dare you speak to me in that manner! Surely you know, as well as everyone else here, my attachment is to your son.'

He did not even have the grace to look contrite. 'My dear, the son is nothing to the father.'

A wave of nausea washed through her. She clamped her hand against her mouth.

One of the gentlemen from the table where Westleigh had previously sat called to him. 'Wes, we are leaving. Are you coming with us?'

He looked at Celia with regret. 'I might as well.' He seized her hand again and kissed it. 'I will say goodnight, madam. You must let me know if you change your mind. I can make it quite worth your while.'

Worth her while? He would pay her as if she were a common prostitute?

'Leave me, sir,' she said in a clipped tone.

As soon as the men left the supper room, Celia rose and went up another flight to Rhys's private rooms. She glanced to the floor above. Were those rooms for Lord Westleigh's use? The idea sickened her.

Rhys noticed when Celia left the game room, but could not follow her at that moment. It was late before he could get away, so late, in fact, the patrons were leaving. Even Xavier bid him goodnight.

Cummings manned the door and would know if she had left.

Rhys made his way to the hall. 'Did Madame Fortune leave yet?' Rhys asked.

'I didn't see her,' Cummings said.

She must be waiting upstairs. Rhys had not expected her to stay. His tension eased and he took the stairs two at a time. He checked the drawing room, but she was not there. He hurried to his bedchamber and opened the door.

She was seated on a chair, resting her head against her hand, her eyes closed.

He crossed the room to her. 'What is it, Celia? Are you ill?'

She raised her head and it seemed that all colour had left her face. 'I waited for you.'

'I am glad.'

Her eyes narrowed. 'Do not mistake this. I waited to tell you what Lord Westleigh said.'

His spirits fell. 'What did he say?'

She stiffened. 'He said you are working for him. That this gaming house is his, not yours.'

Rhys clenched his fist.

Her voice turned raw. 'I will not be back, Rhys. I will not work for Westleigh. I cannot. I detest him!'

Rhys walked over to the side table and poured himself a brandy. 'He lies, Celia. I own this place. It is mine.' He gripped the brandy glass so hard he thought it might shatter. 'And I detest him, as well. Even more for lying to you. For speaking to you!'

'How do I know what is true, Rhys? I do not know who to believe.' Her hand trembled.

He sat across from her.

'This is the truth, Celia.' He ought to have told her this long ago. 'Westleigh brought the family to near ruin with his gambling and excessive spending. Ned and Hugh came to me, needing a great deal of money quickly. They asked me to run a gaming hell for them. They scraped together the initial investment. In exchange, they receive half of the profits. The property is in my name. I paid back the original investment, but I paid it to Ned. None of it goes to Westleigh. I own the gaming house. I am fully in charge of it. Those were my conditions in agreeing to do this for them.' He paused. 'My other requirement was that Westleigh publicly acknowledge me as his son, something he should have done when I was a child.' He glanced away. 'Or when my mother died.' He faced her again. 'That was why I was introduced at the ball.'

She shook her head. 'It mattered that much to you? To be known as *his* son?' She spat out the words.

He did not answer right away. 'There was more to it. There were many people who were kind to my mother when I was a boy. If the Westleigh estate failed, they would suffer. That was why I agreed to run the gaming house. No other reason.' Except his own desire to make his father beholden to him for something.

'But you wanted him to acknowledge you. You wanted to be known as his son.' Her voice was scathing.

He glanced away. 'I thought it the one thing he would most object to.'

She made a disparaging sound. 'That was your restitution?'

It was time he faced the truth. 'The restitution was for my mother. My birth was the ruin of her life. She might have lived a respectable life if it had not been for me. She might have married, borne legitimate children. She might not have died so young.' His throat tightened.

She leaned towards him and placed her hand on his. 'Oh, Rhys. I am so sorry.'

He'd not told her how Westleigh had left him penniless and alone. He was not trying to win her sympathy. He merely wanted her to understand the truth.

She stood and began to pace. 'I cannot be *connected* to him. I cannot. If I am with you, I will be connected to him. And if Adele marries Ned, I will be connected to him.' She turned back to him. 'I will lose her like I lost…everyone else. Because of him.'

He rose and walked over to her, putting his arms around her. 'He can't make you lose your stepdaughter.'

She took a deep, shuddering breath. 'She will become a part of that family. I would not blame her for it—it is the natural course of things. But I want no part of that family. Or of him.'

'Celia.'

Eventually she melted against him. He wanted to kiss away her pain. He wanted to make love to her and show her that now she was not alone. He would not leave her.

But he had connected himself to the one man she could not abide.

Rhys wished he could open a vein and rid himself of any Westleigh blood flowing through him. 'Do not let him come between us, Celia.'

She held her head between her hands. 'I cannot think any more. I am so weary. I just want to go home. This night has brought too much back.'

'It is almost time for your carriage,' he said, releasing her. 'I'll walk you out.'

Like so many nights before this, Rhys escorted her outside and waited with her until she was safely in her coach, although this time it felt as if everything had changed between them.

Because of Westleigh.

Chapter Twelve

The next day Adele insisted upon calling on Lady Westleigh, to pay her respects to the hostess of the ball and Ned's mother. Celia's mother-in-law refused to go with her to *that house,* so the task fell to Celia.

She wanted to refuse. She did not want to be in surroundings that reminded her of Westleigh, where there was a chance she might see him and have to pretend to be cordial.

She and Adele were announced to Lady Westleigh and entered the drawing room, which had been transformed into a ballroom only the night before.

Immediately Celia noticed the portrait of Lord Westleigh that dominated the room. She had to see him after all.

'How good of you to call.' Lady Westleigh extended her hand to them and the ladies exchanged greetings.

There were no other callers at the moment, although Lady Westleigh was with her daughter. Lady Phillipa wore her hair pulled back into a simple knot. It made her scar even more prominent.

'Come sit with me, Miss Gale.' Lady Westleigh patted the space next to her on the sofa for Adele. 'Let me become better acquainted with you. Last night I did not have a chance to really converse with the young miss who has so captivated my son.'

'Oh, my lady, I would be delighted.' Adele was in raptures.

'I will pour tea,' Phillipa said. 'How do you take it?'

At first the conversation was general enough to include all of them. Compliments from Adele and Celia about the ball. Comments about the weather and the next society event, an opera that night.

Lady Westleigh was a puzzle to Celia. Such a gracious lady to be married to a man who did not care about taking a life and leaving a family in tatters.

The lady took Adele's hand. 'I should tell you, my dear Miss Gale, that I knew your mother.'

'You knew my mother?' Adele's eyes grew wide with excitement. 'Oh, please tell me something about her. I miss her so terribly!'

Celia turned to Phillipa, allowing Adele to have

her private conversation with Lady Westleigh. 'Did you enjoy the ball, Lady Phillipa?'

The young woman picked up a piece of needlework. 'It went well, I suppose. I do not attend many balls, but my mother seemed satisfied.'

She did not answer the question.

Phillipa pushed her needle through the fabric. 'You danced with our—our natural brother, I noticed. It was kind of you.'

'Kind?' He'd been a wonderful dancer.

'No one else danced with him.'

Celia had not seen him ask anyone else to dance. She felt compelled to defend him. 'I found nothing to object to in him.' Except his connection to this family.

Phillipa frowned. 'I did not know of him until lately.'

Celia did not want to make Rhys the topic of conversation. She took a sip of tea and felt the eyes of Lord Westleigh's portrait upon her. 'You danced with Mr Campion, I noticed.'

Phillipa shrugged. 'I suspect his mother or mine put him up to it. Our families have known each other a long time.'

Celia did not know what to say in response to that.

'To own the truth,' Phillipa went on, 'I do not like to attend balls or any of the London events.'

'Will you not come to the opera tonight?' It was the event everyone was attending.

'I think not,' Phillipa said.

At that moment Neddington entered the room. 'Forgive me for intruding, Mother,' he said. 'I merely wished to say hello to Miss Gale and Lady Gale.' He bowed to Celia. 'How do you do, my lady?'

'Very well, Ned. Thank you,' she responded, thinking now that he looked like a younger version of his father. Why had she not seen it before?

He turned to Adele and his voice softened. 'And you, Miss Gale?'

She glowed. 'I am very well, sir.'

Celia felt like weeping. She would surely lose Adele when she married this man.

She would lose Rhys, as well.

She glanced at the clock on the mantel. 'We ought to be on our way, Adele.' They'd been there longer than the typical fifteen minutes.

'Will you allow me to see you to your carriage?' Ned asked.

'Oh, we walked. It is such a fine day,' Adele said.

Ned smiled. 'Then might I escort you both back home?'

Adele gave Celia a pleading look.

'That would be kind of you,' Celia said.

Rhys prowled around the gaming house like a bear in a cage. He'd felt like a caged beast since the night before, the night of the ball, the event that had changed everything with Celia. How could he have guessed that Celia would be present at that ball? At any ball?

She was nothing like the aristocracy.

He should have told her his connection with Westleigh right from the beginning—especially after she confessed that Westleigh had killed her father.

He'd used that fact as an excuse not to tell her.

Would she come tonight?

He wanted another chance to make her understand.

To ask her to forgive him.

He wandered to the cashier's office and stood in the doorway. MacEvoy was busy with a patron, but Rhys did not need to speak aloud. He merely raised his brows.

MacEvoy shook his head.

She had not arrived.

Rhys spun around, his frustration growing.

Xavier stood there, leaning against the wall, arms folded over his chest. 'Let me guess. Mac told you matters were unchanged since the last time you checked with him. Twenty minutes ago.'

Rhys scowled at him. 'Were you counting the time on your pocket watch?'

'I probably could have set my watch by you.' Xavier straightened. 'Care to tell me why you are pacing the rooms?'

He was in no mood to go into this with his

friend and hear again Xavier's cautions. 'I'm merely making certain all is well.'

He pushed past Xavier and re-entered the game room.

A few minutes later, Rhys spied Xavier at the hazard table watching the play.

Rhys wandered over to him. 'It seems slow tonight.'

'Everyone is at the opera,' Xavier answered in a good-natured tone, somewhat easing Rhys's guilt for having snapped at him.

A patron threw the dice on the table.

'Nine!' Belinda called.

'I'm out,' the man cried.

'How do you know everyone is at the opera?' Rhys asked Xavier.

'I called upon my parents today,' his friend replied. 'They were bound for the opera and said that was the entertainment for the evening.'

Rhys nodded. 'Your parents looked in good health last night.'

'As always.'

Xavier's parents were, in Rhys's eyes, a rarity—members of the *ton* who were selfless and generous, and not at all concerned with the status of one's birth. Xavier's brothers and sisters had each found their places in society. Xavier had not.

Rhys noticed Xavier's attention shift and his brows rise.

Lord Westleigh had entered the game room.

Celia was at his side, but looked as if she were trying to remove a leech.

'Now what?' Xavier commented.

'Now what indeed,' growled Rhys who crossed the room to get his father away from her.

'Westleigh,' he said in a sharp voice.

His father gave him a contemptuous look. 'Well, well. If it isn't my *son*.'

Through her mask, Rhys saw Celia's eyes reflecting distress. She took advantage of the situation and turned to greet other gamblers who walked in behind them.

'Some whist, Madame Fortune?' Rhys heard one of them ask.

He faced his father. 'What are you about, Westleigh?'

Westleigh made a helpless gesture. 'Whatever do you mean, my *son*?' He smirked. 'Are you fearing I will steal your paramour from you?'

Rhys leaned threateningly into his face. 'Do not plague her. Do you hear me?'

They were attracting some attention, so Rhys walked away from him. He searched for Celia, but she was seated at a whist table with Sir Reginald and another masked couple he strongly suspected were Lord and Lady Ashstone. Ashstone's pockets were deep and Rhys hoped Celia would win a good sum from him.

She raised her eyes and caught Rhys's gaze,

but her opponents gestured to the cards and she looked away.

Rhys wandered back towards the hazard table where Xavier was now in conversation with Belinda, the table's croupier, whose complexion had brightened at his attention.

Rhys approached Xavier from behind and heard him say, 'Let me know if anything seems amiss. Especially if Madame Fortune plays.'

Rhys stepped back quickly, but caught sight of Westleigh intently watching the exchange.

Had Westleigh heard Xavier, as well?

Celia should have skipped the gaming house this night. She was so weary. She supposed the constant late hours were taking a toll. She'd come, she told herself, to win more money, but truly, she had come to see Rhys. Except she doubted she could last long enough to see him. All she could think about was sleep.

She struggled to make it through the whist game. Her play was so badly off that quitting was the only decent thing to do.

'Another game?' Sir Reginald asked eagerly. 'We need a chance to recoup.'

The masked couple playing them were eager to continue.

'By all means,' the lady said with a smile.

Celia scooped up the few counters she had left.

'I must beg off. I fear I am so fatigued that I cannot think straight.'

Her gentleman opponent chuckled. 'All the more reason we wish to play you another game.'

She smiled at him. 'I am no challenge tonight. You both would be bored by me.'

'I suppose you are correct, madam,' the man responded.

She dropped her counters in her reticule and stood. 'Another time, perhaps.'

Her feet felt leaden as she walked to the cashier's room.

She poured out her counters. 'I am done for the night, Mr MacEvoy.'

He looked surprised. 'Early for you, is it not, madam?'

She tried to smile. 'It is, indeed. If—if you think Mr Rhysdale would not wish to pay me, just cash in what is left.'

'You may pay her, MacEvoy,' came a voice from behind her.

Celia turned. Rhys stood there, filling the doorway, his expression indiscernible.

'Forgive me, Rhys. I am so very tired. I cannot stay.' She took four crowns from MacEvoy's hand and placed them in the leather purse inside her reticule.

When she stepped towards the door again, he did not move. She raised her eyes to his and he gave way for her.

But he walked with her to the hall.

'You are fatigued?' He made it sound as if she were making an excuse.

'I am, Rhys. Truly. There is no other reason.'

He touched her arm, an expression of concern on his face. 'How do you plan to summon your carriage?'

She placed the back of her hand against her forehead. 'I had not thought that far ahead.'

He took her arm. 'Come. I'll sort it out for you.'

She was too tired to protest.

They reached the hall.

Rhys said, 'Tell me where your coachman waits for you and I'll send for him.'

She shook her head. 'I do not know where he waits. I think he goes back to the stable.'

'Then I will send for a hackney coach and alert your coachman when he calls for you.'

He'd have to send someone to Piccadilly to a coach stand. It seemed a foolish fuss. 'Rhys, I do not live far from here. Would you have someone walk me home?'

'I will walk you home.' He turned to Cummings and asked for Celia's shawl and his hat and gloves.

When they stepped outside, he asked, 'You do not mind me knowing your address?'

She shrugged. 'You know who I am. It would be a simple matter for you to discover where I live.'

He offered his arm. 'Which way?'

She held on to him, grateful for his strength. 'To Half Moon Street.'

As they walked to St James's Street and turned towards Piccadilly, Celia removed her mask and carried it by its ribbons.

The night air felt cool on her face, reviving her. 'I feel better in the fresh air.'

'Are you ill?' he asked.

'Not ill, I do not think. Tired.' Her limbs felt heavy. 'All I wish is to go to bed.'

Her gaze flashed to him. She realised what she'd said.

He simply kept walking.

Finally he spoke. 'The late nights are too taxing for you.'

They hadn't been. She'd been energised by the success of her gambling—and the pleasures of her affair with him. The fatigue came on all of a sudden.

'I just need a little rest, I expect,' she told him.

In spite of herself she relished the feel of his strong arm under her fingers. It reminded her of how it felt to be held by him.

Her body flared merely at the memory and the intensity of her desire momentarily drove away fatigue. She wanted him so desperately she thought of asking him to take her back to the Masquerade and put her to bed in his room.

And remain there with her.

But an image of Rhys standing next to West-leigh, greeting guests in the ballroom, also flashed through her mind. She tried to shake it away.

She broke the silence between them. 'One could almost like London if it always felt like this.'

'Like what?' His voice matched the night.

'Quiet and still.' A carriage sounded in a nearby street, the horses' hooves and the wheels loud even at a distance. She smiled. 'At least, mostly quiet and still.'

He reached over and touched her hand, but released it and kept walking.

They reached Piccadilly and he gestured down the length of the street. 'It is an impressive sight.'

Gas lamps bathed the street in gold and the busy traffic of the day was reduced to a carriage or two. All the dirt of the day was obscured by the night.

'It is lovely,' she admitted.

They crossed Piccadilly.

'But you plan to leave.' He said this as a statement.

'I am not meant for London,' she said.

They fell silent again.

This time he spoke first. 'I want you to stay.'

She stopped and turned to him, but she could not speak. Instead she reached up and touched his cheek.

He clasped her hand and pressed it to his lips. 'I do not want what we've had to end.'

Neither did she. 'Oh, Rhys.'

He pulled her into an embrace and she could not help but melt against him. Encircled in his arms she did not feel alone.

She rested her head against his heart and was comforted by its steady beat. 'I am not leaving yet, Rhys.'

She felt his voice rumble in his chest. 'Then come to me as often as you can, Celia.'

She pulled away, only to nod her head.

She'd endure the contact with Westleigh and risk the intoxication of gambling to be with him a little longer.

They walked arm in arm along Piccadilly, the night wrapping them in an illusion that there was no one else in the world except the two of them. For the first time since the ball, Celia felt at peace.

They approached Half Moon Street. 'My street,' she said.

They turned on to the street and she wished her rooms were at the far end instead of so close to Piccadilly.

'Here.' She stopped, already bereft at parting from him.

He gathered her in his arms again and lowered his head, touching his lips to hers. 'Come to me tomorrow,' he whispered. 'If you feel well enough.'

He kissed her again and desire flamed through her, its intensity taking more of a toll on her body than her fatigue. All she wanted was to share a bed with him and re-experience the delight of joining her body with his.

She threw her arms around him and hugged him close. 'I will if I can, Rhys,' she cried.

It would be impossible for her to stay away.

Celia knocked lightly on the door to her rooms and listened through it until she heard footsteps approach. 'Tucker?' she called through the door. 'It is Lady Gale.'

The lock turned and the door opened.

Her butler looked surprised.

'Do not be concerned, Tucker.' She walked inside. 'I merely decided to leave early.'

He leaned outside. 'The carriage, ma'am?'

She turned around and glimpsed Rhys walking away, a mere shadow in the darkness. 'No carriage, but I was escorted home. Someone must tell Jonah.'

'I will see to it, ma'am.' He closed the door and turned the lock again.

'You can go to bed early.' She gave a wan smile. 'I am indebted to you for the long hours I force you to keep. Please know how grateful I am.'

He bowed his head. 'I can only admire you, my lady.'

She started up the stairs. Her flesh ached from missing Rhys and her fatigue returned. Suddenly it was like scaling the Alps to reach the first floor.

She opened her bedchamber door and startled her maid.

'Oh!' The woman popped up from a chair. 'I must have dozed. What time is it? Forgive me, ma'am.'

'I do not mind if you doze, Younie.' Celia yawned. 'I am home early. It must only be half-past two. I became so fatigued.'

Younie hurried over to her. 'Are you ill, ma'am? Let me feel your forehead.' She put the back of her hand against Celia's forehead.

'I do not feel feverish,' Celia responded. 'Merely tired.'

Her maid took her shawl from her shoulders and Celia dropped her reticule and mask on a table.

As soon as she was all dressed and ready to crawl into bed, the door opened. 'Another night of gallivanting, I see.' Her mother-in-law strode in.

Celia turned to her maid. 'You may go, Younie. Goodnight and thank you.'

Younie ducked her head down and walked out of the room.

Celia turned away from her mother-in-law. 'I did not hear you knock, Lady Gale.'

'Well, I didn't knock,' the woman answered without apology. 'Was that the man whose bed you are warming? I saw you with him outside.'

Celia rubbed her temples. 'What were you doing at the window at this hour?'

The older woman pursed her lips. 'Why, waiting to see you, of course. Otherwise I'd be asleep.'

Celia swung around. 'Why? Is something amiss? With Adele?'

Lady Gale put her fists on her hips. 'Nothing is amiss with Adele except having a stepmother who is a strumpet.'

Celia's fingers pressed into her temples. 'So you have merely come to lash me with your tongue. I have no patience for it. Leave me, Lady Gale. I will not discuss my private affairs with you. I cannot tolerate you any longer.'

Lady Gale lifted her chin. 'What will you do? Toss me out?'

Celia speared her with her gaze. 'Do not tempt me, ma'am.'

Her tone must have penetrated, because her mother-in-law turned around and left the room. Celia climbed into bed, but now was so agitated by her mother-in-law that sleep evaded her.

By morning Celia was convinced she was ill. When she woke she felt so nauseated she feared she could not reach the chamberpot in time to vomit. She remained in bed the whole day and begged off from attending the social event of the evening.

She also had Tucker deliver a message to Rhys to tell him she could not come to the gaming house that night.

* * *

When she felt equally unwell the next day, as well, she sent a message to Rhys saying she would return when she was recovered.

She missed him. And not only for the lovemaking. She missed watching him walk through the game room watching everything with an experienced eye. She missed sharing supper with him and sharing the trivialities of each night together. She missed being held by him.

Days passed. Sometimes by afternoon, Celia would feel the malaise leave her, but by evening all she wished was to retire early and sleep.

She had apologised to Younie and the housekeeper more than once for not being able to hold down her food and causing them such unpleasantness.

One morning Younie brought her dry toast and tea in bed.

'I do not know why I am not recovering,' she said to her maid. 'I am never ill. Adele thinks I should call the physician, but I keep thinking tomorrow I will feel better.'

Younie put her hands on her hips and frowned. 'You are fatigued. You have nausea. Do you have any aches or pains?'

Celia coloured. 'It might be shameful to say, but my breasts are sore. I've had aches with ague before, but never in such a part of me.'

Younie cocked her head. 'When are your courses due?'

When were her courses due? She could not remember the last time she had bled. It must have been...several weeks ago. About the time she and Rhys—

She blanched. 'Younie, you do not think?'

'That you are increasing?' Her maid lifted her brows.

Celia covered her mouth with her hand. 'It is not possible!'

In all the time her husband tried to make her conceive a child, she'd failed. Failed. She was barren. Gale had called her barren. Even his physician had called her barren.

She hugged her abdomen. Could it be? Could she have a baby inside her? Rhys's baby?

What a miracle! A blessing.

'Younie! Could it be true? Could it really be true?' Was she truly carrying Rhys's child?

'Time will tell, ma'am, but it is my guess.'

For a moment Celia felt like dancing, but only for a moment. Then the reality of her situation descended upon her.

She was a respectable baron's widow and she was pregnant with her lover's child.

'Oh, Younie,' she cried, 'then what am I to do?'

Chapter Thirteen

Celia was too restless to remain in bed. She rose and dressed. The idea of a baby had firmly taken route and her head spun with wonder and fear.

Fear, because it could very well be that she merely suffered from some sort of stomach malady and her bleeding would start any day. She could so easily suffer a crushing disappointment.

But if it were true? She hugged herself in delight.

She would move to a place where no one knew her, a place where she could present the child as legitimate and no one would question it. Mentally she calculated how much money it would cost to give her child a trouble-free life—

She caught herself making plans and stopped herself. Patience, she cautioned herself. As Younie said, time will tell.

To keep her mind busy, she came downstairs to the small parlour where she kept her desk and papers. Her mother-in-law and Adele were out, so it was a good time to go through the bills that had arrived in the last few days. She counted what she owed and tallied her funds.

Being away from the Masquerade Club had hurt her finances. How could bills mount so swiftly?

She had reworked the figures for the third time when her butler knocked on the door.

'A gentleman to see you,' he announced.

She looked up in surprise. 'To see me?' Callers came to see her mother-in-law or Adele, but never Celia. 'Who is it?'

'Mr Rhysdale, ma'am,' Tucker said.

Her face heated. 'Is he waiting in the drawing room?'

'Yes, ma'am.'

Her heart beat faster. 'I'll go there directly. Bring some tea, though, will you?'

'Immediately, ma'am.' He bowed.

She took a breath and pressed her hands to her abdomen before rising from her chair.

As she approached the open door of the drawing room, he turned and her heart leapt in her chest.

She'd never seen him in daylight.

'Celia.' He crossed the room to her and he took her into his arms.

At the same instant, she closed the door behind her. 'I have been worried over you.' He let go to examine her. 'You look pale. You are still ill. What can I do?'

He could hold her again. She'd desperately missed the comfort of his arms, the warmth of his concern.

Instead she smiled up at him. 'I am better. Truly. It is an odd illness that comes and goes, but I think I am over the worst.'

His strong forehead creased. 'What does the physician say?'

She glanced aside. 'I did not consult a physician. It did not seem so serious.'

He surprised her by wrapping his arms around her and holding her close. The sheer glory of it made her want to weep.

A knock sounded and she pulled away. 'Tea.'

Tucker entered and set the tea tray on the table.

When he left, Celia said, 'Would you sit, Rhys? I'll pour you tea.'

He hesitated, but lowered himself onto the sofa adjacent to her chair.

A glance at the biscuits Cook had provided and the scent of the tea made Celia queasy again, but she managed to pour for him and for herself.

She quickly took a bite of a biscuit and swallowed it. 'You should not have come, Rhys.'

He frowned. 'Do not say that. I had to see how you went on. There was no way I could ask anyone.' He lifted the teacup, but set it down again without drinking. 'I chose a time when you were unlikely to have other callers.'

She opened her mouth to ask him what he would have done if she'd been abed? Or if Adele had spoken to him? Or, worse, her mother-in-law? But she bit her tongue.

She was too glad to see him. 'I am truly much better. I—I might even come to the club tonight.' She needed to play cards. She needed money. 'How are things there?'

'The same.' He shook his head. 'Not the same. You are missed.' He took her hand in his. 'I have missed you.'

She warmed to his touch.

And thought of the baby inside her.

But it likely was not a baby inside her, but merely a fanciful dream.

His gaze seemed to caress her face and his hand warmed hers.

He stood again. 'I should not stay long, I know.'

She rose, as well, and he reached out and touched her hair. 'I needed to see you for myself and now that I have—' He pulled her into an embrace and kissed her.

Passion rushed through her, demanding release. She hungrily kissed him back, wanting him inside her, wanting to be joined with him and together climb the heights of pleasure. He pressed her against him and she felt his male member from beneath his clothes.

Most of all, she wanted to be carrying his child inside her.

He broke off and leaned his forehead against hers. 'Come tonight, but only if you are well enough.'

She nodded.

He stepped away and straightened his clothes. With a grin and another quick kiss, he walked out of the room. She ran to the window to watch him leave and catch the last glimpse of him.

To her horror, she saw her mother-in-law and Adele approaching.

The front door opened and Rhys walked out just as they reached the door. He tipped his hat to Adele and Lady Gale before turning in the other direction and striding away.

A moment later Celia heard her mother-in-law's strident voice quizzing Tucker.

Celia walked to the drawing-room door. 'Leave Tucker in peace, Lady Gale. If you have questions, ask me.'

Her mother-in-law marched directly to the drawing room. Celia retreated to the middle of the room and awaited the assault.

Her mother-in-law slammed the door behind her. 'Was that Westleigh's bastard son leaving our rooms?'

How detestable her mother-in-law was!

Celia straightened. 'It was Mr Rhysdale.'

'He had the gall to call upon us?' Lady Gale looked completely affronted. 'How dare he?'

Celia glared at her. 'He did not call upon you. He called upon me.'

The older lady peered at her. Her mouth worked, but no words emerged. She jabbed her finger at Celia. 'I see what it is,' she finally managed. '*He* is the one.'

Celia lifted her chin.

Adele's voice came from the doorway. 'What do you mean, he is the one?'

Celia flashed her mother-in-law a warning look. Adele did not need to know this.

But Lady Gale swung around to her granddaughter. 'He is the one she has been bedding! Imagine it, Adele. He is not only a bastard but a gambler, as well.'

'Lady Gale!' Celia cried. 'You will not speak that way in my presence. Leave the room this instant!'

The old woman tossed her head and in her outrage swirled around as nimble as a nymph. 'That suits me perfectly. I cannot abide the sight of you.' When she reached Adele, she said, 'Come with me, Adele.'

Adele shook her head, instead entering the room. 'What is she talking about, Celia? Is it true? Are you having a—a—liaison with Ned's half-brother?'

Celia put her hand to her abdomen. 'Listen to me, Adele—'

Lady Gale re-entered the room. 'And this illness of yours. This vomiting and fatigue. I know what it is about!'

Celia raised a hand to halt her.

Her mother-in-law took no heed. 'You are pretending to be with child, are you not? What a convincing act. What do you hope to accomplish from that, I wonder?' She marched off again.

Adele stared at Celia, eyes wide, mouth agape. 'Celia! Are you—?'

Celia turned to the girl. 'I do not know why I am ill.'

'You are *increasing*?' Adele was not listening to her.

She tried again. 'It is impossible—'

Adele covered her mouth with her hand. 'You lied to me! You said you were gambling. But you were—were—engaging in lewd behaviour. Or were you doing both? Ned told me his half-brother runs a gambling place.' She tore at her hair. 'Oh! Ned! What will he think of me when he finds out? He will despise me. You have ruined everything! You have ruined my whole life!'

'Adele!' Celia raised her voice. 'Stop this nonsense at once.'

Adele covered her ears. 'I will not listen to you ever again!' She ran out the door and her footsteps pounded up the stairs, accompanied by loud sobs.

Celia collapsed into a chair, clutching her stomach, trying to quiet the waves of nausea, rage and fear that swept through her.

When Ned pulled up to Adele's rooms in his curricle, the door opened and she ran out to him. She climbed into the curricle before he could do more than extend his hand to assist her.

'What is it, my darling?' he asked her.

'Oh, Ned!' Tears poured from her beautiful eyes. 'Please just drive. I wish to be away from here. Is there somewhere we might be alone? I do not wish to see another person.'

As a gentleman, he ought not be alone with her, but he could not resist indulging her every request.

'We should walk, then.' They could be more private on foot. 'I can take the horses back to the stable if you wish.'

She threaded her arm through his and leaned against his shoulder.

When something troubled her, Ned wanted only to ease it, but he did not press her to tell him what distressed her. Better wait until they could be alone.

His horses were stabled at Brook's Mews behind Brook Street. If the stablemen were surprised to see him return so soon, and in the company of a young lady, they gave no indication.

'I will not need them the rest of the day,' he told the men.

He jumped down and reached up to help Adele by placing his hands at her tiny waist and lifting her down. It was so close to an embrace that he felt the blood rush through his veins.

From the mews they walked to the park and found a path leading to a secluded bench overlooking the Serpentine.

'No one will disturb us here, my love,' Ned told her.

She flew into his arms and sobbed against his chest.

'Tell me what is the matter?' he begged, unable to bear this helpless feeling.

'Oh, Ned!' she cried. 'It is all too wretched. I must tell you, because I would not hold back anything from you, not for the world. You must know all, even though—even though—' She shuddered. 'You will despise me and I know you will never want to marry me.'

He became very alarmed. 'Come. Sit with me and tell me what it is.'

He led her to the bench. When they sat, he kept hold of both of her hands.

She took a deep breath. 'I come from a wretched family.'

Was that all? No family member of hers could be more wretched than his father.

'Today I discovered that my stepmother—although I never call her that—she is Celia to me. More like a sister, really, than a mother—' She waved a hand in front of her mouth and was too overcome to speak.

He used a soothing voice. 'I am sure it cannot be as bad as all that.'

She gulped. 'It is worse. I discovered—I discovered today that dear Celia—although she cannot be dear to me now—not after this…' She paused and held her hand against her chest. 'Celia is having an affair with your brother.'

'My brother!' He gaped at her. 'Hugh?'

'Not Hugh,' she snapped. 'Rhysdale.'

'Rhysdale?' He could not wrap his mind around it. 'But did they not just meet at the ball?' Comprehension immediately dawned. 'Oh, my God. She is…' He could not say it.

'She is gambling, as well. She goes out to gamble at night. I think that is how she met him.' Her tone was so disdainful that he dared not tell her why he knew precisely how her stepmother knew Rhysdale.

He collected his wits. 'Adele, this is not so dreadful. Surely Lady Gale has been discreet. And she is a widow. Widows are allowed some licence.'

She gazed at him with wonder. 'Do you mean you will not despise me for this?'

He put his arm around her and held her close. 'I could never despise you. It has nothing to do with you.'

'Oh, you are too wonderful.' She sighed against him and he revelled in the feel of her in his arms.

It almost made him forget the complications Rhys and her stepmother created.

'Oh...' She suddenly sounded more despairing. 'But you have not heard the worst of it.'

It could get worse?

She pulled away. 'Celia is going to have a baby.'

Celia returned to the Masquerade Club that night, but in turmoil, not anticipation. She felt more agitated than she'd been that night of the ball.

Adele refused to speak with her and Celia had been unable to explain to the girl that she could not be increasing. It was impossible. Wasn't it?

Celia had absolutely no idea how to tell any of this to Rhys. How could she say anything until her fears were confirmed once more—that she did not and could never have a child growing inside her?

'Good to see you, madam,' Cummings greeted her as he took her wrap. It was the most he'd ever spoken to her.

'I am pleased to be back.' She hoped it was wise to have returned. Her spirits were extremely low and she was still very tired.

MacEvoy grinned when she entered the cashier room. 'There she is at last. We've missed you, Madame Fortune.'

It touched her that her absence had been noticed, even in this devil's den.

MacEvoy handed her the counters with a friendly wink. 'I'll expect more from you later.'

'I will endeavour to please you, then.' She smiled and dropped the counters in her reticule.

As she approached the door to the game room, she adjusted her mask. She was dressed as she'd been the very first night she'd come here. Only then she'd not known that her heart would leap for joy to catch sight of the man who ran the establishment and that sharing his bed had taught her more about pleasure than she'd ever dared imagine. How unfair of fate to pair him with all that was dark and painful in her life.

But, then, fate had never been kind to her.

She pressed her hand against her stomach and stepped across the threshold.

The noise in the room swirled around her. She scanned the room looking for Rhys, but all she saw were men with red faces and bulging eyes playing at the gaming tables, a few women, masked and otherwise, hanging on to them with every throw of the dice or play of a card. At the card tables players kept emotion out of their faces, but their postures were tense and she knew nerves were exploding inside them.

There was nothing pleasant in view, nothing happy or peaceful. But as much as the scene revolted her sensitive stomach, another part of her was impatient to play.

A man broke away from the hazard table and approached her.

Lord Westleigh.

'Madame Fortune!' He seized her hand and kissed it. 'You have returned! I've despaired of ever being in your company again. Come, play hazard with me.'

She was due for losing at this game; she just knew it. But there was little chance she could avoid it. Others joined him in begging her to roll the dice.

'Very well,' she said, feigning enjoyment.

Another man cried, 'Madame Fortune is back! Quick. To the hazard table.'

The crowd around the hazard table grew larger as she walked closer.

'Shall we allow Madame Fortune to roll next?' Westleigh said loudly.

'I'll give it up.' The man in possession of the dice dropped them into Westleigh's hand.

Westleigh immediately gave the dice to Celia. 'Roll and make us all rich, Madame.'

She rolled, calling out, 'Six,' but made seven. She rolled the second time and made seven again and won. The men and women around her cheered and a thrill rushed through her.

She continued to roll and to win more times than she lost. The betting was high and the winners feverish with excitement. Celia forgot she was tired, forgot that she loathed the sight and sound of gambling, forgot that she'd been looking for Rhys.

But soon it was as if a London fog parted and she suddenly saw him, watching her through the crowd like he'd watched her that first night.

She rolled a losing number.

Amidst the groans of defeat, she lifted her hands. 'That is enough for me, gentlemen!'

Westleigh scooped up the dice. 'One more roll, Madame. Have pity on us.'

She stepped away. 'My luck is turned. It is time to stop.' And time to see Rhys.

The players closed ranks around the hazard table and play continued without her. She backed away and felt a hand on her shoulder.

'Celia.' It was Rhys.

She turned to face him.

His expression was all concern. 'Are you feeling well enough to be here?'

She wanted to say her illness was merely the effect of carrying his child inside her, but that was no more than a foolish dream, one she'd dreamed before and been disappointed. She could say nothing to him about a mere foolish dream.

A week. If another week went by and she did not have her menses, she would dare to believe in it. She would tell him then.

'I am still tired.' And queasy. 'But I think it is a little better today. I need to be here. I need to play.'

He turned impassive. 'Then I will leave you to

play. You no longer require my assistance gaining partners.' He stepped away.

She placed a hand on his arm to halt him. 'May I see you later?'

His eyes darkened and she felt the air between them grow alive with desire. 'Come to my room when you are ready.'

Rhys walked away from her, but turned to watch her. She remained where they'd stood together for a moment, before strolling through the room, greeting others and stopping for brief chats. Finally she joined three others for whist and he was satisfied that she was well settled.

Xavier came up to him and turned to look in the same direction as Rhys. 'She has returned, I see.'

The two friends had achieved a sort of truce while she'd been ill, but now Rhys heard something in Xavier's voice that put him on guard.

'Her illness is improved,' Rhys said in as matter of fact a tone as he could muster.

'She won at hazard again.' Xavier's voice was mild, but Rhys knew his message. 'Quite a winning streak. Unlike any we've seen these last few days.'

Rhys faced him. 'Your meaning?'

Xavier backed away. 'No meaning. A mere observation.'

In spite of himself, Rhys's suspicions were

aroused and he played a version of Xavier's discourse in his head. There was still much Rhys did not know about her. How many more secrets had she kept from him? She needed money. Maybe her need was so great she was driven to cheating. She was skilled enough to know how. Her father had been accused of it.

He stopped himself.

Her father had been killed because of cheating. Certainly that alone would serve as a caution to her. Besides, he did know her. In an intimate way, where secrets were harder to keep.

He glanced towards the doorway and saw Ned and Hugh advancing directly on him.

He met them halfway.

'We would speak with you,' Ned demanded.

Hugh looked as if he were ten years old again and ready to throw the first punch.

Rhys nodded. 'Let us go somewhere private.'

He led them up to his drawing room on the floor above.

Once inside the room, he closed the door. 'Now what is it?'

'How could you do this?' Hugh spat. 'It is abominable even coming from the likes of you.'

Rhys's brows rose. 'Perhaps you might tell me what it is I have done.'

Ned faced him squarely. 'Lady Gale is with child and you are the father.'

It was like a blow direct to his gut.

For a second Rhys could not even breathe. But he knew better than to give away his utter shock. He kept his face still, his expression bland. They obviously held all the aces and he had nothing.

'Who told you this?' He kept any emotion from his voice.

'Miss Gale,' Ned responded. 'And her distress over the matter is sufficient reason for me to call you out.'

Rhys merely raised his eyes to him. 'Are you calling me out, Neddington?'

Ned backed off. 'No. Of course not. But this is badly done of you, Rhys.'

Hugh's hands curled into fists. 'Haven't you done enough to our family?'

Rhys turned his steely gaze on him. 'You are forgetting who you came to when the family needed rescuing.'

'See here—' Hugh shot back.

'Stop it, Hugh,' Ned snapped. He faced Rhys again. 'Do you deny this? That you have been engaging in an affair with Lady Gale, who we now know must be Madame Fortune? That you have got her with child? A respectable woman from a respectable family. Think what this will mean to her stepdaughter.'

'To her stepdaughter?' Rhys laughed. 'You malign both Lady Gale and Madame Fortune and your concern is solely for the stepdaughter?'

Ned's eyes flashed. 'Miss Gale is my sole concern. Do you deny what we say?'

Hugh broke in. 'What are you going to do about it?'

Rhys made himself look blandly from one brother to the other, while inside he was furious with their implication that he was not worthy of a respectable woman. He was furious that they would criticise Celia as if her behaviour would somehow soil her stepdaughter's virginal mind. Mostly he was wounded to the depths of his soul that Celia had not told him herself that she carried his child.

Finally he spoke. 'If any of this were true, I fail to see how it is your concern. Do not come here and shout insults at me and to ladies who are not present to defend themselves. And stop spreading gossip like a set of garrulous hags.'

'Everyone knows you are having an affair with Madame Fortune!' Hugh cried.

Rhys countered, 'They suspect. They do not know.'

Hugh sprang at Rhys.

Ned held his brother back. 'Are you denying this, Rhys?'

'I am not crediting any of it with more comment,' Rhys replied in a firm voice. 'One thing I will tell you. Do not speak with Madame Fortune about this. I will not have you throwing out accusations and speculations against patrons who have chosen to be masked and anonymous. You will keep silent on this manner or you will answer to me. And, do not forget, you need the money I provide to you.'

'It is our money,' Hugh cried. 'We invested everything we had left in this.'

'And I have paid back that investment,' Rhys responded. 'We are even now.'

'You still owe us!' Hugh leaned into Rhys's face.

Rhys pushed him away. 'If I hear one more word of this from anyone else, I'm holding you responsible and these doors will be closed to you.'

'But this is our gaming house!' Hugh cried.

Rhys swung so close his face was inches from Hugh's. 'This is my gaming house. That was the bargain. I decide who may enter and who will be banned.'

Ned pulled Hugh away. 'We've said our piece. Let us go now.'

Rhys drove them towards the door. 'Remember my warning. Keep silent on this or answer to me!'

They left the room and he slammed the door shut behind them.

Chapter Fourteen

With Ned and Hugh gone, Rhys had no need to
hold in his rage. He prowled through the room,
wishing he were in some seedy tavern in the East
End so he could pick a fight and break some furniture, smash some glass.

Why had she not told him?

With a growl he pulled the door open and ran
down the stairs, slowing only when reaching the
last step. Cummings glanced up at him in surprise.

'Cummings, ask Madame Fortune to come upstairs as soon as she is able,' he ordered.

Cummings gave him a queer look, but nodded.

Rhys returned to the drawing room to pace and
contemplate what in the room he might smash
against the wall.

She said she was barren.

Had she lied to him about that? To what purpose? Having a child would shame her and, in his station of life, make no difference to him.

Except it did make a difference to him.

He gripped the back of a chair.

No child of his would come into the world in shame. No child of his would bear the burden of being called bastard.

It seemed a long time until he heard her footsteps on the stairs. He waited in the doorway.

She climbed the stairs wearily and a wave of worry washed over him. She was still ill.

She glanced up and saw him waiting for her. 'Rhys?'

He turned and re-entered the drawing room.

She followed, pulling off her mask. 'What is it, Rhys?'

He supposed he looked like thunder. He composed his face. 'Neddington and Hugh just called upon me.'

She gave him a wary look. 'And?'

He stepped close to her and leaned even closer. 'They said you are carrying my child.'

She blanched. 'I—'

He seized her arms for a moment, but immediately released her. 'Were you planning on informing me of this fact?'

'It—it cannot be a fact,' she countered. 'I was told by a physician that I am barren, that I would never conceive.'

He seethed. 'Then why say so to Miss Gale?'

'Adele,' she whispered in an exasperated tone. She raised her head to Rhys. 'I told her it could not be true, but she would not listen.'

He held her arms again and looked down into her eyes. 'But it is true, is it not? Tell me now.'

She glanced away. 'I can only say that—that I am late in bleeding.'

'Then it might be true,' he persisted.

She bit her lips and pain contorted her features. 'It might be,' she said in the tiniest voice.

He made an angry sound and released her again, swinging away and putting some distance between them.

Celia reeled under the force of his anger, so unexpected.

So crushingly disappointing.

She blinked away sudden tears and straightened her spine. 'Do not concern yourself, Rhys. If it is true, I ask nothing of you. I have enough money to care for a child.' Or she would after a few more weeks of gambling.

He swivelled back, fire shooting from his eyes. 'Do you think I am trying to shirk responsibility? Is that the sort of man you think I am?'

She was taken aback. 'Why else be angry about my possible condition?'

He seized her wrists and pulled her close. 'I am angry you did not tell me. You might have done so this morning when I called and we were private. I am angry that you excluded me from this.'

She tried to pull away. 'How could I say a word of it when everything I know speaks against it?' Her throat grew tight. 'I cannot hope it is a child.'

He released her, his expression full of pain. 'You do not want it to be true.'

The grief of many years' duration enveloped her once again. 'I want it to be true with all my heart.'

He reached out to her again, this time tenderly touching her arm. 'Then we have no conflict, no scandal. We can marry. You and our child will want for nothing.'

'Marry?' No. Never. Marriage was misery, a prison.

But this was Rhys. She might wake every morning in his arms, see his smile when sunshine filled the room. She might walk with him to the shops, sit next to him at the opera, share every meal with him across the table from her.

A knock sounded at the door and Cummings's voice carried into the room, 'Mr Rhysdale. Come. There is trouble in the game room.'

He looked at her with regret. 'We'll continue this.'

He left with Cummings, leaving the door ajar. Sounds of raised voices reached her ears. She tied her mask in place and followed him.

From the game room door the scene unfolded.

One man lunging after another, Xavier and another man holding him back. 'You took my money! All of it! I am ruined! It is out of all fairness!'

The other man leaned threateningly towards him. 'Are you calling me a cheat? I play a fair game!'

Rhys stood between the two. 'We'll have none of this. No fighting.' He turned to Xavier. 'Take him away.' To the other man, Rhys said, 'Calm yourself, sir. I suggest you cash out and leave. Tempers are too high at the moment.'

'I won't be accused of cheating!' the man cried. 'I demand satisfaction.'

'I will have you banned if you do not calm down.' Rhys pushed him away. 'He is upset at losing, nothing more.'

Xavier and the other man dragged their charge out of the game room. As they passed by Celia, the man continued to wail, 'I am ruined! What am I to do? I am ruined.'

Rhys meanwhile stuck with the other man, waiting for him to pick up his counters and a vowel written by the loser. He walked with the man past Celia, out the door, presumably to the cashier.

The other patrons turned back to their games and soon the sounds of wins and losses returned in its familiar cadence. Celia grew cold as she watched their faces. At the hazard table all eyes were riveted on the roll of the dice. At *vingt-et-un,* the players were spellbound by each turn of a card, at faro, the dealing box. Yet one man's life was ruined and another man was willing to risk death for some dubious code of honour.

The room held perhaps seventy players and it seemed to Celia that each of the men wore her father's face. She closed her eyes only to see him again returning home with smiles and gifts, swinging her mother around and swearing that life would be easy from then on. She blinked and he was now weeping into her mother's lap, begging for forgiveness for losing money for rent, for clothing, for food.

Lord Westleigh sidled over to her. 'Might I interest Madame in some more hazard? A little luck is in order, do you not think?'

She gaped at him. The scenario played out before her eyes a moment ago might have been the way it had occurred with her father. Did not Westleigh remember that night? Should she ask him if her father won? Was that why Westleigh accused him of cheating? Was that why her father had challenged him to a duel? Should she ask how it felt for Westleigh to shoot the pistol and see her father fall? Or how he lived with himself for merely running away? He'd hid behind some gentleman's code of silence and had never been held accountable for the crime.

'No hazard, sir,' she managed.

'Then let us have some supper.' He took her arm.

She recoiled. 'No!'

He gripped her harder. 'Come now, madam, you must know I have developed a regard for you. You would do very well to take advantage of that fact.'

'Take advantage!' The very sight of him sickened her.

'I would pay handsomely for some…private time with you. You would not regret the money or the experience.' He leered at her.

'Release me, sir,' she demanded. 'I'll not bear your insults.'

He pulled her closer. 'Do not say you prefer that bastard Rhysdale? He is nothing compared to me, I assure you. A mere hireling. You cannot prefer him to me.'

She lowered her voice, so angry at him it trembled. 'How dare you call him a hireling! And I do prefer him to you. I prefer any man to you. Do not ever approach me again. For any reason.' She wrenched out of his grasp and walked out of the game room.

He caught her in the hall and pinned her against the wall, leaning down into her masked face. 'You will regret rebuffing me, madam. I have ways of retaliating against such insults.' His mouth stretched into a malevolent grin. 'Perhaps I will unmask you. You would dislike that, wouldn't you.'

When he let go of her to reach for her mask, she pushed hard on his chest, knocking him off balance.

She hurried to get away from him. As she neared the cashier's office. Rhys had entered the hallway, escorting the winning gentleman out. He gave her an apologetic glance, but she could not meet his eyes, nor tell him what just happened to her at the hands of Westleigh. She walked into the cashier's room.

MacEvoy looked up at her. 'Cashing out, Madame?'

'Yes.' She could hardly speak.

When she made her way to the hall, Westleigh was nowhere to be seen.

Xavier emerged from Cummings's coat room.

'Is Rhys in there?' she asked.

'He is. He is calming the fellow down,' Xavier responded. 'Do you wish me to get him for you?'

She shook her head. 'But I must beg a favour from you.'

'Of course.' He inclined his head graciously.

'Walk me home.'

It took all of an hour to calm Mr Poole enough to release him to go home without the intention to kill himself on the way. It also took a loan from

Rhys of one hundred pounds, money Rhys suspected he would never see again.

But he did not want the pall of suicide hanging over his gaming house. Besides, the man had a wife and children. They should not have to pay for the man's sins.

Poole had to endure a strong lecture from Rhys regarding the duty a man owed to his children. It was a lecture that had special meaning to Rhys now and he was eager to settle matters between him and Celia.

As soon as Poole walked out of the house, Rhys ran upstairs to the drawing room, but Celia was not there. He checked the bedchamber. She was not there, either.

He returned to the hall.

Cummings stood in his usual place.

'Did you see Madame Fortune?' he asked.

Cummings shook his head.

Rhys checked the game room, the supper room and the cashier. MacEvoy told him she'd cashed out.

He returned to the hall just as Xavier opened the front door and entered.

Xavier held up a hand. 'She asked me to walk her home.'

'Did she say why?' Was she ill again?

Xavier walked over to him. 'She barely said a word. Something upset her. That was evident.'

He waited for Xavier to say more or to indicate

that her leaving was somehow proof that her intentions were nefarious, but Xavier said nothing.

Rhys's impulse was to rush out and run to her rooms to demand to speak with her, but it was nearly three o'clock in the morning.

He would see her when it was day and a civil time to call. He'd not wait a moment longer to discover why, after he had proposed marriage to her, she fled from him.

Chapter Fifteen

Ned spent the morning poring over his father's accounts with his father's secretary, attempting to decide which bills to pay and which to defer. Thanks to Rhys, the task was now tedious rather than desperate.

It was a task his father ought to be performing, but, ever since Ned and Hugh had discovered the dismal state of their financial affairs and confronted their father with it, their father had washed his hands of his responsibility, as if the bearers of the bad news were responsible for the problems.

Now, though, Ned had even more to worry over. Rhys had not confirmed or denied an affair with the younger Lady Gale, nor even if Lady Gale was Madame Fortune, which Ned strongly suspected. It agonised Ned that he and Hugh had managed merely to muddle matters rather than rescue Adele from this vexing problem.

Ned tallied a list of numbers for the third time, getting yet another total, when the butler knocked on the door.

'What is it, Mason?' Ned asked.

Mason bowed. 'Your mother requests your presence in her sitting room.'

What now? Ever since Rhys called that day and made certain his mother was informed of the crisis, she'd demanded to know every detail of every decision he and Hugh made. And every problem they encountered.

He did not wish his mother to know this new scandal Rhys had created, not when it so involved and affected Adele.

He handed the ledger to the secretary and left the library to climb the stairs to his mother's private sitting room.

To his astonishment, when he opened the door to enter, she was there, his Adele, sitting next to his mother on her chaise longue.

'Adele!' He went straight to her, clasping her hands in his and looking into her beautiful eyes.

'Do sit, Ned,' his mother said impatiently. 'Miss Gale has been telling me an extraordinary tale. We wish to know what you have done about it.'

Adele's lip trembled. 'I have told your dear mother *everything*. I simply had to talk to someone and I could think of no one but her.'

'I see,' he said non-committally. He'd wanted to handle it without his mother's intervention.

'Did you speak to Rhysdale about it?' his mother asked. 'He must marry Lady Gale, of course. I hope you told him so.'

He frowned. 'Rhysdale would not speak to us of it. He called it gossip and all but tossed us out.'

'It is not gossip!' Adele cried. 'It is my life! I know that Celia is going to have a baby. Our maid verifies that it is so…' She paused as if reconsidering her words. 'Or, rather, she admits it is *possible*. Celia has all the signs, Younie said. You can ask her yourself. She came with me.'

Ned's brow knit in confusion. 'Lady Gale is with you?'

'Not Lady Gale!' Adele rolled her eyes. 'Younie. Our ladies' maid.'

His mother waved a dismissive hand. 'Rhysdale denies it?'

Ned shrugged. 'He did not confirm or deny it.'

'Then it must be true.' His mother nodded with certainty.

That logic escaped him.

'What I cannot understand…' Adele put a finger to her flawless cheek '…is how it could be true? How can Celia be carrying a baby when she was barren all those years with my father?'

'Maybe it was your father who could not…' how to put it delicately? he wondered '…father a child.'

Her eyes grew wide. 'But…but there is me! I am proof there was nothing wrong with my father.'

'Not necessarily so,' interjected his mother.

'What do you mean?' Adele turned to her.

His mother did not answer right away. 'I told you that I knew your mother, did I not?' she finally said.

Adele nodded her head.

His mother went on. 'She confided in me.' She gave Adele a very sympathetic look. 'Your mother was unhappy in her marriage to your father.'

Adele's expression darkened. 'I know that. My father was not a nice man. I remember him shouting at her when I was a little girl.' She glanced away in thought. 'He shouted at Celia, too.'

Ned's mother patted her hand. 'He was a cruel and thoughtless husband.' She grasped Adele's hand. 'You mother sought comfort elsewhere.'

Adele looked appalled. Ned wished his mother would stop. Surely this was no comfort to the poor young woman.

His mother went on. 'One Season, here in Mayfair, she fell in love with a fine gentleman, an army officer of good family, but nothing else to offer anyone. They had several months of happiness before he was sent to the Continent to fight the French.' She continued to hold Adele's hand. 'When news came to her that he'd died fighting the French in Holland, you were already grow-ing inside her.'

Adele's eyes widened. 'Do not tell me!'

His mother turned very sympathetic. 'I am sorry to tell you, my dear.'

Ned reached over and took Adele's other hand. How difficult this must be for her. Had she not had enough to bear?

Adele squeezed his hand and broke out into smiles. She looked from his mother to him and back to his mother again. 'Oh, this is marvellous news. I disliked my father very much. I am glad I am not his daughter. I only wish I could have known my real father—' Her voice cracked and tears fell from her eyes.

'I will tell you all I know of him, but this is enough for one day,' his mother said to her.

Adele hugged his mother and all Ned could wish was that he could feel her arms around him, as well, but that, of course, would not be proper.

Perhaps if he could contrive to see her alone?

She glanced at him and concern filled her lovely face. 'Do you object very much, Nedding-ton? I mean, I am not really the daughter of a baron. Does this change your opinion of me?'

He seized her hand again and pressed it to his lips. 'Nothing could change my opinion of you.'

His mother clapped her hands as if summon-ing recalcitrant children. 'We are still left with the problem of Adele's stepmother and Rhysdale.

Perhaps I should call upon Lady Gale and speak to her about this.' She turned to Adele. 'As your future mother-in-law, it might be seen as my duty.'

Celia sat in her bedchamber nibbling on toasted bread and sipping tea. The events of the night before returned to her mind, even though she wanted to banish them. Rhys's offer of marriage. The nightmare that was the gaming house. Its winners and losers.

Lord Westleigh.

Her stomach heaved and she quickly bit down on another piece of toast. The queasiness was manageable as long as she could keep some food down.

Her butler knocked on the door. 'A word with you, ma'am?' he asked.

'Come in, Tucker,' she responded. 'What is it?'

'Ma'am, I thought you should know that the new Lord Gale is at this moment in the drawing room. I am of the impression that the Dowager Lady Gale summoned him. They are in deep conversation about something.'

Celia pressed her fingers against her temple.

'What is she up to now?' she said below her breath. She looked up at Tucker. 'Is Adele with them?' Had Lady Gale not given up the scheme to marry Adele off to her cousin?

'No, ma'am,' replied Tucker. 'Miss Gale went out with Younie a while ago.'

Where would Adele have gone with Younie? That was a worry. Adele had been so upset with Celia the previous day she would neither speak to nor listen to Celia. Who knew what she was thinking today?

Celia stood. 'Thank you, Tucker. I will attend to it.'

Tucker left and Celia sat at her dressing table and hurriedly twisted her hair into a chignon. She pinched her cheeks to put some colour into her face and rushed out the door, not caring if her morning dress was presentable enough for Cousin Luther.

When she approached the drawing-room door, she slowed her pace, strolling in as if by accident rather than design. 'Why, Lady Gale. Luther. What a surprise.'

Lady Gale looked lightning bolts at her.

Luther rose and did not look any more pleased to see her. 'Good morning, Celia. We have been talking about you.'

Her gaze darted to her mother-in-law. 'I dare say you have.'

Luther pointed to a chair. 'Sit down. Now you are here, I wish to talk to you.'

She advanced to the seating area, but stopped some distance from their chairs. 'I prefer to stand.' There was nothing that would entice her to sit and be scolded as if a child.

His lips pursed. 'As you wish.'

Besides, if she stood, he also had to stand. That would make it easier for him to leave.

He shifted on his feet. 'Lady Gale informs me that you have been very indiscreet and that you are attempting to entrap the owner of a gaming hell into marrying you.'

Celia glanced at her mother-in-law. How cruel and heartless could that woman be? First to tell this tale to Adele and now Luther.

Celia put on a bold face. 'Lady Gale has been busy telling stories.'

Luther baulked. 'What? Do you say it is not true?'

She straightened. 'I do not feel compelled to say anything.'

He raised his nose at her. 'As the head of the family, I believe you owe me an explanation for this scandalous behaviour.' He shook his head in dismay. 'Imagine *trying* to marry a gamester. It is the outside of enough.'

A shaft of pain impaled her at the thought that Rhys wanted to marry her. She'd been unable to face him the previous night, but tonight, she must.

Not that Luther had any say in what she did.

'Head of the family?' She shook her head. 'You are not the head of *my* family. I owe you nothing.'

'See here, Celia!' His cheeks puffed out.

Her temper was lost. She went on. 'And if you were any *decent* head of the family, you would take responsibility for those who need your protection. Adele and her grandmother should have been allowed to stay at Gale House, at least until you bring a wife there. Or you should have given them the dower house. What's more, you should have financed Adele's come-out and seen that her future was well settled. Adele and Lady Gale should have been your guests at the town house, not forced into rented rooms.' Her arm swept across the room.

'Celia!' her mother-in-law snapped. 'I will not have you speak to Cousin Luther in that manner.'

She turned her glare onto Lady Gale. 'Do not you speak to me at all.'

Lady Gale drew back as if struck.

Luther pounded the air with his fist. 'Your husband left his property and finances in such a sorry state that I am strained to the limit. You expect me to dole out more money?'

She shot back, 'A baron takes care of those in his charge. Or he should. The title comes with responsibility, not just property.'

Luther fussed at his collar. 'I do not need to stay here and listen to these insults.' He turned to Celia's mother-in-law. 'I planned to make an offer of marriage to your granddaughter, ma'am, but you may rest assured that will never happen now. I wash my hands of the lot of you.'

'Spoken like a true gentleman,' Celia said sarcastically.

For a moment he looked exactly like her husband. He looked as if he might strike her, which Gale had done. Once.

Instead, Luther started for the door.

Celia's mother-in-law rushed after him. 'Luther! You cannot credit anything she says. I beg you to reconsider.'

He threw up his hands. 'I said I wash my hands of you.'

As soon as the two of them had left the room, Celia collapsed in a chair. Her legs trembled, her stomach heaved and she could taste vomit in her mouth. She fought to keep her food down.

She rested both hands on her abdomen. If only this were indeed a baby, then at least she would not be alone.

It would be some comfort.

Celia did not know how long she sat there, but the sounds of her mother-in-law pleading with Luther faded and she heard the front door close. Soon after, the sounds of the mantel clock ticking and an occasional carriage passing by were the only sounds she heard.

The knocker sounded and Tucker's voice reached her ears.

Another caller.

She ought to have retreated to her bedchamber when she'd had the chance, so she might have avoided anyone.

Tucker rapped at the door, still slightly ajar

from Luther and Lady Gale's hasty departure. 'A gentleman to see you, ma'am.'

She turned, knowing instantly who she would see.

He stepped into the room. 'Hello, Celia.'

'Rhys.' She rose. 'Do come in.'

He walked towards her and the air changed around her. Her body came alive to him with a yearning she knew could never be satisfied. Why should this man capture her heart, of all men?

'I will skip the niceties, Celia.' His face was serious. 'Why did you leave last night? What happened?'

She turned away. 'I do not know how to explain.'

He took her arm and turned her back. 'I suggest you try.' His eyes flickered with pain. 'Explain why you left me moments after I told you I will marry you.'

She opened her mouth in an attempt to explain what settled like a pit of fear inside her, but voices from the hall distracted her.

A moment later the door opened and Adele walked in. Behind her were Lady Westleigh and Ned.

'Celia, Tucker said you were in here—' Adele stopped cold when she caught sight of Rhys. 'Oh.'

A wave of nausea hit Celia, but she had to ignore it. She curtsied, instead.

'Lady Westleigh.' She and Rhys spoke at the same time.

'Lady Gale,' the woman responded. 'Rhys. It is just as well you are here. We ought to get this sorted out.'

Tucker stood at the door, looking apologetic.

'Some tea, if you please, Tucker,' Celia said.

From behind him she saw her mother-in-law approaching. 'I heard voices. Who is here?'

Tucker gave her a sympathetic look before turning away.

Her mother-in-law strode in.

Adele stopped her. 'Grandmama, you must be civil.'

Her grandmother gave the girl a scathing look.

Rhys nodded to her and she turned her head away, instead greeting Lady Westleigh. Ned said a stiff hello to Rhys.

'Shall we sit?' invited Lady Westleigh as if she were the hostess.

Adele and Ned sat together on the sofa. Lady Gale settled in one chair and Lady Westleigh in another.

Both Rhys and Celia remained standing.

'To what do we owe the pleasure of your visit?' Celia asked Lady Westleigh.

'Adele told me about this situation of yours,' the lady answered. 'I will help devise a plan that will minimise any scandal to the family.' She turned to Rhys. 'Rhysdale, you are crucial in how we must manage it.'

Celia felt him stiffen as her ladyship spoke.

'Adele has been busy,' he remarked in a low voice only Celia might have heard.

Lady Westleigh went on. 'Now, the only thing to do, of course, is for you to marry—'

'Do not be ridiculous,' Celia's mother-in-law piped up. 'This is all a sham. She is not increasing. It is impossible. She is unable to conceive. It is a proven fact.'

Rhys put his hand on Celia's arm, a steadying gesture that surprised her as much as her mother-in-law's unrelenting abuse.

Lady Westleigh immediately swung to the dowager. 'Why do you say that, ma'am?'

The older woman straightened. 'Because my son told me so. A physician confirmed the diagnosis.' She inclined her head towards Celia. 'She was a great disappointment to him.'

Lady Westleigh shook her head. 'I dare say the problem was not your daughter-in-law's, but your son's.'

Celia's mother-in-law huffed, 'Of course it was not my son's problem. He already sired a daughter.'

'Grandmama,' Adele broke in. 'Papa was not my real father. My mother gave birth to me after a love affair with an officer.'

Her grandmother clasped her heart. 'It isn't so—' She protested in every way manageable.

But her words did not penetrate through the blood pounding in Celia's ears. She touched her abdomen. She'd been so afraid to hope, but now hope turned to possibility and possibility to certainty. The magic and wonder of it made her want to throw herself in Rhys's arms. He'd given her this life growing inside her. There was no other man she would rather be the father of her child.

Her mother-in-law's words finally penetrated. 'My son was a virile man. Her womb was as dry as an old woman's!'

'Ma'am!' Rhys gave Celia's mother-in-law a fierce look. 'I demand you apologise to her. Do you hear me? I will not tolerate it.'

'*You* will not tolerate it?' her mother-in-law went on. 'You dare speak to me that way when you are nothing but a—'

'Bastard?' He said it for her. 'Madam, none of us choose our birth, but we do choose our behaviour. I've known women forced to live on the streets who have more grace and kindness than you.'

Lady Gale gave a disparaging laugh. 'I wager you would know countless women who live on the streets—'

'Lady Gale!' Celia cried. 'Leave this room now or I will have Younie pack your trunk and I will personally escort you out of the house.'

Adele shrieked and covered her mouth with her fist.

Her mother-in-law rose and, grumbling outrage and insults, flounced out of the room.

As soon as the door closed behind her, Lady Westleigh again spoke. 'Well, that was unpleasant. But perhaps now we can address the problem at hand.'

Rhys put up a hand. 'No, Lady Westleigh.'

Celia quickly added, 'I appreciate your concern, my lady, but I have no intention of discussing anything.'

'Lady Gale—' Ned sounded outraged '—this affects Adele and that reason alone gives me the right to speak with you about this. My mother, as well.'

Celia turned to him. 'I am not going to discuss it with you or your mother. Adele should have come to me first.' She turned to her stepdaughter. 'I tried to speak with you yesterday, you recall.'

Adele crossed her arms over her chest. 'I did not wish to speak with you.'

'No, you preferred the ravings of your grandmother to anything I might say.' Celia gave her a penetrating look. 'And then you carried tales about me.'

'See here, Lady Gale,' Ned cried. 'She came to me and to my mother. There is nothing to object to in that.'

They were Westleighs and Celia wanted nothing to do with any of them. If it made Adele happy to join that family, so be it, but Celia was not obligated.

'Your family is not my family,' Celia said to Ned. 'Adele should have respected that.'

'You are maligning my dear Ned,' wailed Adele.

'She is not maligning Ned,' Rhys broke in. 'Stop acting like a child.'

'See here, Rhys!' Ned pressed his hands into fists and leapt from his chair.

Celia faced him. 'Ned, if you had an ounce of sense in your head, you would marry Adele now. You'd get a special licence and marry without delay. I dare say even with your financial difficulties, you have more resources to care for her than I have. You do not even have the courage to officially declare yourselves betrothed. It is wrong to leave her in such a precarious position.'

Ned fumed. 'I have good reasons! Besides, you cannot tell me when Adele and I should marry. That is for us to decide.'

Celia nodded. 'And you cannot tell me what I should do. That is for me to decide.'

Lady Westleigh stood. 'Your point is well taken, Lady Gale. We have been unforgivingly presumptive. Do forgive us.' She turned to her son. 'Ned, we should take our leave.'

He gave his mother a pleading look. 'I would like some time to speak with Adele.'

Celia turned to Rhys. 'Would you escort Lady Westleigh home?'

He gave her a questioning glance.

She spoke more quietly. 'I will see you later. We can talk then.'

Celia needed time. Time to think of her child, time to think of what was best to do.

Rhys bowed to Lady Westleigh. 'Ma'am, I would be honoured to escort you.'

Lady Westleigh nodded to Rhys. 'I accept. That is very kind of you.'

'I'll walk you both out,' Celia said.

As they stepped out of the room, Tucker approached with the tea tray.

Celia shook her head. 'We do not need tea now, Tucker. Lady Westleigh and Mr Rhysdale are just leaving.'

He nodded and carried the tray back to the hall and placed it on a nearby table. He went to retrieve Lady Westleigh's wrap and Rhys's hat and gloves.

Rhys took Celia aside. 'Come tonight, Celia. We must talk this out.'

She nodded, but did not know what she would say to him when the time came.

Chapter Sixteen

That night Rhys told Cummings to send Celia up to the drawing room as soon as she arrived and to summon him immediately.

She arrived at her usual time and Rhys left the game room to go to her.

When he entered the drawing room, she was standing in the centre of the room, waiting for him. In the candlelight her white shimmering gown made her look as if she were a vision created from his dreams.

She smiled tentatively. 'Do you think we will be disturbed this time?'

He frowned. 'Not for anything.'

He walked over to her as if under a spell, his body craving her almost as much as his soul. He did not wish to need her so much. He prided himself on not needing anyone. If one was alone, one had nothing to lose. Suddenly he risked losing this woman.

And their child.

He would never do what his father did. He would never abandon her or their child.

Rhys tried to pour all those emotions into an embrace.

She sighed and melted against him and, as their bodies entwined, the need to join with her grew to an even greater intensity.

He bent his head and placed his lips upon hers in a hunger that shocked him.

But her returning kiss felt like regret.

He broke away from the intense contact and held only her arms. 'I have missed you, Celia.'

Her lips trembled. 'I have missed you, too.'

So why had she left after he'd proposed marriage to her?

He released her and walked over to the decanter on the table. 'Brandy or port?'

She pressed her stomach. 'Neither. Just the thought of spirits makes me feel out of sorts.'

He turned back to her. 'You are still ill?'

'I am now thinking it might be because of a baby,' she said. 'My ills are expected, I am told.'

'Do you now believe you are increasing?' He poured himself some brandy.

'Yes.' She walked over to the table where his stood and fingered the wood. 'Lady Westleigh made me dare hope.'

'Hope?' He was more confused than ever.

Her eyes filled with tears. 'It is a miracle for me.'

He gulped his brandy and stared directly into her eyes. 'Then finish what we started this afternoon. Explain why things are not right between us.'

She turned away.

He drained the contents of his glass and pressed on. 'Explain why you will not simply say you will marry me and give our baby my name. Is it because of my birth?'

She turned in surprise. 'Not at all. I never even thought such a thing.'

'Then why?'

She averted her gaze again. 'I do not know how to say it.'

His insides twisted in pain, but he kept his expression blank. 'Celia. Just say it.'

She took a breath. 'I went down to the game room. And the men there—the ones you were sent to deal with—it was so much like what happened to my father and Westleigh.'

He could see that. 'You must know, though, that what happened had nothing to do with you or me.'

She held up a hand to stop him from interrupting. 'After you took the men out of the room, everyone went back to gambling as if nothing had happened. One man ruined. Another wanting a duel. And they all went back to the games. And then Westleigh came up to me and wanted to play hazard...' She stopped.

Westleigh.

What was she not telling him? What had Westleigh done?

'What did Westleigh do?' His voice deepened to a growl.

She made a nervous gesture. 'Nothing.'

He did not believe her.

She paced in front of him. 'It is merely that— that this is your world. It connects you to Westleigh, but I cannot be connected to it.'

He burned inside. 'You connected yourself to it.'

'Yes,' she admitted, 'but before I knew of him. And out of necessity. I needed—still need—the money. I loathe this—*him*—I loathe all this represents.'

'I am here out of necessity, as well.' Did she think he was given a choice? It was gamble or starve. 'But you are being less than truthful. You enjoy the play.'

'That is it,' she agreed. 'That is the seduction. The fever. It robs everyone of their senses. It is what killed my father.'

'I am not your father, Celia.' Rhys never played cards with emotion. 'Cards are nothing more than a tool to me. A means to an end.' Survival once;

now something more. 'I know when to play on and I know when to cash out.'

She shook her head. 'You cannot control luck, Rhys. No one can. All it takes is a turn of luck. I've lived this all during my childhood. I'll not subject my child to such a life.'

'And if I said I would give it all up?' He'd always intended to give it up. He had figured three years would do the trick. By then the Westleighs' fortunes would be solid and he would be wealthy enough to buy a factory or a ship or something.

She gave him a direct look. 'Do you know how many times my father promised to give it up?'

He stepped towards her, seized her arms and held her gaze. 'There is a difference between those men like your father and those like me. I am a gambler because when I had nothing, it was an honest way to get food to eat. When I won, I ate; when I lost, I didn't. I learned how to win. I learned how to survive and eventually I learned how to thrive. I will not go backwards. So do not hold up my gambling as a reason not to give your child a father.'

She averted her face. 'There is another reason.'

'And that is?'

She met his eye again. 'Westleigh. You are connected to Westleigh.'

He let go and swung away. 'He should not be considered at all!'

She would refuse to marry him because he was fathered by Westleigh? How ironic. When a boy he'd hoped his father would once call him son. Now that he accomplished it out of spite, doing so meant losing the woman he loved and a child he could call his own.

Rhys felt the pain of it as if a thousand sabres cut into his flesh. 'Westleigh keeps you from me? Am I again to be punished because of my birth?'

She reached out to him with sympathy on her face. 'Not because of your birth. Because you chose to entangle your life with his.'

He turned away, too angry at her—at himself— to trust what he would say or do next. 'Then we are done here.' He looked back with a sardonic smile. 'I must return to my gaming hell.'

She picked up her mask. 'Do you object to me playing tonight?'

That she would gamble after that speech of hers, after rejecting him for his gambling life, a life that was providing her needed funds, was a final sabre thrust.

'You are still in my employ, Celia.'

He walked out.

She'd hurt him and it agonised her. Almost as much as having to turn away from him for the sake of her child.

Rhys was a good man, a man to love. She'd

never know his like again and her heart shattered at the thought that she had rejected him when she wanted him more than she could bear.

It was the gambling she did not want, *could* not want around her child. She could not bring a child into the sort of childhood she'd endured.

Gambling, its seductions and its perils, was the real villain. Now it had dealt her another blow. It had robbed her of the man she loved.

Celia tied the mask to her face and peeked in the mirror above the mantel to see if it concealed her identity well enough. The bone-weariness she felt tonight had little to do with her condition. She was exhausted from the battle she'd waged inside herself, the battle her heart had lost.

She walked down to the cashier's office and picked up her counters. She made her way to the game room, pausing in the doorway while its sounds and sights enveloped her. Lifting her chin, she walked through the room, looking around.

Looking for Rhys.

She found him conversing with a masked woman and her partner at whist. He lifted his gaze to her as she moved past him and her heart ached inside her chest.

'Madame Fortune!' a gentleman cried. 'Come! Play some hazard. I'm in need of a little luck.'

Some others joined his plea.

A man came up to her from behind and leaned

into her ear. 'Do play hazard, my dear. See if your luck still holds.'

It was Lord Westleigh.

She straightened her spine and took another man's arm. 'If you insist. I will play hazard.'

Her first roll was a loss and the dice passed to another player. When it came around to her again and she reached down to scoop up the dice, Westleigh beat her to it.

He took the dice in one hand and grasped her hand in the other, dropping the dice into her palm.

'Best of luck, Madame Fortune.' He smirked.

She expected to lose again, but she won the toss.

A shout rang out from the crowd, 'Madame Fortune has found her luck!'

The next bets placed were overwhelmingly with her next roll. Westleigh bet with her, as well.

With the crowd's enthusiastic encouragement, she rolled again and again, not always winning, but more often than not. More often than seemed likely. In spite of herself, it roused her excitement and she was eager for the next roll. Even Xavier's intent scrutiny did not deter her. The counters piled up and more and more players pushed their way to place their bets.

Rhys appeared next to Xavier, watching her play. She froze, dice in hand. She might be winning, but she was losing him a great deal of money.

Bets were already placed and her next roll called. She had no choice but to roll, telling herself she'd stop after this.

She'd called seven and the dice fell into a three and a four. A cheer went up and the wagerers collected their counters.

Westleigh picked up the dice from the table and bounced them in his palm. 'They are weighted!' he said in a loud voice. 'I declare. The dice are weighted.'

She stared at him.

'Watch,' he said pointedly to Rhys and Xavier.

He placed one die on its corner and tried to make it spin. It fell immediately to the number four. He tried to spin the other die. It, too, failed and fell to a two.

Loud rumblings went up from the crowd.

'Weighted dice,' Westleigh intoned.

The voices grew more outraged.

'But, I never—' Celia tried to protest.

Rhys broke in. 'The hazard table is closed.' He walked around the table and seized Celia's arm. 'Come with me, madam.' He inclined his head to Westleigh. 'You, too, sir.' He turned to Belinda. 'Pay the winners, then you and Xavier come find us.'

'Rhys, I did not cheat,' Celia tried to tell him. He nearly dragged her through the room. 'I know nothing of fixing dice.'

But she did instantly understand her part in it. She'd chosen favourite numbers, not realising that the dice themselves were training her which numbers were more likely winners. She also knew that Westleigh had somehow planted the dice.

But why would he do such a thing? It lost money for the house and his family if he planted weighted dice.

Xavier had suspected her all along, though. He often watched her at hazard and she'd even admitted to him that she counted cards at *vingt-et-un*. Counting cards was not cheating, precisely, but it did put her in a class beyond the typical player.

As they reached the door, Ned and Hugh were walking in. 'What is this?' Hugh asked.

His father looked triumphant. 'She was caught cheating.'

Ned gaped at her. 'Cheating!'

Rhys led Celia to the hall. Westleigh and his sons followed.

Cummings became very alert when they all strode in.

Rhys said to him, 'We will be in my private drawing room. Tell Xavier and Belinda to come to us there.'

'Yes, sir,' Cummings responded.

Rhys practically dragged her to the room where he had just embraced her and kissed her and where she had spurned him.

Once inside the drawing room with the door closed, Ned blurted out, 'My lady, what more scandal are you going to bring to your family?'

His father's brows rose. 'My lady? Who is she?'

Celia did not want Westleigh, of all people, to know her identity, but, even more, she did not wish for someone other than herself to reveal it.

She pulled off her mask.

He looked at her blankly.

'Do you not recognise her?' Ned looked aghast. 'She is Lady Gale.'

Westleigh still appeared mystified.

'Miss Gale's stepmother,' Ned tried. 'You met them both at the ball.'

'He still doesn't know!' groaned Hugh.

Westleigh protested, 'I cannot be expected to recall every person ever introduced to me.'

Celia broke in. 'Perhaps he would know me better as Mr Cecil Allen's daughter.'

Westleigh's eyes flickered with comprehension.

'Yes,' she said in a low voice. 'I hoped you would remember him.'

Xavier and Belinda walked in the room.

'Sit, everyone,' Rhys said.

Westleigh shot him a withering glance, but did as he was asked. He turned to Ned and Hugh. 'She was using weighted dice at hazard. I dare say the house had some big losses.'

'If the dice were weighted, I knew nothing of it,' Celia retorted.

'I didn't know.' Belinda turned to Rhys. 'I put out new dice each night, as you ordered.'

Westleigh pointed to Xavier. 'You suspected Madame-whoever-she-is, did you not? You've watched her play.'

Xavier nodded. 'I did suspect her.'

Celia looked from him to Rhys. 'I do not cheat. It was not me.'

Rhys and Xavier both remained standing and Rhys gave nothing away in his expression.

He had every reason not to believe her. He knew she needed money, knew she was the daughter of a gamester, knew her father had been accused of cheating.

She also had hurt him.

'Who, then?' Hugh asked.

Rhys's brows rose.

Celia turned to Belinda. 'Have I always won at hazard?' she asked.

Belinda's forehead furrowed. 'Mostly.'

'But always?' Celia persisted. 'Was there not a time I did not win so much?'

The young woman seemed to be thinking hard. 'Only for a little while once.'

'What was different about that time?' she asked.

Belinda shrugged. 'I can't think of anything.'

Celia leaned forwards. 'Was Lord Westleigh with me that time?'

'When you lost?'

Celia nodded. 'When I lost.'

Belinda glanced away. When she turned back, she said, 'I can't remember him there that time.'

Rhys picked this up. 'When Westleigh was there, did he touch the dice?'

'What is this?' Westleigh sounded outraged. 'Do not accuse me. I am the one who showed you it was she who played the bad dice.'

Rhys turned to him. 'Where would she procure the dice?'

Westleigh's eyes shifted as if he was composing the answer. 'Why, from her father, of course. He was a cheat.'

Xavier looked pensive. 'Westleigh was always with her. He was always asking her to play hazard. And he always touched the dice.'

'You cannot remember all that!' Westleigh raised supplicating hands. 'Besides, what reason would I have to cheat? The profits come to me anyway. I have no motive to steal from myself.' He laughed, but his laugh rang false.

Belinda looked puzzled.

Hugh glared at his father. 'Except that the profits are under Ned's control, not yours. You have no money except what Ned gives you. You are cheating to have more money to gamble with!'

'You cannot prove that.' Westleigh pointed to

Rhys. 'You just want to blame me. You sleep with her. Everyone knows that. You are behind this. So you can keep her in your bed.'

Rhys appeared to ignore him. 'It should be easy to discover proof,' Rhys said to the others. 'Whoever has the original set of dice is the culprit.'

Celia stood up and stretched her hands out to her sides. 'Search me.'

Rhys walked over to her, and, as he did so, she removed her gloves and handed them to him. There were no dice in her gloves. She had no sleeves in which to hide the dice.

Westleigh harrumphed. 'She would not put dice in her gloves. She dropped them down her dress.'

Rhys signalled to Belinda. 'Would you step out of the room and check her dress?'

When the two women walked out, Westleigh continued his barrage. 'Who is to say she did not drop the dice on the floor or conceal them in the table? You want to refute what I say, but I saw her rolling the weighted dice. I called your attention to it. Why would I do so for any other reason than an abhorrence of cheating? She is cheating our gaming house, after all.'

Rhys let him go on, but only with difficulty.

Celia would not cheat. It went against everything he knew of her, everything he'd countered when Xavier suggested she was not to be trusted.

She was being set up and he knew precisely who was behind it.

He caught Xavier's eye. Xavier was perhaps the only one who could tell how near Rhys was to murderous rage. He would control it. He'd spent a lifetime perfecting control of his emotions.

He'd settle his accounts with this man once and for all. This man had made a fatal mistake. He'd involved Celia in his dealings, and in the most hurtful way possible.

Hugh looked over at his father. 'Would you stubble it, Father? Your accusation of this woman does you no credit at all. What do you have against her?'

'She prefers the son over the father,' Xavier said.

That was it, Rhys thought. Westleigh had decided to make Madame Fortune a conquest, because Rhys had warned him off. Westleigh had moved from complete indifference towards his bastard son to resentment and rivalry.

The two women returned.

'I could not find anything,' Belinda said.

Celia did not appear steady on her feet. Rhys crossed the room to her and gave her his arm for support.

'This is too taxing for you,' he murmured.

She gave a dismissive wave of her hand. 'I am managing.'

He helped her back to her chair.

'Touching display,' Westleigh said sarcastically.

Rhys swung around to him, losing his composure momentarily.

Ned spoke first. 'This is enough, Father.'

'Stand up, Father,' Hugh ordered. 'It is time to search you.'

Westleigh's eyes bugged out in alarm. 'Me? Why me? This is an outrage. I will tolerate no such thing. You forget who I am.'

Hugh released an exasperated breath. 'We know precisely who you are. Stand up.'

'I will not!' Westleigh gripped the arms of his chair.

Hugh commenced to search his father's sleeves while the man sat in the chair and tried to wave him away. Westleigh gave up the fight as Hugh searched though the pockets in his father's coat and waistcoat and patted him to see if he could feel the dice underneath his clothing.

He moved away, his hands empty.

Celia spoke in a weary voice, 'Check around his chair.'

Ned crouched down and felt the carpet under Westleigh's chair. He looked up and shook his head. Hugh reached behind his father, who tried to prevent access. 'This is a humiliation!' Westleigh cried.

But Hugh pulled his arm out from behind his father and lifted the dice in the air for all to see.

'Oh!' exclaimed Belinda. 'The dice.'

'You are an abomination,' Ned said to his father.

'Which is worse?' Rhys asked Ned. 'What you lately accused this lady of, or your father cheating his own sons and attempting to put the blame on an innocent person?'

Ned glanced away, chastened.

Xavier inclined his head towards Westleigh. 'What will you do with him?'

'I am not certain.' Rhys knew what he would like to do with him, but that punishment belonged to the Middle Ages. 'Would you and Belinda return to the game room? You can reopen the hazard table with new dice.'

'What shall we say to the patrons?' Xavier asked.

'Say only that we do not tolerate cheating and that we have stopped it.' He was not certain what other action he wished to take.

After Xavier and Belinda left the room, Rhys turned to Ned and Hugh. 'Are you able to keep your father in your custody and return him here tomorrow?'

'You are not going to accuse me of cheating! I will be ruined,' Westleigh ranted. 'I will ruin you first. I will take this gaming hell to the devil and all of you with it. I have powerful friends.'

Rhys had no doubt that Earl Westleigh did indeed have powerful friends, but the code of honour for gambling was sacred among the highest reaches of the *ton*. Would they tolerate even a friend who cheated his own sons at hazard and tried to place the blame on a woman?

'You have contrived to make me look guilty,' Westleigh went on, 'because of *her*. You do not want it known that you were duped by a common cheat.'

Rhys leaned into the man's face and his rage turned his voice low and treacherous. 'Do not say another word about her.'

Westleigh flinched, but quickly recovered. He waved a finger at his two legitimate sons. 'Do not believe this man! You traitorous pups. I am your father. You owe your allegiance to me!'

Hugh wheeled on him. 'You were cheating *us,* Father. You knew the profits went to us.'

'And to him!' Westleigh pointed to Rhys. 'Besides, I needed more money than you provided me.' He glared at Ned, but quickly caught himself. 'But I did not cheat. The weighted dice are not mine.'

'Rise, Father,' Hugh ordered. 'We are taking you home.'

Westleigh's two sons pulled him out of his chair and each held one of his arms.

Rhys turned to Celia. 'I will see them out.'

But he would return to her afterwards to assure himself that these stressful events had not done an injury to her health.

As he followed the three Westleighs down the

stairs, he had to admit that Celia had the right of it. Gaming houses were ugly places where greed and desperation drove men to unseemly acts. Rhys might be able to control himself and his emotions around gaming and gamblers, but he could not control others. The veneer might be pretty, but a gaming house was not so different than the desperate streets he'd been thrown into at age fourteen.

When they reached the hall, Westleigh demanded, 'I want to cash out. I need to cash out.'

'Let us just give the cashier the whole lot,' Hugh said to his brother.

On their way to the cashier's office, the game-room door opened. Westleigh seized that moment to break free.

He ran into the game room and shouted, 'Rhysdale is making an unjust accusation. He says he will accuse me of cheating. But you all saw it! It was Madame Fortune!'

Rhys dashed into the room after him.

Westleigh swung around to him. 'I will not be unjustly accused! I demand satisfaction!'

'Here! Here!' some of his cronies shouted. 'Cannot have this!'

One gentleman stepped forwards and said, 'I will be your second, if you wish, Westleigh. It is an outrage. We saw her cheating with our own eyes. Now we know why she always won. How many other cheats are here, I wonder?'

The patrons started to glance at each other in sudden suspicion.

'Lord Westleigh planted the weighted dice on Madame Fortune,' Rhys shouted above the din. 'There is no false accusation here.'

Westleigh smiled a malevolent smile. 'Let us settle this with a duel.'

'A duel! A duel!' others shouted.

'What say you?' Westleigh challenged Rhys. 'We can settle this like gentlemen—'

Chapter Seventeen

Celia heard the shouting from below and feared something had gone wrong. She hurried out of the drawing room and down the stairs, tying her mask to her face as she went.

She reached the doorway of the game room in time to hear Westleigh say, 'Pistols at dawn, Rhysdale?'

'No!' Her voice pierced through the room.

She ran to Rhys's side and grasped his arm. 'No, Rhys! You mustn't do this.'

He pulled her fingers away. 'I will manage it. Trust me.'

Westleigh laughed. 'Madame Fortune, have you come to admit to cheating at hazard?'

Celia's heart pounded. She could stop this! All she had to do was admit to cheating.

She stepped forwards, but Rhys held her back.

'You, Westleigh, are still trying to blame her,' Rhys said. 'Even your sons saw proof of your lies.'

'You set me up!' Westleigh cried. 'You and— and your lover here.'

'Nonsense,' Rhys countered. 'What gaming-house proprietor conspires to lose money?'

Several men nodded their heads.

'You have not answered my challenge, sir.' Westleigh returned to that horrible question. Would Rhys accept a duel?

Because of her.

Rhys glanced around. 'Forgive me, gentlemen. You may know this better than I, but is a gentle-man allowed to issue a challenge to one such as me? I am certainly his social inferior.'

'You are his natural son,' one man blurted out.

The murmurs of the crowd grew louder.

'And I am older than you,' Westleigh said. 'That more than cancels out the inferior blood of your mother.'

Celia's gaze darted to Rhys. Surely he would react to such an insult.

But if he felt the blow, as she had, he did not show it. His face was as composed as if he were strolling through the room watching the gamblers.

'What say you, gentlemen?' Westleigh asked the crowd.

'I say pistols at dawn,' one man shouted.

Others cheered.

Ned walked up to his father and seized his arm. Hugh hurried over and grabbed the other one.

'We are leaving now!' Ned said.

As they pulled him past where Celia and Rhys stood, she heard Ned say, 'Are you mad? We could have kept this quiet and now all London will know of it. A duel, Father? With your son?'

'He's naught but a bastard, Ned,' Westleigh said.

She knew Rhys heard, as well.

Xavier walked up to him. 'That was unfortunate. What will you do?'

'Meet him,' Rhys said.

She grasped his arm. 'No, Rhys! I will not let you!'

He took her chin in his fingers and lifted her face to his. 'I must, Celia. But trust me in this. I know what I am about.'

It was akin to what her father had said to her mother— *It is something I must do.*

'Please, Rhys!' she begged.

He walked her into the hall. 'Celia, you were barely able to stand on your feet a while ago. You must be exhausted. When does your coachman come?'

'Not for an hour.'

He touched her cheek. 'Go upstairs. Lie down. Rest. I need to be visible in the game room. I cannot be seen as hiding from what just occurred.'

She nodded. 'But promise me you will not fight a duel.'

'I cannot promise that.'

Celia was too tired to argue. She walked up to his bedchamber and took off her mask and let down her hair. She kicked off her slippers, climbed onto his bed and fell asleep immediately.

She woke to his arms around her and rolled over to face him. All the candles had been extinguished and the only light came from the glow of the coals in the fireplace. He was shirtless and his face was shadowed with beard. He was warm and comfortable.

And comforting.

His eyes opened for a moment and he gathered her closer, so that her head rested against his heart, lulling her with its rhythmic beat. She wanted to stay in his arms for ever.

But she pulled away. 'What time is it? My carriage.'

He gathered her close again. 'I sent your coachman away. I told him to leave word you were staying here tonight.'

She ought to protest. Her mother-in-law and Adele would have fits of apoplexy.

But she could not care. Not when he held her, when the scent of his skin filled her nostrils, and the even sound of his breathing lulled her into an illusion that everything was as it should be. Everything was wonderful.

She fancied she could feel his baby inside her and she thrilled anew with the wonder of it. She imagined them as a family, saw herself rocking their baby to sleep while she and Rhys quietly conversed about the day.

But it would never be that way. Because she refused to listen to tales of men and women winning and losing, elated and despairing. She could not live in fear of bad luck or challenges to duels.

She did not want him to face Westleigh with pistols. Rhys could die as her father died. It was the greatest cruelty that he would not refuse for her sake, if for no other reason.

And even if he did not die, what would happen to him? An earl might escape arrest, but the proprietor of a gaming hell would certainly be hanged.

He purported to know how to play the odds, but in this case the odds were stacked solidly against him.

She clung to him tighter as tears rolled down her cheeks.

She must discover where the duel was to be held. She would stop it. Somehow, she would stop it.

She might not be able to live with Rhys and his gambling ways, but life would be unbearable if he did not live at all.

* * *

If it was wonderful to fall asleep in Rhys's arms it was glorious to waken in them. When Celia opened her eyes he was already gazing at her. They each lay drinking in the sight of the other for several long moments before he closed the space between them and kissed her.

Silently, he helped her out of her clothing and made love to her. Quietly. Gently. So gently that she thought she would shatter under the sheer beauty of it. He stroked her body as if worshipping it, and every sensation inside her lit up like the illuminations at Vauxhall Gardens. She'd missed him so terribly that her desire burned white-hot for him.

She would have taken him fast and hard. Her body urged her to do that very thing, but his pace remained lazy and leisurely, as if they had all the time in the world.

As if this would not be their last time.

As if he were not intending to engage in a duel at the next sunrise.

When he entered her, she moaned in relief. He'd already driven her to a fevered state with his hands and lips. Now her body could take over, meet his thrusts and urge him to go faster.

But, still, he built the passion slowly and she finally surrendered to his pace, savouring every moment, every sensation.

Even her climax built slowly, like a stack of wood meant to last most of the day instead of the flash of brush she'd initially craved. Once released, it seemed as if the culmination of their lovemaking would have no end. Inside her she felt him spill his seed while she still convulsed with unbelievable pleasure.

An act like this had resulted in a new life, a baby for Celia to love. She said a prayer of thanks that her child had been created out of love. That in itself was a miracle.

He collapsed beside her, holding her as if she would disappear if he let go.

That was not too distant from the truth.

'How are you this morning, my love?' he asked.

He'd never before used such an endearment. 'I feel very well,' she responded. 'I think you have found a cure for the morning sickness.'

He stared into her eyes. 'Then let me treat you every morning.'

He kissed her again.

Later they sat across from each other at the small table in his bedchamber. She was wrapped in a banyan he'd lent her to wear. He was in shirtsleeves and trousers.

Over a cup of hot tea, he continued what he'd begun after lovemaking. 'We could make a marriage work for us, Celia,' he insisted. 'The gaming house is temporary. No more than three years or so and I'll be done with it.'

He thought he was telling the truth, she knew, but she'd heard her father promise to quit gambling over and over. *Tomorrow I'll quit. Just one more game. A chance to recoup.* If he won he could not interrupt his winning streak. If he lost, he still needed one more game. Then it would start all over again.

But even that would be preferable to his death.

She lifted her chin. 'Give up the duel with Westleigh and I will marry you, Rhys.'

He frowned at her. 'I cannot.'

'You could! You could admit to him and the world that Madame Fortune was cheating. She could vanish, then. All who know I am Madame Fortune would have good reason not to tell anyone.' She gave him a pleading look. 'I do not mind giving up being Madame Fortune. It could work.'

He shook his head. 'I am going to stop Westleigh once and for all. He has had this coming for a very long time.'

Did he mean to kill Westleigh? She shuddered. 'I burn to have my father's death avenged, but not at the risk to your life.'

He did not waver. 'I said before, you must trust me on this matter.' He rose. 'And do not use marriage as a bargaining chip. Either you wish to marry me or you don't. But you know marriage would be best for the child.'

'I am not so certain.' She raised her eyes to his. 'I lived that life, Rhys.'

He reached across the table and took her hands. 'You need to trust me, Celia. If I tell you I will give up the gaming house in three years, I will.'

It was not that simple, Celia thought.

He went on. 'If I say I will come out of the duel without a scratch, I will.'

Celia pulled her hands away. 'How can you promise that? You cannot.' Her voice broke. 'My father promised the same thing.'

'Trust me.'

'Tell me how you will do it,' she countered.

He shrugged. 'My plan is not yet in place, but it will be. This duel will solve everything.'

Celia wanted to believe him. She supposed her mother wanted to believe her father, too.

'No. I will not listen.' She waved his words away. 'A duel is too big a risk.'

'Everything in life involves risk, Celia.' He spoke in a low, firm voice. 'The best we can ever do is stack the odds in our favour. Trust me to do that.' His gaze was intense. 'I am not your father. I've never trusted my life to fate. I've made my own luck against all the odds. That is what I will do and can do again.'

She wanted to believe him.

One thing she knew. She'd always been a victim of fate.

No more.

If he could make his own luck, so could she. She had no intention of leaving his life to fate. Somehow, she would stop this duel.

It was about noon when he sent her home in a hackney coach. She walked slowly into her set of rooms, passing Tucker in the hall.

'Good morning, ma'am,' he said in a concerned tone.

'Do not worry,' she responded to his implicit question. 'I am well.'

She walked straight to her bedchamber, but Adele appeared before she made it inside.

'Celia, I must tell you something.' Adele's voice was still cold.

'Very well,' Celia said. 'Come into my room. You can help me change my clothes.'

Adele followed her inside. 'Younie is here somewhere. I'll get her to help. I only need a minute of your time.'

Adele would not even help her with her laces?

Celia stepped into her dressing room and managed to remove her dress by herself. She put on one of her morning dresses. 'What is it you wished to tell me?' she asked, walking back out to the bedchamber.

'Ned and I are getting married. As soon as he can procure a special licence. I need you to secure my guardian's permission.'

So they were following her advice. 'I will send a letter today.'

'Good.' Adele started towards the door, but stopped before opening it. 'After my wedding, I will be moving in with Lord and Lady Westleigh until Ned and I can find rooms of our own.'

'And your grandmother?'

Adele lifted her chin. 'She does not wish to live with you or with me. We are not relations, she says. She wishes to retire to Bath. Ned will pay for her.'

They both would be free of the woman.

And Celia would be free to leave London in perhaps a matter of days.

Unless she agreed to Rhys's proposal.

Assuming he lived.

Anxiety clenched her insides. 'Will you see Ned today, Adele?'

'No,' the girl answered mournfully. 'He sent word that he has business to attend to. He will not see me tomorrow, either.' She narrowed her eyes. 'I do hope his absence is not due to some trouble you or your lover have caused.'

Adele's barb hurt.

Celia spoke quietly. 'That was not well said of

you, Adele. Nothing I have done was meant to hurt you, but you deliberately wound me.'

Adele looked chastened for a moment, but she cried, 'You are going to have a baby out of wedlock!'

Celia put a hand on her abdomen. 'I am going to have a baby. What greater happiness could there be for me?'

Adele's expression remained obstinate. 'Why did you ask about Ned?'

She certainly was not going to confide in Adele. 'No reason. I merely wanted to know your schedule for the day.'

Adele opened the door. 'I am calling upon some of my friends. Younie will accompany me.' She walked out.

Celia went in search of Younie. She had decided to make a call of her own and needed Younie to help her dress again.

Younie helped Celia into a walking dress and she soon was off again, walking through Mayfair to the Westleigh town house. She knocked upon the door and was admitted by the butler.

A few minutes later she was escorted to the second floor and announced to Lady Westleigh. Fortunately the lady was alone. Even her daughter was not present.

Lady Westleigh remained on her chaise longue

when Celia was admitted into a small parlour. The lady's private sitting room, Celia suspected. It was a very feminine room, with upholstered chairs in blue brocade and gilded tables with white marble tops. Celia immediately felt comfortable. She could not imagine Lord Westleigh setting foot in such a room.

'Ma'am, thank you for receiving me.' Celia curtsied.

Lady Westleigh nodded. 'I confess I am surprised to see you.' She gestured for Celia to sit.

'May I enquire whether your sons or your husband are at home?' Celia asked.

Lady Westleigh raised her brows. 'They are not. They all went out. I confess they sounded as if in a quarrel.'

Celia could believe it. 'I am guessing you do not know of any of this, but your husband has challenged Mr Rhysdale to a duel.'

'A duel?' Lady Westleigh sat up straight. 'Whatever for?'

Celia explained the circumstances. 'I must stop this.'

'Certainly we must,' the lady agreed.

A footman served tea.

Lady Westleigh said to him, 'Tell Mason I wish to see him.'

The butler presented himself shortly. 'You asked for me, my lady?'

Lady Westleigh spoke in an officious tone. 'It has come to my attention that my husband is fighting a duel at dawn. I want you to tell me where it will be held.'

The man blanched. 'I am certain I do not know such a thing, my lady.'

Lady Westleigh did not back down. 'And I am certain you do. One of the valets will have heard of it and I am certain it was mentioned in the servants' quarters. It is imperative you tell me.'

Chapter Eighteen

⁓⁓⁓⁓

At first morning's light the next day, Rhys and Xavier stood on Hampstead Heath, fog swirling around their ankles.

'I wonder how many duels have been fought here?' Rhys mused.

'It is popular with those of us with no imagination.' Xavier, as Rhys's second, had had to attend to all the details of the duel. 'It is not too late to get out of this.'

Xavier had suggested the same thing as Celia. Blame Madame Fortune and have her disappear. But Xavier lacked the imagination to use this duel as an opportunity.

'Westleigh will pay this day. Madame Fortune did nothing wrong.' He walked the spot where they would take their positions.

'You don't truly plan to shoot him?' Xavier asked. 'He is your father, after all.'

Rhys turned as he would turn to fire. 'I intend to finish it here.'

They heard a carriage approaching.

'They are here.' Xavier shivered. 'Blast. It is as cold as winter this morning.'

Rhys turned at the sound. 'The coldest summer anyone recalls,' he remarked.

A curricle emerged through the mist and a moment later two men climbed down. It was not Westleigh who had arrived, but Ned and Hugh.

Rhys nodded to them. 'You came after all.'

Ned shivered. 'We said we would.'

Ned and Hugh had called upon Rhys the day before and discussed the duel and its likely aftermath. They had parted in agreement, which surprised Rhys.

It also surprised him that he'd come to a grudging respect for these two men with whom he shared a father. Ned might make a cake of himself over Miss Gale, but he took his responsibilities to his family and his people very seriously. Hugh, as volatile as Rhys was controlled, none the less did not suffer fools gladly. Neither of them exhibited the self-conceit of their father.

'Our father is not here yet?' Hugh asked, his tone contemptuous. 'Perhaps he will not show.'

Rhys was probably the only one who knew that

their father had fought a duel at least once before. 'He will show.'

Sure enough, the sound of a carriage reached their ears. It, too, came through the mist and stopped nearby. Westleigh and his second climbed out of the carriage, the surgeon after them.

Rhys looked back to where he would stand in a few minutes. The sky was lightening by the minute.

Time to deal the cards and play the game.

Rhys and Xavier walked towards the new arrivals, followed by Ned and Hugh.

His second drew Xavier aside for the final task. Loading the pistols.

'What are you doing here?' Westleigh gave his sons scathing glances.

Hugh smiled. 'We would not miss this.'

Westleigh waved a hand at him as if he were an annoying fly. He turned to Rhys. 'Do you have anything to say to me?'

'Only that you are a fool.' Rhys spoke calmly. 'Did you not recall that I spent almost a decade in the army? I am very used to killing.'

Westleigh's brows knit.

'And I am steadier and thinner than you.' He looked Westleigh up and down. 'You'll make a bigger target.' He let Westleigh contemplate that for a moment before adding, 'And since you made the challenge, the weapons are mine. I will be firing a pistol I've fired many times before.'

Westleigh wiped his forehead with his sleeve. 'All that is to no purpose.'

'Suit yourself.' Rhys folded his arms across his chest and waited for Xavier and the other man.

Westleigh tossed the two seconds worried glances. As Rhys had suspected, Westleigh had hoped he would back out. He underestimated Rhys's resolve.

Ironically, only Celia and his brothers believed he would truly go through with it.

The two seconds approached them.

'We agreed the duel will allow for one shot each at thirty paces. No shooting into the air,' Westleigh's second said.

Xavier opened the case containing the duelling pistols. 'Choose first, Westleigh.'

Westleigh tossed Rhys one nervous glance and his hand shook as he selected a pistol. Rhys remained impassive.

'Take your positions,' Xavier said.

Rhys walked at a brisk pace to the spot he had chosen. Westleigh breathed hard to keep up. They stood back to back and Westleigh's second counted the paces. '…nine. Ten. Eleven—'

Ned and Hugh sprinted to Rhys's side and paced with him.

Westleigh's second paused, but Xavier gestured for him to continue.

'Twelve. Thirteen. Fourteen. Fifteen. Turn and fire!'

Rhys, Ned and Hugh turned quickly, as if they were one unit.

Westleigh turned, as well, but his arm faltered when he faced, not only Rhys, but his heir and his spare, as well. 'See here! This is not how it is done.'

Rhys's arm was raised and his aim steady. 'You would know precisely how it is done, would you not, Westleigh?'

Westleigh gestured with his free hand. 'Get them away.'

'Fire, Father,' Hugh said. 'We are not moving.'

'We chose to watch from here,' Ned added.

'Do not fire,' his second cried. 'What if you hit one of your sons?'

'That is the point, is it not, Westleigh?' Rhys held his aim. 'To shoot a son? You are bound to succeed, are you not? Who knows? With luck you might even hit me.'

'You are traitors,' Westleigh cried. 'Siding with him.'

'Should we side with you, Father?' Hugh asked. 'A liar and a cheat? A man who hides his guilt behind a skirt?'

'You cannot shoot your own sons,' his second cried. 'The scandal will ruin you.'

'Shoot, Westleigh,' Rhys called again. 'Or shall I fire first? I am an excellent shot.'

Westleigh's arm trembled.

'Do not do it!' his second begged.

His legs began to shake, as well.

Rhys's arm did not waver. 'You can end this another way.'

Westleigh's face contorted. As the sun lightened the sky it showed a sheen of perspiration on his brow.

Rhys was unshaken. 'Apologise. Confess that it was you who cheated, then leave the country and never return.' He wanted Westleigh far away. Out of his family. Far from Celia. He wanted her to never see the man again. 'Or fire so I can kill you.'

Westleigh fired the pistol into the air and collapsed to his knees. 'Very well. I did it. I planted the dice and blamed Madame Fortune or whoever she is.'

Rhys, Ned and Hugh strode over to him.

From the mist came a cry, 'No!'

The men turned to the sound.

A woman appeared, running towards them. 'Rhys!' she cried.

'Celia,' Rhys whispered. He stepped in her path.

She came to a halt, then vaulted into his arms. 'I thought he'd shot you.'

'No one is shot.' He held on to her. 'Celia, what are you doing here?'

'I came to stop you,' she cried.

He touched her stomach. 'You should not have exerted yourself. I told you to trust me. It is all over. All over. I have fixed it.'

Ned and Hugh pulled their father to his feet and another woman appeared.

Ned peered at her. 'Mother?'

'She would meddle,' Westleigh mumbled.

'You sorry creature,' she spat.

Rhys released Celia and faced Lord Westleigh. 'Here is what you will do. You will leave today for the Continent. You will stay there. You'll have an allowance large enough for comfort, but if you gamble it away or waste it on carousing, there will be no other money. You will leave your family alone, with Ned in charge and empowered to act on your behalf in all matters. What say you?'

'You had better agree,' Lady Westleigh demanded.

Westleigh nodded. 'Yes. I agree. I'll do as you say.'

'Your word as a gentleman?' Rhys persisted.

'I give you my word,' Westleigh said.

'Louder,' Rhys said.

'I give my word as a gentleman!' he shouted.

Ned and Hugh walked him past his second. The man made a sound of disgust and signalled to the surgeon to come with him. They left in the carriage.

Xavier walked up to Rhys and Celia. 'Lady Gale, I am not surprised to see you.' He bowed. 'I would have expected no less from you.' He turned to Rhys. 'Well done. Quite clever, actually.'

Rhys grinned. 'I suppose it violated some part

of the gentleman's code, but, as we all know, I am no gentleman.'

'Rhys,' Ned called to him. 'We'll take charge of Father. Hugh and I will take him directly to our solicitor in the curricle. We'll be on our way to Dover by noon and to Calais on the morrow.'

'Take him in the carriage with me,' Lady Westleigh said. 'Rhys can take the curricle back to the stables.'

'I'll take our horses back,' Xavier said.

Before Rhys knew it, everyone had left them, except Ned's tiger. He helped Celia into the curricle and the tiger hopped on the back.

'Where do I take you, Celia?' he asked.

'To your house.' She caressed his cheek. 'I believe I can trust you at the Masquerade Club.'

He peered at her. 'Are you saying you have reconsidered?'

She nodded and put her arms around him. 'I trust you will do as you say.'

Epilogue

~~~~~~

London—April 1820

Rhys walked through the game room watching the play. The Masquerade Club was as popular as ever—and as profitable. It was hard to believe that so much had happened in under a year.

Change had come to the monarchy in this year, with the mad king's death and George IV inheriting the throne.

But there were even more important changes in Rhys's life. His friend Xavier was still at his side, but also were his brothers. Ironically, he was now accepted as a Westleigh, after all, but only because his father was gone, still banished to the Continent and keeping his word to leave his family in peace.

Best of all, Rhys had married Celia.

At Ned's insistence, they'd been married by special licence in the drawing room of the Westleigh town house on the same day and place as Ned and Adele's wedding, very shortly after he'd almost lost Celia because of the duel.

But he'd managed to rid them all of Westleigh, save the Westleigh estates, and convince Celia that he was a man of his word. In return he'd been given happiness greater than he ever thought possible.

He glanced towards the game-room door. To his surprise Celia stood there. She never came downstairs during the night's play, not since she'd grown so large.

A memory flashed of his first glimpse of her in her mask and deep red gown that now would never contain her full breasts and rounded abdomen.

She braced herself against the door jamb and signalled for him to come to her. He was already heading there.

He touched her arm. 'What are you doing down here?'

She smiled. 'I don't want to alarm you, but I think it is time.'

'Time for what?' he asked.

She looked him in the eye. 'Time for our baby to be born.'

He blanched. 'Indeed?'

She nodded. 'I had Xavier send for Lady Westleigh and the physician.'

'You should not have risked the stairs.' He took her by the arm. 'We must get you back upstairs.'

They'd prepared one of the rooms upstairs for the birth, with a comfortable bed, a tiny cradle and a window for fresh air.

He helped her up the stairs and stayed with her, letting her grip his hand when the contractions came, wishing he could ensure that nothing went wrong.

Lady Westleigh arrived and immediately took charge, telling even the physician what he should do.

'You must leave, Rhys,' she told him.

'Do not waste your breath arguing with me over it,' he told her. 'I am staying with her.'

'I want him to stay,' Celia managed as yet another contraction came.

He endured twelve hours of witnessing Celia in more pain than he could ever imagine, even after being in battle. Finally Lady Westleigh, not the physician, declared that it was time for the birth. Rhys let Celia grip his hand as hard as she wished as she bore down, trying to push the baby from her body.

Finally, after yet another of her agonised cries, another sound erupted. The cry of a newborn baby.

'You have a son,' Lady Westleigh announced.

'A son,' he rasped.

Celia laughed in relief and reached out for her baby.

Later when she, the baby and the room were cleaned up and she put the baby to her breast, Rhys sat back and just gazed at his lusty-lunged son and his beautiful wife.

He made a wager. He wagered this baby would never be hungry or alone, not if Rhys could help it. He would always be loved. Rhys also wagered that Celia, too, would always be loved and that he'd give her the security she had lacked as a child.

He knew the odds of winning these wagers were extremely high.

'Is he not the most handsome baby you have ever seen?' Celia said. 'And so clever to learn how to nurse right away.'

'He is as wonderful as his mother,' Rhys replied. He leaned down and kissed the baby on top of his head. He kissed Celia, too, a kiss of thanksgiving that she and their son had come through the ordeal so well.

'I love my family,' he murmured, kissing her again.

* * * * *

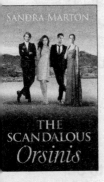

Join the Mills & Boon Book Club

Want to read more **Historical** books?
We're offering you **2 more** absolutely **FREE!**

We'll also treat you to these fabulous extras:

- Exclusive offers and much more!
- FREE home delivery
- FREE books and gifts with our special rewards scheme

Get your free books now!

visit www.millsandboon.co.uk/bookclub
or call Customer Relations on 020 8288 2888